SOUL PURPOSE

Cheers!
Diane Cobalt

DIANE COBALT

ISBN: 9780578997773

Cover Image courtesy of Canstockphoto, dndavis, IgOrZh and Artixty

Cover by Joleene Naylor

ALSO BY DIANE COBALT

Fatal Impact

Fatal Move

Fatal Race

TO MY DAD:

who was my cheerleader and my role model.
Thank you for your wisdom and encouragement and for proving to me that love is more powerful than death.
I miss you every day!

TO MY GRANDDAD:

Thank you for raising Dad and keeping in touch with Margaret's side of the family. I will always remember you as a kind, soft-spoken gentleman who exemplified integrity.

AND TO MARGARET:

Thank you for bringing Dad into the world
and for inspiring me to tell your story.
Though you weren't here long enough,
you left behind an amazing legacy.

"To live in hearts we leave behind, is not to die."

—Thomas Campbell

PROLOGUE

March 16, 1934

It was almost seven thirty in the evening. Mort and Agnes Miller were driving out in the country on a paved, two-lane road. They were heading to their home in Illinois after a long day attending Mort's aunt's 90th birthday party in western Indiana. The stars and full winter's moon provided the only light along their way.

The usually talkative couple had been silent for the past few miles, tired because they had left home almost before the sun had risen that morning. Suddenly, a piece of paper hit their windshield. "What the hell?" Mort asked as he slowed his pickup truck. "Agnes, look at all those papers blowing across the road!"

"Is that a person lying in the other lane?" Agnes shrieked.

Mort pulled his truck to a stop, leaving his lights on so he could survey the situation. "Looks like it. And that appears to be glass and a hunk of metal beyond the body." He swung open his car door and motioned for Agnes to stay put. Seconds later he returned, out of breath. "It's a woman. She's badly hurt. We've got to get her help!"

From her side of the car, Agnes craned her neck to see the woman. "What are we going to do, Mort? We can't just leave her in the middle of the road. What if another car comes along? Is she even alive?"

"I don't know. I don't know what to do. I didn't touch her. I don't want to move her, but if another car comes along, she'll get run over! Hell, we can't leave our car stopped here and risk getting hit ourselves." Mort scanned the side of the road to see where he might safely move his truck. "There's a huge drainage ditch across the way so that won't work, but we are in luck. The grass on this side of the road is fairly flat." He climbed back into the truck and moved it into gear. "I'll just park it over here."

Agnes couldn't take her eyes off the woman lying in the center of the lane on the other side. "Take off your shirt, Mort."

"What?"

"Just take it off. Surely that bright red shirt will help us wave over any oncoming cars. Then we can send someone back to town to get help."

Mort hastily stripped off his shirt, not even reacting to the prickly, cold night air. Before he could determine the best way to safely move her body, another car's headlights appeared in the distance. Mort positioned himself between the car and the woman and frantically waved his red shirt.

Agnes was right. The driver saw the red fabric and stopped to help. As fate would have it, the driver was a doctor. Before sending Mort and Agnes back to town to call an ambulance, the doctor instructed Mort how to help him move the woman to safety. Despite what appeared to be a massive head injury, she was somehow still breathing.

"Doc, are you sure you want me to leave you here?"

"Yes, but first get my black bag out of my car, will ya?" The doctor gently picked up the woman's wrist. Her wedding ring glinted in the headlights from his car.

Agnes had decided she could no longer just sit in their truck and wait. She slowly approached the doctor. "Is there something I can do to help?" The unique sweet scent of honeysuckle tickled her nose as she approached the woman's body. How odd, Agnes thought. It was way too early in the spring for that shrub to flower.

The doctor looked up at Agnes. "Can you drive that truck? Because if you can, I need you to go to the nearest home or place of business and call an ambulance. There's a town a few miles up the road. I need your husband to help flag down any other cars coming our way."

Agnes nodded, noting the woman's ring shining in the darkness. "She can't be out here alone. Looks like she's married. Where's the car that belongs to that piece of metal?"

As Mort handed the doctor his bag, the doctor looked around and saw the glass and a crumpled car door. "Good observation. If we can stabilize her, maybe we can look around for the car." He looked at Agnes. "She's still breathing and has a pulse, but has lost a lot of blood, so please hurry. Maybe we can still save her."

Agnes shrugged off her coat and draped it over her husband's bare shoulders before getting in their car to head to the nearest town.

"Ma'am? Can you hear me?" the doctor said to the woman on the road. "You've been in a car accident. Can you squeeze my hand?"

Are they talking to me? "Hey, where's Ike?" We need to get home to William before his bedtime. Why can't they hear me? I need to get up and find my husband. It doesn't feel like I'm in our car. Why can't I move my hand? Why is it so cold? "Please help me get back to my little boy!"

• • •

An hour earlier, Margaret and Ike had been laughing as they left one of their favorite restaurants and headed toward what they still referred to as their "new" car, a 1932 Ford. A good friend of Ike's had sold it to them shortly after their now fifteen-month-old son, William, was born. "You'll be needing a sedan now with three of you," the friend had advised. But Margaret's favorite part of the car was the convertible top, which she hoped to use in another month or two when the central Illinois weather would warm. Ike's favorites were the deep red leather seats, a luxury they wouldn't have been able to afford had his friend not given him a deal. They contrasted nicely with the car's navy blue exterior.

Ike held open the passenger door and Margaret slid in. "I'm still not used to how slippery these seats are," she laughed. "But they sure do make it easier to get in and out."

Her husband of five years entered the driver's side and started the engine. "I believe the leather seats were a smart choice. If William spills anything on them, they'll be easy to clean."

Margaret smiled at her always practical husband. She took his hand as he steered the car out of the parking lot. "This little jaunt was so much fun. I'm so glad Doodles and Bub were able to meet us. And you had a successful business trip to boot judging by all those papers in the back seat. Leaving William for a few days was difficult, but good for me!"

Ike grinned. "Yes, it was. And I'm glad Frances was available to take care of our little guy."

"Oh my, yes," Margaret nodded. "Your sister is a saint. I'm not sure what we'd do if she lived out of town. My folks would have gladly made the trek from St. Louis if it had not been such short notice. They just need so much lead time with Daddy's job."

Dusk had come and gone and now a full moon hung overhead. As Ike maneuvered the car onto the two-lane highway, the lights of the town faded into the distance. "It's a nice evening for this time of year. Look at all the stars in the sky," he commented.

Margaret checked her watch. It was almost seven. "I'm kind of wishing we hadn't stopped for dinner. We're probably not going to make it home before Frances tucks William into bed for the night," she lamented. "I have missed his sweet kisses and smile so much."

"He definitely favors his mother in those regards," Ike replied. "I bet we'll make it back home before our son is in bed. I know how much you like rocking him to sleep. I watched you the night before we left. You promised him you'd return."

"That I did! I hope you're right about getting home in time. Frances will kill us if we wake him up just to give him a kiss goodnight."

"That she might," agreed Ike. "Big sisters tend to be kind of bossy. But anyway, how often do we get to see our best friends? Why if it hadn't been for Doodles, I probably wouldn't have met you."

"Probably? You definitely wouldn't have met me! If Doodles hadn't dragged me to that fraternity party you all threw my freshman year, how would we have met?"

"Maybe I would have run into you at the business school," Ike said thoughtfully.

Margaret shrugged and smoothed out her dress. "Unlikely, given the fact you were two years my senior. We had no classes together."

"True, my love. And let's not forget Doodles' motive for attending our fraternity function."

"Bub!" they both said in unison.

"Why did they have to move to Cleveland? It's just too far away from us," Margaret asked.

"That it is," agreed Ike. "But I wouldn't be surprised if some day they get back to Illinois. They'd be even closer if he could find a job in Chicago."

"Hmm… you have some friends up there. Maybe you could help him find something?"

Ike smiled. "That would be nice, now, wouldn't it?"

Margaret eyed her husband suspiciously. "Why Ike Stearns. Do you and Bub have something up your proverbial sleeves?"

Ike snuck a look at Margaret out of the corner of his eyes and just grinned.

Half an hour later Margaret grew tired of looking at the blackness of the night. "How much longer do you think until we get home?"

"Well we just passed Danville so I'd say about three quarters of an hour."

Darkness surrounded them as they continued down the two-lane road which had narrow concrete shoulders. It had been awhile since they had seen the lights of a car come towards them. Margaret reached for her purse which she had laid on the floor next to her feet. Chewing a stick of gum might help her pass the time.

As she straightened with the stick of gum in her hand, Ike yelled out, "What the heck is that?!" A black coal truck seemed to appear out of nowhere. It was stopped in their lane. Ike swung the steering wheel hard to the left to prevent them from hitting the vehicle and in his efforts to avoid crashing into the truck, Margaret's door was sheared off, providing no barrier to her body sliding out of the car and onto the road. As the Ford crossed the oncoming lane of traffic, it hit an embankment. Ike was thrown part way through the windshield before the car came to rest in a second ditch almost a quarter mile from where Margaret lay on the road.

CHAPTER ONE

June 2, 2017

Whoever came up with the phrase "The mother of the groom should wear beige and keep her mouth shut," should be shot. Really? The author had to have been the bride's mother, maybe even my own mother who actually ended up wearing beige to my wedding when she apparently didn't have to!

Beige is not my color. I hold it and other earth tones one step above the drab hue of gray. When I'm not wearing black, I prefer to don bright or deep, rich colors. So, when my son's fiancé chose brown dresses with pink sashes for her bridesmaids, I felt even more pressure to move into the beige world until her mother selected a beige ensemble and I was off to find a deep berry-colored gown.

During one of my many dress hunting excursions, I was heading out of a department store when I was sure I heard my dad's voice, not in my head, but actually talking to a clerk. This would not be anything to panic about if it weren't for the fact that my father has been dead for over sixteen years!

I shake my head to clear the memory. The rehearsal and following dinner start in just over an hour and so far, I've done a pretty good job of keeping my mouth shut, at least as far as my future daughter-in-law and her mother know! I really can't complain. Libby is my favorite of all the girls my younger son has dated—and there have been many over the years. She's a darling, petite blonde with piercing blue eyes and a radiant smile, complete with dimples. I have no doubt that my grandchildren will be more beautiful than the Gerber baby.

I've been through this mother-of-the-groom role before. Our older son, Brock, married the most perfect young woman just three years ago. The wedding was in another state so my husband and I hosted a rehearsal dinner in unfamiliar surroundings. (And just for the record, I wore a sapphire blue dress to that wedding.) Tonight's dinner is at one of our favorite restaurants in Dallas which eliminates a lot of anxiety. In fact, the three of us: Wynn, my husband; Brock and I have been planning parts of Chase's rehearsal dinner since he was ten. I can't wait to see how this all plays out. But here I am sitting in our family room in my robe, hair and makeup done, listening to the ticking of our mantle clock and wondering where all those minutes of the past twenty-five years went.

These are the last few hours of my role as mother of the groom. I hear Chase start the shower upstairs. He moved home about a month ago when the lease was up on his bachelor pad in LA. He and Libby will be moving into a small home when they return to California from their honeymoon. Maybe that's it—why I'm feeling so melancholy. Chase has been home long enough for me to get used to having him around again and now he's minutes away from leaving our home permanently. Yes, that's it. My sole purpose for over twenty-five years has been to raise my two sons to be outstanding husbands. Now, today, it appears I have finished my job.

To be fair, my husband and sons would remind me that I am an author and that I surely have more books to write. I've always loved to write, to create and convey stories that sometimes just "pop" into my head. Despite the fact that I've published three suspense novels, I still have a hard time claiming the title of author. I'm not on the New York Times' Bestsellers List and I don't have an agent. While more people have read my books than I ever would have imagined, I'm still unknown.

After all these years, I feel now if I were to write my life story, it would be time to type: "the end." To be clear, I have no intention of ending my life, I just don't feel I have any special purpose anymore. My most interesting, challenging days are in my rearview mirror and what stretches before me is a mundane country road leading nowhere.

If I weren't so organized, I wouldn't have time to be thinking about this, at least not right now. And right now, I can't afford to cry and ruin my makeup because then I will have to redo it and I will run late. I am NEVER late.

The door from the garage into the kitchen opens and my knight in shining armor bursts through just in time to prevent me from being late. He holds two garment bags in his hands. Relief spreads across his face. "Two tuxedos, this time the correct designer." He walks across the room and kisses my neck. "Where's Chase?"

"Upstairs showering."

"Great! I'll run up and leave these tuxes in their rooms for tomorrow, then get showered myself." Wynn heads down the hall and calls over his shoulder, "Oh and I talked to Vincent at St. Martin's and he was able to get plenty of the Bogle Phantom wine."

Now I'm smiling. The last detail for tonight's rehearsal dinner is complete. Chase and Libby aren't big wine drinkers, but ever since Chase starred as the Phantom in his high school's production of "The Phantom of the Opera" it has become their favorite wine. It will be a fun reminder to Chase of where he got his start now that he is starring in his own TV sitcom.

I still don't think of Chase as a TV star. Maybe when the show airs it will sink in. He and Libby decided to get married before his show goes into production the end of next month. Chase has always wanted to be on TV or in the movies ever since he had one line in his first musical his sophomore year in high school. I remember him watching the Emmy Awards and saying some day that would be him going to get an award. Wynn and I had laughed and suggested he have a Plan B for how he would support himself on that potentially long journey.

"Just be sure to remember to thank the important people in your acceptance speech," I hinted.

"Right," Chase responded. "First God, then my high school director, my elementary school director...and oh of course... Granddad." He had pointed above, then turned his attention back to the TV.

I cleared my voice. "And?"

I can still picture the impish grin on his sweet face. "Hmm... am I forgetting someone?"

I tilted my head.

"Oh, that's right. I'll thank my mom!"

But it was really his thanking his granddad, my dad, that always got to me.

My dad died when Chase was nine and Brock was thirteen. Dad was only seventy, but had spent a lot of time with both boys. They had looked up to him when he was alive and they still look up, only now to heaven.

I rise from my perch on the couch and head back to our bedroom to put on my dress. There's no time to get sad thinking about my dad and wishing he were here for the festivities. After sixteen years, you'd think I'd get used to him being gone.

The three of us are dressed and ready to go fifteen minutes early. "Let me get a quick picture of the two of you," Wynn says. My darling husband is a picture-taking crazed fanatic. Notice I didn't say photographer. His pictures always look great, but he always takes an annoying number of shots. Tonight though, neither Chase nor I object.

"My turn to take one of you two," I announce after Wynn snaps four shots.

We go outside by our pool. The same pool where I taught Chase to swim when he was barely two years old. I look at the screen on the camera at father and son. Wynn at fifty-eight, is still as handsome as the day I met him at SMU. He still has a head of thick hair with more black than gray although the gray is gaining every day. Chase is six feet tall, three inches taller than his dad. Chase's once strawberry blonde hair is now a medium brown and despite the fact that his eyes are piercing blue and Wynn's are hazel, he looks a lot like his father.

Chase smiles as I press the button on the camera. "Let me take one of you and Dad and then I've got to run and pick up Libby." Wynn and I quickly pose while Chase takes a few shots of us.

"Did you put the top down on the car?" Wynn asks him as he heads inside.

"Yes, I did, Dad. Thanks for letting me borrow it."

"We'll see you at church," I call after him.

A few minutes later, Wynn drops me off at the front entrance to our church and heads off to park the car. It still amazes me that Libby is not only a local girl, but is also a member of our church. Her family, the Andrews, moved here her senior year in high school. She and Chase graduated the same year but then parted ways without really knowing each other. Libby went to the University of Oklahoma and Chase headed to the University of Texas, a huge rival of OU's. The two might have never met again if Libby hadn't started a program for special needs students at our church. Chase's love for helping others started when he was in junior high where he participated in Partners P.E., a program that paired student volunteers with special needs students. So, when he found out the summer before his senior year in college that our church was looking for volunteers for this new area of ministry, he quickly signed up. His preschool teachers predicted Chase would be a minister or an actor and that summer he was a little of both.

I recall vividly the day he came home from his training session with the program's leader, Libby Andrews. "Mom, First's Kids is going to be great! This girl, Libby Andrews, who started the program, is phenomenal!" His blue eyes sparkled. "She wants me to be her assistant since I had all that experience with Partners P.E. I won't be home for dinner tonight because we're meeting to plan all the details." Chase started to go upstairs, then stopped and looked at me over his shoulder. "Oh, and did I tell you she's smokin' hot?" His grin said it all.

Libby started the First's Kids program five years ago. It now serves about 100 area special needs children ranging in age from five to eighteen. After graduating from OU, Libby continued running the program while getting her PhD at SMU. Chase was fortunate enough to have had a few acting roles locally and helped her until his agent convinced him he needed to move to the West Coast if he was serious about furthering his acting career.

Chase had hated leaving Libby behind while he got "established," which meant doing community theater and waiting tables. About the time he had persuaded Libby to move to LA he landed the lead role in a new sitcom and then proposed to Libby. She was sad to leave her job as director of First's Kids, but decided to start a similar program at a Methodist church in an LA suburb which would also provide counseling services to special needs kids and their families.

It seemed like only a few minutes had passed by from the

time Sarah Andrews, Libby's mother, had greeted me at the door of our church until the rehearsal was almost over. Wynn and I are sitting in the traditional grooms' parents' location: front pew on the right side. I nudge my husband and whisper, "I think we should scoot out and get to the restaurant. Brock and Meredith just left." Wynn nods as we quietly get up giving a small wave to the bride's mother.

St. Martin's restaurant is located on lower Greenville Avenue in Dallas. Greenville Avenue has been known for its bars and restaurants since Wynn and I were in college. Everything from casual burger places to swank, hip cafes can be found lining this street.

We pull up to the valet stand in front of the restaurant. The valet opens my door and I step onto a red carpet that leads to the door of St. Martin's. As our guests arrive, they have been instructed to line both sides of the red carpet so when Chase and Libby arrive, they can emulate the paparazzi. The red carpet was Brock's idea, and as I approach the restaurant door, I see he and Meredith smiling.

"Now who's really the star tonight, Mom?" Brock grins. "You just might outshine the happy couple." He gives me a hug.

"Not a chance," I reply.

It always strikes me as ironic that Chase may be the movie star in the family when so many of my friends have commented over the years that Brock is movie-star handsome. Chase is striking and very good looking, don't get me wrong. But Brock is tall, dark and handsome with his dark brown hair, olive complexion and my dad's eyes...pools of melted milk chocolate.

The early evening sun is still bearing down and I am beginning to sweat. "Dad and I are going inside to check on things," I tell Brock. "Make sure you text me when they arrive."

Brock looks up from his cell phone. "He just texted me that they are leaving church now so you probably have about fifteen minutes, Mom."

"Perfect." Wynn and I enter the dimly lit restaurant.

"Ah, Mr. and Mrs. Parker, welcome," Vincent, the manager greets us. "Follow me and let me know if there's anything you need."

We pass down the narrow aisle in front of the bar and wave to the bartender before entering the private dining room. I study the tables, ticking off items from my mental checklist: rectangle table at back with six places all facing the rest of the room, six round tables with eight chairs each, podium with microphone, private bar stocked with Phantom wine, oblong floral spray on the head table, clear bowls with pink gerbera daisies floating in them surrounded by lit candles on each of the round tables, programs at each place, flat panel TV to show the video…oh shit! "The DVD!! Wynn, I forgot to bring the…"

"No, you didn't, sweetheart. It's right here," Wynn's voice soothes me as he extracts the disc from his jacket pocket.

"Thank you." I take a deep breath. "I think everything is perfect. Do you notice anything missing?"

"Looks good to me. Now let's go back outside so we don't miss their arrival."

"Any last-minute details we need to attend to Mrs. Parker?" Vincent asks in his smooth Hungarian accent as we make our way past the bar towards the front entrance.

"It looks great! You did an amazing job. Thank you."

Outside, the red carpet is fully lined by our guests—most holding their phones and some with cameras—ready to snap pictures. It isn't long before Chase and Libby pull up in our convertible. The valet hustles over to open Chase's door while Brock helps Libby out of the car and offers her his arm.

"Hey, Bro," Chase shouts, hurrying over and grabbing Libby's other arm. "She's my girl!" Brock smiles, releases her arm and gives the thumbs up to the "paparazzi" whom Chase hasn't noticed. Instantly, flashes are popping.

Brock walks towards the restaurant door in front of the happy couple and holds up his hand. "Sorry folks, we're not doing pictures today! No pictures, please." But the guests, who had been previously instructed to ignore Brock, continue snapping away.

Chase bursts out laughing. "I think that's my line."

It was one of our family's private jokes that went back to Chase's high school days. While we were vacationing in Florida, the boys went to the beach. Two girls approached the boys and asked Chase if he would take their picture with Brock. Although offended, Chase obliged. For days, we wondered what famous person they mistook Brock for. And every day after that when the brothers went to the beach, Chase would ask Brock if he was "doing pictures" today.

I overhear Libby laugh at the attention as she and Chase make their way into the restaurant. "Now I know how Kate Middleton felt when she married Prince William."

"Ah, but alas I cannot bestow upon you the royal title you

so richly deserve, my love," Chase replies in a clipped British accent. "Your fairest beauty overwhelms me and you are doth my queen."

"Ok, ok, enough of the Shakespeare," Brock interrupts. "Let's get this party started."

Dinner goes smoothly. The only thing better than the delicious food is the laughter and joyous conversation oozing from the room. As the dessert plates are cleared, Wynn steps up to the podium. He motions to Brock for aid in quieting the happy guests. Brock stands and hold his water glass in the air as he clinks his spoon against its side. It takes a few minutes for the chatter to die down.

"Margo and I are so blessed to be welcoming Libby into our family. Chase, once again your lucky stars have shone down upon you in your ability to woo Libby into agreeing to become your wife."

"I think the word is 'con', Dad," Brock interrupts.

Wynn pauses for a moment as if weighing his choice of words. "Woo, con, maybe charm's the better word. At any rate, Margo and I have enjoyed getting to know Libby and her family: Sarah, Jim and Haley. We welcome them all to the Parker family." "Cheers!" fill the room.

"Normally, I would have given my speech and toast before we started dinner, but having been the father of two boys for over twenty-five years, I learned a long time ago that anything beyond the quick blessing our pastor offered earlier, would be ignored until appetites were satisfied. So, without further ado, I will turn over the festivities to our older son and Best Man, Brock."

Brock nods and smiles. I catch his eye and he winks at me. The two of us have been awaiting this moment since Chase was ten! I can't believe we've kept this secret for so long and more were added to our treasure trove throughout his life. We always planned to reveal them at his rehearsal dinner.

"I attended most of my brother's shows and programs. And I admit, there were several musicals I just didn't understand... especially the ones you were in at UT. So tonight, we have our own little program for you to watch, Chase. No, we haven't put together a musical, just some surprises. But first, I'd like to welcome Libby to our crazy family. I've always wanted a sister and sometimes with all Chase's drama, it seemed like I had one!" Laughter erupts in the room. "But now..."

"I'm here...I'm here..." comes a sing-song voice from one corner of the room, and then again from another corner. Brock acts startled.

"Oh no! Sorry about this, folks. It happens at the most inopportune..."

The restaurant manager enters the room on cue. "Excuse me, Mr. Brock? This arrived for you." He hands Brock a plain trifold note card. Brock carefully unfolds the note and looks at Libby.

"I will take Libby as my bride or awful things will occur. Signed OG."

The manager dims the lights and presses the play button on the DVD remote. The screen stays black for a few moments while the ominous organ music of "The Phantom of the Opera" fills the room. Then Chase's masked face fills the screen. The video continues with a montage of pictures from both Chase and Libby's childhoods set to various songs from the musicals Chase appeared in. There is much laughter and "aws" from the wedding party. I'm glad the lights aren't on and that Wynn is holding my hand. Tears are racing down my cheeks and dripping onto my dress. I don't dare look at Sarah, but I imagine she is crying as well. Brock and I chose the song "Point of No Return" to end the video. The lights come up and Brock is holding Chase's Phantom mask.

"Well, Libby, it seems that this is your point of no return. You have made...your...choice and you have chosen well. My best wishes and heartfelt condolences to you on spending the rest of your life with my brother." The room explodes with laughter and applause. "Oh, and here's a gift from me to you, Libby. It might come in handy on your wedding night." The females giggle and the males whoop and holler. Brock hands Libby a pink striped Victoria's Secret box.

Libby is blushing, and of course, Chase is moving his eyebrows up and down. My future daughter-in-law opens the box and delicately extracts a dilapidated brown teddy bear.

"Wilson!" shouts Chase as he grabs his long-lost bedtime companion from Libby's hands. He grins at Wilson, then knits his brows together. "What the...so where have you been keeping him all these years, Bro?"

Uh oh. I can't tell if Chase is truly upset with this surprise or is just acting.

"Don't you remember? He ran away. Mom and I sent him a wedding invitation and he just couldn't wait to see who took his place. I hope three's not a crowd for you, Libby." Brock barely gets the words out before he doubles over laughing. Shouts for the whole story echo around the room.

Brock holds up his hand to quiet the group. "I gave Wilson to Chase when he was first born and Chase gave me a Big Brother shirt." Brock holds up the tiny shirt. "Well within a year, I had outgrown the shirt, but suffice it to say, Chase didn't outgrow Wilson. He slept with Wilson every night, took him on vacation, took him to school for show and tell—yeah the professors at UT loved that." The audience howls. "But seriously when Chase was what, thirteen?"

"No, I was only eight."

"Hmm. Okay, I'll be nice and go with eight. When Chase was eight and went to camp at Pine Cove, I told him Wilson had to stay at home. Chase didn't like that one bit and threw a big hissy fit. I was not about to let my little brother be the only one in his cabin who brought a teddy bear. So, I ended up having to hide Wilson and I hid him so well that when Chase returned from camp, I couldn't find Wilson. Mom and Dad couldn't find him anywhere. And we concluded that he must have ended up in a pile of clothing we gave to the Salvation Army. We told Chase that Wilson ran away to teddy bear camp. Well…when I was cleaning out my closet before I went to college, I found Wilson. I asked Mom what I should do and she said to give him back to Chase at his rehearsal dinner."

"Oh, fine, blame this on me!" I chime in.

"Ok, we decided together. Now that you have Wilson back, missing ear and all, is the wedding still on, Chase?"

At this moment, Chase jettisons Wilson through the air hitting Brock in the face.

"Well, folks, that answers my question." Brock lifts his champagne glass that Vincent had just finished filling during his speech. "To Libby. Welcome to our family and best wishes for a lifetime of drama...I mean happiness with my brother."

"Cheers!" add the guests, raising their glasses.

CHAPTER TWO

June third dawns brightly albeit noisily. Birds are chirping right outside our bedroom window as if they are discussing details of Chase and Libby's wedding day. I turn my gaze from the ceiling fan to my beloved husband, Winston Parker the third, or Wynn as we all call him. He remains in a blissful slumber. I can't help but smile. Today will be the first day in eighteen years that June third will be remembered with joy instead of overwhelming sadness.

When Libby and Chase first called to announce the date, I had cringed internally, grateful that they couldn't see my face. June third was the day when cancer claimed my dear, sweet father's life. The day it had taken him away from his wife, daughters, sons-in-law and four grandchildren. It was a day irrevocably etched in all our hearts as the day a saint's soul had been called to greater glory, leaving behind an immense void in all of our lives.

Several hours after the initial phone call proclaiming the wedding date, Chase had called back.

"Mom?" he began.

"Hi, Sweetie," I struggled not to say anything about the date…in case he'd forgotten.

"I wanted to talk to you when Libby wasn't around. She's the one who picked the date. We have to be back in LA by June eighteenth because we start shooting the series on the nineteenth. We want to have time for a honeymoon and with her job, we couldn't get married any sooner."

I took a deep breath. Of course, he hadn't forgotten. "Chase, it's fine. I appreciate your thoughtfulness and concern. But really, this is a gift. You know Granddad wouldn't want us to be sad and you know how much he loved celebrations. So this is perfect! Now June third will be a positive date!"

Chase was silent and when he spoke his voice cracked. "Thanks, Mom, for making me feel better about this."

I now stretch and then sit on the edge of the bed. Wynn's arm squeezes my shoulder. "Ready for the big day?"

I twist my body towards his and smile. "Yes. You?"

Wynn nods. "Let's get this show on the road!"

I look at the clock on my nightstand. "Brock and Meredith will be up soon and the groomsmen will be here in an hour for one last pancake breakfast. I'd better get dressed."

"Whoa there, Margo. Not so fast!" Wynn grabs my waist. "Last pancake breakfast? You're not planning on ever making pancakes for just little 'ole me again?" He sticks out his lower lip for effect.

"Of course, I'll still make pancakes for you, silly boy!"

Within our family of four, my homemade sour cream

pancakes have become legendary. Twice a month on Saturday mornings, I made my grandmother's recipe. It wasn't until the boys went off to college that they realized how much they missed those pancake breakfasts. I had told them over the years that I would share the recipe only with their wives and that was only if I liked the girl!

Meredith will be helping me this morning, claiming she needs more practice to get them as good as mine. I gave the recipe to Libby last night.

During their college years both Brock and Chase brought home their buddies and girlfriends for Saturday morning pancakes. Surprisingly to me, a few of them were not impressed... definitely an indicator of their future relationship to our family. Brock's "evil girlfriend" hadn't liked them at all. And one of Chase's roommates ate them without making a comment. By the end of that semester, Chase and his other roommates were ready to kick the guy out. The boys often joked that any future wife or life-long friend would have to pass the "pancake test." The groomsmen who would be at our table this morning had all passed with flying colors and I can't wait to have a kitchen full of hungry, happy men! This certainly would be a day to treasure!

An hour later, Meredith begins heating up the griddles and Brock is setting the dining room table. "Gee Mom, I don't think we've ever had pancakes in the dining room."

I pause. "I guess we never have. You'll have to add one more chair."

"Just put it next to your mom's place," Meredith adds, "so I can get to the kitchen easily."

Meredith is such a sweet, kind daughter-in-law and is perfect for Brock. She is vibrant, bubbly and most important, wants what's best for her husband. I am certain that God put her in his path and I thank Him daily for it.

The doorbell rings. "I got it," calls Chase as he bounds down the stairs.

"Good morning, Mrs. Parker," Michael Shannon, a swim team friend of Chase's greets me as he walks into the kitchen. "Do I smell pancakes?" He hands me a bouquet of stargazer lilies.

"Oh Michael, they're beautiful! And one of my favorites. Thank you!"

"No, thank *you*! Your pancakes are worth a whole room full of flowers."

I smile. Michael and Chase grew up together swimming on the same summer swim team. Although they went to different high schools, they still like to hang out together when time allows.

"Chocolate chips in your pancakes?"

"Yes, please."

The doorbell rings again. This time Brock answers it. Standing on our front step are three of Chase's fraternity brothers: Will, Jake and Sterling. "Where's the groom?" Jake asks in his booming theatrical voice.

"Follow me," Brock says as he leads them to the kitchen.

"Exactly where I'd expect him to be...near the food," Sterling adds.

"Margo, should I put the first batch on the griddle?" asks Meredith.

"Yes, let's get started. Wynn, would you start the bacon and sausage?"

The doorbell rings again. This time it's Phillip, Chase's best friend from high school who is staying with his parents down the street.

"Wow, does it smell good in here! I hope I'm not too late, Mrs. Parker."

"You're right on time, Phillip. Breakfast will be ready in a few minutes." Before I know it, the boys are pushing back their chairs from the table and taking their plates into the kitchen.

"Thank you, Mrs. Parker. Those were awesome pancakes," Sterling announces.

"Yes, the best in the world," says Jake.

"You should open a restaurant," suggests Will.

"You're welcome guys. Now you better scoot or you'll be late for your tee times."

Chase kisses me on the cheek as he, Wynn and his brother head out the door. "Thanks, Mom. I'll miss these mornings!"

"Go! Shoo! Have fun," I smile brightly. The door barely closes behind them before the first tear of the day tumbles over my lower lashes. If I could just have those few precious hours back. I shake my head. I guess I'll just have to freeze the image of their smiling faces.

Before I can turn around, I feel Meredith's hand on my shoulder. "We probably should be going soon ourselves."

I wipe my tears away with the back of my hand. "Yes. I appreciate you going to the salon with me. Libby invited me to the spa, but I feel better going to my stylist. But I'm sure it's not too late for you to change your mind and join them."

"Oh, I barely know those girls. And besides, I don't get to spend enough time with you anyway."

"Brock is one lucky guy, Meredith. Let me dry these few dishes and we'll be on our way."

• • •

I really try relaxing in the salon chair, but I can't help running through my "to-do" list one more time. It's fairly short...a perk of being mother of the groom. I glance at the clock. It's already one o'clock.

"What do you have left to do?" asks Joel, my amazing stylist who has taken care of my wavy, graying hair since before Chase was born. He begins flat ironing my hair.

"We have to be at the church at four for pictures. You're doing my makeup. All I have left to do is put on my dress and jewelry." My stomach sinks. "Shit!"

Joel wisely stops straightening my hair and holds the flat iron away from my head. "What did you forget?"

"To get my grandmother's ring out of the safe deposit box at the bank which closed at noon. I've worn that ring to all of the boys' special occasions. Great!"

Joel cocks his head to the side. "Do you have something else of hers? A necklace or earrings?"

"No, just the ring. I can't believe I didn't think about wearing it to the rehearsal dinner last night."

"Well if that's the worst thing that happens today, then everything should be fine." Joel reaches for his hand mirror and gives it to me so I can view the back of my now shiny straight hair. He spins me around to face the larger mirror. "At least you don't have to worry about the weather ruining your hair today," he reminds me as he spritzes a little spray on my hair. "I hope you don't outshine the bride."

I smile up at him. "Thanks!"

The men have already returned by the time Meredith and I pull into the garage.

"That was fun, Margo. I love Joel. I wish I could take him to Tulsa with me!"

"I love you, Meredith, but not enough to let you steal my hair stylist."

Meredith laughs. "I'm heading upstairs to get ready."

As I head towards our bedroom, I can hear our shower running. I open the door to see Wynn soaping his hair, singing away! I inspect my hair and makeup in our mirror and decide I need a little more color on my cheeks. As I roll open the drawer that holds my blush, a purple box catches my eye. Grabbing it as if the house is burning down, I open it to reveal my grandmother's ring! "How in the world did it get in here?" I comment aloud. "I would never put jewelry in this drawer."

Wynn exits the shower and is toweling off. "What did you say, Sweetheart?"

"Look!" I grab the tiny box and once again push the button to release the top.

"Yes, your grandmother's ring."

"Did you put it in that drawer?"

"No, Margo. I haven't..."

"Did you go to the safe deposit box and get it out today?"

"No. Did you ask me to?"

I shake my head. "I swear that's where it was. I thought I had forgotten to get it out and here it is!"

Wynn smiles. "You've had a lot on your plate this week. You probably got it out and forgot you'd done it."

"But I never would have put it in that drawer." I am adamant.

"Like I said, you've had a lot on your mind. At least it's not still in the safe deposit box!"

"True. And while I'm thinking about this, I need to talk to Brock. Is he here?"

"He should be. He went to do an errand for Chase. But I'll bet he's back now."

Clutching the purple crushed velour box, I head back to the kitchen. Sure enough, there is Brock having a snack. I kiss his cheek.

"I should have known you'd be where the food is! How was golf?"

"Hmm, it was fun. I won," he replies as he stuffs another cookie into his mouth.

"Um, do you think you could have let your brother win on his wedding day?"

"Ha! He could be eighty years old and on his death bed and I wouldn't let him win!"

Brock grabs the milk jug from the refrigerator, pours himself a glass and heads to the kitchen table. I sit down across from him. "While I'm thinking about it, I want to tell you about this ring." I open my hand to reveal the purple box.

"I know. It's your grandmother's ring. Granddad's mother."

"That's right. And my dad gave it to me when I was twenty-five. Since I don't have any daughters, I want this to go to my oldest granddaughter when she turns twenty-five."

"Okay. And why are you telling me this now? We don't even have any children."

I shrug. "Well, in case I'm not here, I just want you to know my wishes."

Brock grins. "Well, let's just plan on you giving it to her." He stands and takes his empty milk glass to the kitchen sink. "I better go upstairs and get ready. See you in a few!"

I nod and stare at the open box. The brilliant cut diamond is in a square platinum setting. It's very unique, much like I imagine my grandmother was. I slip it on the ring finger of my right hand and stare at the reflection as it catches the late afternoon sun. I may be getting old, but I know for a fact that I hadn't retrieved it from our safe deposit box. While I don't believe in ghosts, there really seems to be no other logical explanation for this.

• • •

A few hours later, Wynn drops me off under the portico of our church. When I reach the front doors, I see my sister, Melissa, and her two daughters standing just inside.

"Hi, girls," I greet them giving each one a hug. "You all look gorgeous!"

"As do you," Melissa says as she hugs me back. "I thought we'd get here early in case you need anything or have forgotten anything."

"Like when I forgot my slip the day of your wedding?" I reply.

My sister grins and shrugs. "Well, I wasn't going to bring it up…"

I smile back and take a deep breath. "Thanks for coming early, just in case. But so far, I think I have everything. There should be a pew reserved for you right behind ours."

Melissa nods. "Girls, why don't you go check on that."

My nieces, happy to have something to do, enter the sanctuary. I see Wynn talking to Melissa's husband just outside the front doors. When I return my attention back to my sister, I notice she is frowning.

"She's not having a good day," she tells me, referring to our mother who is suffering from dementia. Melissa shakes her head. "There's just no way I could bring her."

"Don't worry about it. We knew that it was a longshot that she could be here." I look at my watch. "I'm due in the bride's room. Sorry I have to go. Thanks for being here!"

"If you need anything, I'll be right here."

I walk down the hallway and knock softly on the door to our church's bride's room and stick my head inside. The room is bustling with activity. "Just want to report that the groom is here and is eagerly awaiting his bride. You look absolutely stunning, Libby!"

My future daughter-in-law pads bare-footed to me and gives me a hug. "Thank you, Margo. You look beautiful."

"You're just in time for the something old, something new, sixpence in your shoe ritual," Libby's mom announces. "So, I'll start with something old." Sarah Andrews reaches into her purse and pulls out a cloth pouch. "While not in their original box, these pearls were worn by your great grandmother, then your grandmother and finally me at our respective weddings. And as most of you in this room know, all three of those were happy unions and were blessed with many children. Libby, I'm delighted to pass these pearls of happiness on to you." While Libby holds up her hair, Sarah unfastens the clasp and drapes the pearls around Libby's neck.

"Thank you, Momma," she smiles, gently placing her hand on the necklace while admiring it in the mirror.

For a minute I fear that Sarah is going to cry. But she holds her emotions in check. "You are most welcome, precious child. Now before I cry and ruin my makeup, let's move on to something new."

"Oh, that's me," says Haley, Libby's younger sister. "I have your garter." The other bridesmaids whoop and holler. Haley pretends she's going to shoot it in the air, but at the last minute carefully hands it to her sister.

"Thanks. I'll put it on now." More whoops fill the room.

Sarah discreetly checks her watch knowing the they have a schedule to follow. "Ok, ladies, let's continue. We only have ten minutes left before that drill sergeant of a wedding planner comes knocking on that door saying it's time to march out of here. Now who's loaning something to our bride?"

"I am," comes a voice from across the room. The sea of bridesmaids parts to reveal an elderly woman with snow white hair sitting in an over-stuffed chair.

"Oh Granny," Libby grins as she makes her way over to the other side.

In her grandmother's hand is a small porcelain box. "Your grandfather gave me these diamond earrings when your mother was born. They're unusual because of the heart shape. They've always been my favorites. I'd love for you to wear them today... but I want them back."

Everyone laughs. "I'd be honored. And I promise to give them back." Libby takes the earrings and carefully secures them onto each ear.

"My turn, my turn," comes a tiny voice. "I have something blue." Kennedy, Libby's flower girl, steps forward.

Libby carefully stoops down. "What do you have?"

At five years old, Kennedy is ecstatic to be in a wedding, wearing a long dress and hanging out with the "big" girls. "Well I told Mommy you didn't need anything blue cause your eyes are blue. But she said they don't count! So, we got you this glass blue bird to put into your bouquet." Kennedy hands her a blown-glass blue bird about two inches in size.

Libby takes the bird. "Gosh, that's so pretty. I'll put it in the very center of my bouquet."

"Will Chase see it there? Cause he has pretty blue eyes too?"

"I'll make sure he does." Libby stands.

"Okay, you have something old, something new, something borrowed and something blue," Sarah announces.

"And I have the sixpence for your shoe," I add holding up the sixpence I had in my shoe when Wynn and I were married.

Libby beams. "Thank you. I feel so blessed to be marrying your son." She hugs me and takes the sixpence. "I don't think I've ever seen one of these."

"It might be more comfortable if you put it underneath the liner in your shoe," I suggest.

Sarah bends down to pick up Libby's right shoe which is in the corner of the room. "Good idea. I'll just peel back this lining and..."

"What's the matter?" Libby asks her mom.

"There's already a coin in here. It's one of those state quarters. It looks like the state of Illinois...2003. Well that is odd. I'll just remove it and replace it with the sixpence."

"No! Leave the quarter in there." My voice sounds funny and I feel like I can't breathe. Everyone is looking at me.

I can almost smell the chlorine in Loos Natatorium. And I can definitely still see the somber expressions of Brock and Chase at the All-Star swim meet that took place the month after my dad died. Brock had refused to go to the meet at first because his granddad wouldn't be there. Chase, at nine years old, didn't quite feel his grandfather's death as heavily as his thirteen-year-old brother and it had been Chase who had convinced his older brother to go and swim his best. They both won several gold medals that day, but were in tears after the meet. Wynn had herded them to the car while my sister and I collected their towels and duffel bag. When I pulled up the last towel from the bleacher where we had been sitting, two, shiny new quarters were underneath. "Are these yours?" I asked my sister, Melissa.

"Uh, no." She picked them up and looked at them. "Hey, how 'bout that! They're Illinois quarters! Don't the boys collect these?"

Illinois was where my sister, parents, and I were born and raised. Our dad had started the boys' collections of the fifty state quarters. As soon as a new one came out, he gave one to each of them.

My sister handed them to me. "What a coincidence!"

I don't believe in coincidences, but I carefully put them in the small, side zippered pocket of the bag. The next morning, I remembered the quarters and hoping they hadn't gotten lost, unzipped the pouch and removed *three* quarters...all the same circa 2003. They were brand new.

"Margo, are you okay? You look as white as a sheet." Sarah interrupted my thoughts, her hand on my shoulder.

"Um, yes. I'm fine. Libby, please keep that quarter in your shoe. It means something to Chase."

Libby frowns, puzzled and tilts her head. "Oh, did he put it in my shoe?"

I shake my head and thankfully, before I can respond with an explanation, the wedding planner sergeant appears announcing that the ceremony is about to begin.

CHAPTER THREE

The wedding went off without a hitch, unless you count the flower girl tugging on Libby's train and announcing in a loud voice, that she wanted to marry Chase, a hitch. Everyone laughed as Haley, the maid of honor, gently pulled Kennedy back and whispered something in her ear.

The following day, the Andrews held a lovely brunch in their gorgeous backyard. The newlyweds made a brief appearance before heading to the airport. And now it's Monday morning and I'm making my "To-Do" list. The wedding festivities have concluded, but some of the chores that go along with it remain. I need to return the groomsmen's tuxes and the unopened bottles of wine from the reception. Chase asked me to mail several boxes to their new home in California and there's something else I need to do, but at the moment I can't think of what it is so I head to our bathroom to brush my teeth and put on some lipstick. Grabbing my toothbrush, I spy the purple, crushed velour case that holds my grandmother's engagement ring. That's what

I couldn't remember! I want to return it to our safe deposit box. Before I forget, I grab a pink sticky note and write, "To my oldest granddaughter on her 25th birthday. May you cherish this ring that belonged to your great-great grandmother as much as I do. Love, Margo." I stick the note on the bottom of the case and place it in my purse.

I finish getting dressed and brush my teeth and put on some lipstick. As I head to the garage, I note that Wynn is in his usual spot: three feet in front of our TV set watching the recording of last night's hockey playoff game. I know from years of experience that he won't hear me if I tell him I'm heading out so I approach him and tell him face-to-face that I'm leaving to make the returns.

"Oh, okay. Just put the tuxes in my car. I'll take care of returning them. And let me take the wine bottles back too. I don't want you lifting those." He kisses me on the cheek and turns his attention back to our TV.

"Thanks. I'm going to the safe deposit box. Do you need anything out of it?'

He shakes his head. "No. I'm good."

I realize that's more reaction than I thought I would get from him, so I head to my car.

Fortunately, the bank where we have our safe deposit box is only a few blocks from our home. Ruby, the customer service representative, has me sign the log to verify my identity and then lets me into the vault. She takes my key, inserts hers and swings open the door pulling out our large, rectangular box. It's a little heavy and I am happy for her help in placing it on the table in the vault. She leaves and I flip up the latch opening the lid. I reach into my purse and grab the case holding my grandmother's ring. Several documents inside our box have shifted and I need to move them to the other end in order to find room for the purple container. As I place some of the contents to the side, a yellowed document folded in thirds slips out of an envelope marked, "Margaret's Service." I don't recall ever having seen this before.

Carefully, I unfold the sheets of typing paper which are held together in the upper left corner by a very small slit in the paper which has been folded, a predecessor to a paper clip. My hand begins to shake as I realize this is the transcript of my grandmother's funeral. It's quite lengthy, too long to read while I'm in the vault, so I gently place it in my purse. I replace the other documents and snuggle in the ring case next to them before securing the latch and lifting the safe deposit box into its slot, turning my key to secure it.

Shipping Chase's items can wait, I want to read this document. I return home to an empty house. Wynn must have left to do his chores. Before opening the envelope holding the service transcript, I replace the safe deposit key in my bedstand drawer. I'm always afraid I'll forget and leave it in my purse or pocket and won't be able to find it.

As I sit down at our kitchen table, her funeral service in my hand, I remember my great aunt telling me that my grandfather had been unable to attend his wife's funeral because he was still in the hospital with broken bones from the accident. She even showed me a professional portrait with the casket open in the background and huge floral sprays lining both sides of the funeral home walls. I take a deep breath and begin to read.

Funeral Service of
Margaret Bennett Stearns
March 19, 1934
Organ Prelude: Handel's "Largo"
Two stanzas of "Abide with Me"
Readings by the Minister
A Soprano Solo: "My Jesus, As Thou Wilt"
The Funeral Address: The Reverend Henry Northwood

On November 13, 1906, the home of Mr. and Mrs. Clark Bennett was made happy by the arrival of a baby girl, to whom the proud parents gave the name of "Margaret Bennett." This girl grew up in the city of St. Louis, and very early showed qualities of unusual leadership. She started into school. Her talents seemed to burst forth anew in unusual attractiveness during her career in the Cleveland High School where she was the recipient of repeated high honors. Margaret, very naturally, wanted to continue her studies in some university but counseling parents and friends persuaded her that a practical business training would be better at that time. With characteristic enthusiasm, she threw herself into the studies prescribed by the local business college that she attended and completed her course far in advance of the normal schedule and then secured a position with the Board of Education.

Friends of hers told her about the University of Illinois. How grateful we are to those friends! In the second semester after her matriculation, she was received into the Kappa Delta Sorority, which association proved to be one of the precious treasures of her life. Her outstanding record in the University is well-known to those who gather here today.

She was selected for "Mortar Board" in her junior year. She was a member of "Torch", Alpha Lambda Delta Freshman honorary, Beta Gamma Sigma business honorary, and Phi Chi Theta business fraternity where she served as secretary and treasurer. Other honors were hers. She served on the staff of the "Illini", Woman's Editor of the "Enterpriser", General Chairman of the "Mother's Day" festivities in 1931. She served also in the Panhellenic Council and the Woman's League.

The dean of the business school says of Margaret: "In my work of eleven years at the University of Illinois, as Dean of Women, there is no young woman whom I would place ahead of Margaret Bennett Stearns, in her fine influence among the younger women of the University, in her scholarship and in her fine campus responsibility."

We are told that in ancient times, great caravans bearing sweet spices would travel across the deserts from one country to another. But even days afterward, other travelers noted that a sweet fragrance still remained marking the fact that the caravan had travelled that way. Margaret Stearns' life is like that, and in her going from us, fellow-travelers are conscious of the redolent perfume of a gracious and unselfish life that still abides.

On December 19, 1931, Margaret Bennett was married to Ike Stearns. In his personality, there are the qualities of an upright, clean, industrious, genteel, modest, devoted partner. We would pause in this service, today, and recognize our respect and love for him. To this union, fifteen months ago, a baby boy came to bless the home.

As I contemplate the tragedy we face today, with a mind and a heart as stunned as yours, I realize how feeble our words are to meet adequately the needs of this and other hours of grief and sorrow.

My mind goes back to an incident in the New Testament where the Master of Men, Jesus Christ, was meeting in an upper room in Jerusalem with some of his friends. He told these friends that he was to leave them soon and as they broke bread, confusion and sorrow captured their hearts. They could not understand why someone so needed and so young should be taken from them. They asked him questions from their anguished hearts to which, in one particular, he gave this strange reply: "What I do thoust knowest not now." The phrase "Thoust knowest not now" clings in my thought as a sort of text that we might apply to our own need in this hour. We do not "know now." We face a great mystery. But even as those friends of the Master, years ago, did not fully understand the fact that to them was a great tragedy, so we facing our trial, may take the same words as applying to our situation. We do not "know now."

Despite this fact, there are certain things that were imperative to those in sorrow. Even though they did not understand, there were certain things that they needed to realize.

They must not quit! The work that their Friend had stated and had carried on so valiantly must be continued. The work was far from complete. They simply must not quit now even though their leader and friend had gone on ahead. We, too, feel as we contemplate the interests and the influences of this good young woman that we must not quit but that we, too, must carry on in some of the fine idealisms that were hers. This we simply must do!

There is another thing that we must do that comes from that New Testament story. These friends of Jesus, confused as they were, had need to realize that there were certain resources available for them. The resources of faith in a good God who was working with them even in the hours of struggle, trial and confusion. It is so easy to forget our resources of spiritual faith. May this hour recall to us the fact that there is a power working with us whose comradeship and help may be appropriated for this hour. May we lean hard on faith in God today.

My heart joins with yours in the desire to extend a hand of friendship to all the stricken hearts of the families involved in this tragedy...to the parents, the brothers, the sisters, the loving husband and little boy.

Tribute by Dean of Women, University of Illinois
Benediction, Reverend Northwood
Organ Postlude

What an amazing woman! What a tragedy! I can only imagine the grief Margaret's parents and husband felt. My sweet, kind grandfather lived through the unfathomable loss of his young wife, leaving him to parent their fifteen-month-old son, my dad. Granddad could have chosen to become bitter after that experience. Yet, a kinder man, I have never met. I can attest to every adjective mentioned about Ike in that service. I'm sure the words used to describe my grandmother were just as accurate. I'm so thankful this document of her funeral service survived so that I could know her in some way.

I hear our garage door open, signaling Wynn's return. I carefully replace the papers back in their original envelope and put them in my bedstand next to the safe deposit box key.

CHAPTER FOUR

I can't believe it's been almost two weeks since Chase and Libby's beautiful wedding. They enjoyed their honeymoon in Hawaii, came back for a few days and are now making the long trek to LA to start their married life together.

In my right hand I am clutching a small bouquet of gerbera daisies and in my left a bottle of water. I put them both down on my father's grave while I lift the metal urn that is attached to his headstone. "You should see how happy they are, Daddy," I say out loud as I pour the water into the vessel and remove the flowers from their plastic wrapping. "But then I'm sure you saw them...how did you get the quarter in Libby's shoe?" I stand. "I wonder if she ever thought to show it to Chase." I let out a huge sigh. "And why am I talking to you here? I've never believed your spirit is in that casket. Well, just for the record, happy Father's Day."

I gather the empty water bottle and florist paper and walk the few steps to my car. It's a beautiful day, not too hot, and I think about opening the sunroof on my Lexus and then remember I need to stop at the nearby mall to look at swimsuits.

In less than five minutes, I am pulling into a place in the parking garage outside of Dillard's at NorthPark Mall in Dallas. I quickly make my way up the escalators to the second floor where the swimsuit department is located. It's my lucky day! They have the suit I want in the color and correct size. I can avoid trying on a new style.

The clerk hands me my bag and receipt and I descend back down the escalator to the ground floor. I step off and turn left, then left again, making my way through the men's department. And as habit has formed over the years, I look at the paisley sports shirts noting how much my dad would have liked them. As I pass the men's fragrance counter, I get a whiff of the cologne my father used to wear. Briefly, I stop at the counter, scanning the brightly colored bottles hoping to identify the brand he wore. I loved that scent. It smelled like musk and cedar and was slightly spicy. Dad never applied too much, just enough to provide a hint if you were next to him. Would it be wrong for me to buy it for Wynn? Since I can't find a bottle that looks familiar, I continue past the men's dress shirts towards the parking garage.

"Do you think I could get away with wearing that one under a black sports coat?"

My heart stops at the sound of his voice and I squeeze my eyes shut. I shake my head to clear it. That cemetery visit had not been a good idea.

"No? You're probably right. Too casual," the familiar voice seems a little louder this time.

"What about this one, sir?" the male clerk asks.

I take a deep breath and head in the direction of the conversation I'm overhearing. As I approach the middle of the shirt section I spot two eyes staring back at me, the pair of chocolate brown eyes in the kind face belonging to my dad.

He tilts his head and his bushy white eyebrows push together in a frown. "Are you all right, Hon?"

I glance quickly to my right, then left to see if anyone else would see me if I start talking to a figment of my imagination. Just that term, "figment of my imagination," I learned from my father when I'd wake from a bad dream, certain the boogie man was hiding in my closet. Now the very man who comforted me had become a "figment of my imagination." I swallow hard, not sure if I can even speak. The clerk must have stepped away. "Daddy?"

"Yes?"

"What are you doing here?" Still no one around.

"Trying to find a new shirt to go with my one remaining sports coat so I can take you to dinner."

I stare hard at the figment. I squeeze my eyes shut again and open them. He's still here looking just like he did about three years before he died: full head of wavy white hair, parted on the left side, broad forehead, wire framed glasses, large shiny nose, thin upper lip curled upward into the smile that always made me feel safe. "I'm sorry, Daddy. I didn't know we had a dinner date." Fine. I could play this game with my imagination. I could even hear my dad telling me as a child that I had a vivid imagination...like it was a bad thing. And right now, he would be correct. This is a bad thing. Wynn would be calling the men in the little white coats *if* I tell him, which of course I won't! But maybe, just maybe, I can enjoy some bonus time with my dead father.

"Well, I just thought since Wynn is out of town and you're not teaching your water aerobics class...which by the way you're really good at. Those women really love you. Anyway, I digress, I thought you'd have time to go to dinner with me. But if you have other plans..."

I look again to see if the clerk may be approaching, but no one seems to be around. "Of course not. I mean, I'd love to go to dinner with you. But..."

"But what?"

I drop my voice. "You're dead. You've been dead for ..." *Am I really talking out loud to a dead man?*

"Can I ring those up for you, sir? Or are you still looking?" asks the male clerk who appears out of nowhere.

"Well, what do you think, Margo?"

Maybe I should call the men in the little white coats. Save some time. "The blue shirt." Oh shit. Had I conjured up a dead sales clerk too? This was rapidly getting out of control. Rather than react, I opt to watch this play out. How would a dead man pay for something?

"The blue one it is then," Dad answered handing the shirt to the clerk and following him to the register.

I quickly follow, not wanting to lose sight of him...half expecting him to go "poof!"

"Will this be all for you today?" the clerk asks.

"I think that will do it," Dad confirms.

"And would you like this on your Dillard's card?" Aha! This is where my figment will implode.

"Uh, no. I don't have a Dillard's card." *Of course you don't, you're dead!* Dad reaches into his back pocket and pulls out a wallet, the same wallet I remember him carrying. "Do you take American Express?" he asks, extracting his gold card.

"Why of course, sir." The clerk takes the card and swipes it, puts the yellow sticker on the price tag for return purposes and neatly folds the shirt in some tissue paper and places it in the gray plastic bag, identical to the one I am carrying. "Would you like your receipt with you or in the bag?"

"In the bag's fine." Dad takes his purchase and turns to me. "I made a reservation for seven o'clock if that works for you."

This is classic Dad. The man who never considered going to dinner without first securing a reservation. "Sure. Where are we going?" I could see out of the corner of my eye that the clerk was watching us. He didn't seem alarmed. But then again, maybe he wasn't real either.

"How does Trader Vic's sound?"

When Dad brought me to Dallas my junior year in high school to tour SMU, we ate dinner at Trader Vic's. It closed shortly after that, then reopened briefly right before Brock had gone to SMU. But now it has been closed for over a decade. And now my figment is going to evaporate!

"Oh, Daddy. That would have been fun, but it's closed."

"Hmm. Well they must have just reopened because they took my reservation."

I'm not sure what to say.

"Just meet me there at seven, Margo," he smiles.

Oh no! He is about to leave me! I'm not ready for this to end. "Wait! Don't go!"

Dad looks confused.

"I mean, can I give you a hug?" This would be the ultimate test. He would disappear as soon as I touch him. Dream over. Forget this ever happened.

"Well of course you can!" Dad steps towards me and wraps his arms around me. I put my head on his warm chest and breathe in. Same aftershave, same oily skin scent. I pull back expecting him to be gone, but he is smiling down at me. "Now I know you want to go home and change. I'll see you at seven at Trader Vic's."

"You're sure, Dad? You're sure you'll be there? This isn't the last time I get to see you?"

He chuckles. "I'm sure."

CHAPTER FIVE

The spring of my junior year in high school, Dad and I flew to Dallas so that I could tour Southern Methodist University. We stayed at what was once a Hilton hotel situated catty-corner from campus. Adjacent to the hotel, facing Mockingbird Lane, was Trader Vic's restaurant. Trader Vic's originated in Oakland, California in 1934 and in its heyday had over thirty restaurants world-wide. Dad explained to me on that trip that he and Mom had eaten at the original one in California and suggested we try this one. The unusual Polynesian atmosphere complete with large Tikis just inside the front entrance are still crystal clear in my memory.

Dad and I were seated that night at a corner booth. The lights were dim and candles flickered on every table. Dad ordered a strawberry daiquiri which came in a large, hollowed out coconut with two straws. After the waiter set down the drink in front of Dad and walked away, Dad slid the coconut between us. "What? Dad, I'm too young to drink down here,"

I said realizing he wanted me to try it. Although the drinking age in Texas was lower than in Illinois, I was still a year too young to be considered legal.

"You're in my presence so it's just fine. Go ahead and have some."

I gingerly took a sip, unsure of what to expect. "Hmm...it's good." I smiled. "I don't taste any alcohol."

Dad took a sip. "This is a good one. Uh, say, Mom doesn't need to know about this, okay?"

I nodded, having thought the same thing. "Understood." My father was not afraid of the law in this circumstance, just my mother!

The traffic light at Mockingbird Lane and the service road turns green and I shake my head to concentrate on my driving. After crossing the northbound service road, I make an immediate right turn into the parking lot in front of what used to be Trader Vic's. There's a salon where the once grand Tikis welcomed customers. And my heart sinks when I see no sign of my father outside. My overactive imagination had gotten the better of me. Had I really believed that suddenly the building's exterior would have the Trader Vic's sign and that Dad would be patiently awaiting my arrival? *Good one, Margo! Maybe your next stop should be at your favorite psychotherapist's office. Or better yet, just go directly to the loony bin. What are you going to do now, Miss Smarty Pants? Go into the salon and get a manicure?* But what if I don't go in and Dad's waiting inside for me?

Feeling more than a little foolish, I pull my Lexus into a parking place, press the button to turn off its ignition and open my car door. After I exit the car, I brush my thumb over the door button to lock it. I take a deep breath and turn to head to the salon and there, standing by the salon entrance, is a quite dapperly dressed man, my dad!

"Well hello there," he greets me. "You're right on time." He's acting as if we are going into the salon.

I reach up and kiss him on the cheek, not only because I love him but mainly because I need to verify, he's real. Inhaling deeply, I again smell his familiar aftershave. "Um, Dad, this is a salon, not a restaurant."

He looks up at the sign and shrugs. "Let's go in and see. After you," he waves me in the doorway while holding the door.

I put my foot across the threshold and find myself looking at the two Tikis that greeted thousands of Trader Vic's customers throughout the years.

"Guess that sign outside was old," Dad says giving me a wink.

"Ah, Mr. Stearns, so good to see you again. Please. Follow me," the maître 'd greets us. I was only aware of the one time that Dad had eaten here. Surely, they wouldn't remember him thirty plus years later. *Wait, Margo! Look around! Maybe we're the only ones here because this place DOES NOT EXIST anymore!* But there are other customers here…at the bar and at the tables. In fact, it is crowded. Where had they parked? Were they staying at the hotel?

"Is this okay?" the maître 'd asks pointing to a corner booth, the corner booth we sat in all those years ago.

"Perfect," my dad grins.

I slide into the booth, determined to enjoy every minute of this fantasy. In fact, I am probably dreaming. Dad scoots in next to me. The maître 'd unfurls the napkins and places them in our laps. "Your waiter will be with you shortly."

Dad, who is wearing the blue shirt he purchased at Dillard's underneath his black sports coat, turns and looks at me. "I hope traffic getting back down here wasn't too bad."

I had been so lost in thought, I hadn't even noticed. "It was fine."

"Good, good! What are we drinking tonight? Maybe share a strawberry daiquiri with me? Or would you prefer one of your own?"

So, he remembered too! "Sharing one is fine. I have to drive home after this." I look up and the waiter is already setting down a hollowed-out coconut with two straws in front of us. We haven't even ordered!

"Always such great service here," Dad announces. All I can do is nod. He takes a sip and then motions for me to do the same. Hesitating, I put my lips on the straw, expecting it to evaporate. But it doesn't and the icy drink tastes good on my tongue. I know I dream in color, but I've never tasted anything in my dreams. Maybe there won't be any calories?

Noticing that I am unusually quiet, Dad puts his hand on my shoulder. "This must be very strange to you, Hon."

I look around at the people sitting at the table next to ours. Can they see us? Are they ghosts? And does Dad mean it's strange to be eating at a restaurant that hasn't been open in years? Or that I'm dining with my dead father?

I turn to look him in the eyes, those beautiful milk-chocolate eyes I grew up with. "Strange doesn't begin to describe this,

Daddy." My voice is barely a whisper. "The last time I was here was when Brock was a junior in high school. In fact, we sat at this very table. Trader Vic's had just reopened. Friends of ours were investors. I was hoping they'd stay open, but after a few years, they had to shut their doors. This isn't real. It can't be. We are eating in a restaurant that doesn't exist."

Dad tilts his head and grins. "If I pinch you, would you believe it's real?"

My face must be white. "It was you, wasn't it? You pinched Brock that night when he and I were eating here."

My son and I had just toasted my dad with our drinks when Brock had audibly yelped. "Ouch!" he had turned behind him to see what might have caused the sensation in his upper arm, but only the wall was there. He had turned back to me and several minutes later, it happened again. "What the…?"

"It must be your granddad," I had suggested. "He wants us to know he's with us." I hadn't really believed it until now.

Dad laughs. "I didn't mean to pinch him hard. I just wanted you to know I was here."

"But we couldn't see you."

His eyes soften. "No, but you can now. And that's what matters."

"Who else can see you?"

"Well, everyone that I want to see me can. Certainly, everyone in this restaurant." He is very matter-of-fact.

"If Brock or Chase or Melissa were here, could they see you?"

Dad shifts. He looks uncomfortable. "Well, that's a good question and not an easy one to answer. For now, the short answer is no. No, they can't see me. But they're not here. You are. And you've been looking for me, haven't you?"

The logical side of my brain kicks in. "You mean they can't see you because they haven't been looking for you?"

"It's not exactly that simple. And I know you're not going to like it when I tell you that you don't have the ability right now to comprehend the complete answer."

"I can try."

"In due time, Hon. I know you must have a ton of questions for me. You trust me, right?"

"I always have."

"Then for tonight, let's just enjoy being together in this fabulous restaurant of yore."

And until the main course arrived, we chatted as if he were still alive. But in the back of my mind, I knew we didn't have tomorrow as we had taken for granted so many years ago. This was my chance to ask the numerous questions I had since his death.

The waiter places our dinner in front of us and asks Dad to cut into his filet to make sure it is cooked to his specifications. It is and the waiter leaves.

"How are your prawns?" Dad asks.

"Delicious."

"I thought about having the Mahi Mahi, but as you know from our trip to Hawaii, Mahi is excellent only if it's fresh. And since the ocean isn't too close to Dallas, I thought I'd stick with beef. It's been years since I've had a good steak."

Like since he was alive? Or do they eat in Heaven? I decide to begin my interrogation. "So, Dad, have you been able to see what's been happening on Earth since you…died?"

He finishes cutting his next bite of steak and pauses. "Well, the short answer…if there is such a thing…is yes and no." He pops the next piece of steak into his mouth and smiles.

"Could you elaborate on that less than crystal clear answer?"

"In terms that you can understand, let's say I have the best seat in the house for family events."

"So, you were at Chase's wedding?"

Dad smiles. "Of course. And I think you knew that. By the way, that was some rehearsal dinner you and Wynn put on. Very creative. Brock's wedding was so joy-filled. I loved being there too."

I am elated to the point of feeling like I'm about to burst. All of those significant family events that I told myself Dad was with us, he really was! "And you were the one who put that Illinois state quarter in Libby's shoe!"

Dad actually laughs. "That was a good one, wasn't it? I'm glad I got to see the expression on your face. It was my way of letting you know I was there. I wonder if Chase got to see it later."

"I forgot to ask him when they were in town after their honeymoon. But neither boy has ever forgotten about the state quarters you left after their big swim meet. If Chase saw it, I'm sure he's put it somewhere safe."

"That was a big meet for them…the first one I'd missed. I was deeply worried that Brock wouldn't even swim that day. And look how well he did. Chase too, had an incredible meet. I was literally on cloud nine that day!"

"I don't suppose you'd be willing to share how you actually got those quarters underneath our towels or the one in Libby's shoe?"

Dad tilts his head. "Not tonight." He takes his napkin and wipes the corner of his mouth. "I will tell you that I am pleased with both boys' choices in wives. Their weddings were spectacular. Almost as spectacular as yours."

"Oh, Daddy, that was a beautiful day. Do you remember what I told you right before you walked me down the aisle?"

He reaches over and pats my arm. "That I'd always be your hero."

Before the tear that is threatening to sneak out the corner of my eye can make its way to my cheek, the waiter appears to clear our plates. "Did we leave room for dessert this evening?"

"Of course, we did. Banana fritters with the vanilla ice cream sound good to you?" Dad asks me.

"My favorite."

"Great. Make that two and two cups of coffee, please."

My dad always ate dessert. For some reason the calories never found their way to him like they do to me. But I don't want this evening to end. I wish there were an infinite number of courses coming!

The desserts and coffee arrived and I realized I hadn't even begun to scratch the surface with my questions. "As a follow-up to my question about what you can see here on Earth, aren't you sad you can't be with us physically?"

"No. And Margo, you really need to start living in the moment! How's your dessert?"

His unexpected, abrupt response seemed to instantly melt the ice cream I'd just put in my mouth. "I don't understand. Don't you miss us? Didn't you want to participate in the wedding festivities, for example?"

"But I did…just in a different way than you understand."

I thoughtfully worked on finishing my dessert and coffee.

Dad put down his spoon. "Time and loss are viewed very differently in Heaven. When you have an infinite number of days to live, the years you spend on Earth seem like just a moment. The losses you feel can seem insurmountable. It's one of the cruelest things on Earth that can happen…someone you love is taken from you. You've only seen a fraction of your life, the time you've spent here. Until you experience that other side, you can't totally understand anything. Remember when you were frustrated when Brock and Chase seemed so misguided as young adults?"

I nod. "Yes. They thought they had graduated from college and knew everything and they really knew…"

"Nothing. That's right. And neither do you…know everything that is. And what was your answer to that dilemma?"

"That they needed to trust Wynn and me. We've been around a lot longer than they have. Why aren't we their trusted advisors so they don't have to learn things the hard way?"

The waiter silently places the bill next to Dad who pulls his American Express Gold Card out of his weathered wallet and places it on the tray. He crosses his arms and looks me in the eye. "Maybe it's time to take your own advice."

Although he says it in a kind and loving way, I'm taken aback. I admittedly don't know everything, but I think after fifty-four years of life, I've learned a thing or two...and one of those was to trust my father implicitly.

"You're right...as usual."

Dad slides out of the booth and I begin to panic. I have more questions I need him to answer and more things I want to say. I follow him to the front door which he holds open for me and I step into the parking lot, immediately turning to make sure he's behind me. He is.

We walk over to my Lexus. "Nice wheels," Dad comments as he holds my door open for me.

I nod. "Yes, it drives so smoothly on the Dallas streets. That's why I continue to lease this brand."

"Mind if I ride home with you so I can check it out?"

Oh, thank God, the evening isn't over. "Of course. I'd love for you to! Um, would you like to drive?" (My dad almost always drove whenever we were together and he loved cars. In fact, one of our last discussions before he died was about which car I was going to get when my lease ran out.)

"I'm afraid my license expired some time ago," he answers raising his eyebrows as if I should have figured that out.

"Right," is all I can think to say as we get in the car.

CHAPTER SIX

I accelerate as I enter Central Expressway and carefully merge into the oncoming traffic. When I am safely in the lane I prefer, I glance over to the passenger seat. Dad's still there. Good! This dream isn't over yet.

"Nice ride," he comments, "I'm not surprised you like the feel of the suspension. Although this is a sports car, it rides like a luxury sedan."

He knows me too well. "Wynn keeps reminding me that it is a sports car. With all the potholes in the roads, especially in Dallas, I will probably stay with a Lexus vehicle when this lease is up."

"It's got a lot of get-up-and-go and it seems to handle nicely. I assume Wynn runs it through the car wash once a week?"

Dad not only loved cars, but also loved *clean* cars. Almost every Saturday morning when I was young, we would head to the doughnut store which happened to be located next to a car wash...the kind where you got out and watched the car go through the process from the inside of the building. "Maybe more like once every two weeks, Dad. He's not quite as persnickety as you were...are."

"I'm still persnickety. Just because I've...moved on...doesn't mean I've lost my personality."

"What does it mean? 'Moving on' as you call it?"

"Well, I really don't have time to truly answer your question. It's quite complicated and yet exceedingly simple."

"Uh oh. This sounds like your answer to my math homework questions."

Dad chuckles. "I've never thought about it that way. And you ask a very good question, one that I've never had to answer."

"Because you haven't had a conversation with anyone here on Earth?"

"Correct. I have not."

"So, am I the first person who's been able to see you?"

"I think your exit is coming up," he replies. I'm so involved in questioning my dad that I'd almost missed the turnoff. I ease the car into the right lane to exit the freeway. We are less than ten minutes from my home.

"You didn't answer my question."

"And it's another good one. You always did ask good questions, Hon."

"Part of *my* personality that will not change." I glance over and see the grin spread across his face.

"If you mean as I am appearing to you now, then the answer is no. I have not appeared to anyone else this way."

"How else would you...appear?" I turn on my indicator and make a right turn into my neighborhood.

"Let me answer your question with a question. Have you ever seen something that reminded you of me? Or that you thought could be me?"

Can he read my mind? How does he know? *Maybe this is because you've concocted him in your brain and you're telling yourself this story!* "There have been several times over the years that I've seen a bird and thought it might be you," I grudgingly reply.

"Like the seagull in Naples who flew in and sat on the side of the pool when only you were in it?"

It was him!! I nod. "Yes, for example."

"Then I appeared to you. You even talked to me as I recall."

Yes, I did. I make the last right turn onto my street and slow as I approach my driveway. "Yes, I did talk to you."

"And what made you think that seagull was me?"

"You didn't leave. Most birds would have flown away as soon as I said something. You tilted your head and just watched me. We spent a lot of time together in that pool swimming laps and playing with the boys when they were young. Maybe I just needed to feel your presence." I press the button on my rearview mirror to open the garage door.

"Yes, we did spend a lot of time in that pool. You felt my presence because I was able to briefly come to you as that bird, something you were familiar with. Birds are a good tool to use. But very few of those I left behind have even thought that way."

I pull into the driveway and put the car in park. "Very few? I'm not the only one?" *Good, maybe I'm not crazy.*

"You're not the only one."

I wait for him to give me the short list of names, but I am only met with silence. "I take it you're not going to tell me who else thinks they've seen you as a bird or some other entity?"

"Would you want me to tell them that you've seen me?"

I stop to ponder this. On one hand, I'd feel relieved that I could talk to someone else about a common thought: that we'd seen Dad as a bird on an occasion or two. But on the other hand, it might make me look like I have a screw loose. And most important, it might make those other few not feel the special feeling that Dad had chosen to appear only to them. "I see your point."

"I will tell you that you wouldn't be surprised who they are. You can probably figure it out."

I am pulling into the garage. It's easier to maneuver my car because Wynn's is not there since he is out of town. I am so busy thinking about how to ask my dead father to spend the night that I forget to respond to what he just said. I turn off the car and open my door, turning to him as I do. "Would you like to come in? You are welcome to stay as long as you like or maybe I should say as long as you can." That sounds so much better than begging him not to leave.

Dad opens his door. "You don't think I'm going to let you go into an empty house alone at night, do you?" He almost sounds offended.

"Of course not, Daddy. I just...I'm just not sure what all of the rules are for this visit from Heaven."

I get out and walk over to his side of the car to enter my house. He stands aside so that I can go in and turn off the alarm. I punch the button to close the garage door and go inside, quickly tapping in my alarm code on the panel. I turn around and he's gone.

"Dad? Daddy? Please come back. I didn't even thank you for dinner. Am I going to get to see you again?" But I am only answered by the hum of our refrigerator and the ticking of the mantle clock. I yank open the door into the garage. The door is down and it's dark inside. "Dad?" I call hopefully. Nothing, not a sound.

I walk through our downstairs flicking on light switches as I go. Everything's as I left it a few hours earlier. I wish I hadn't eaten all of my meal. That way I'd have a to-go bag with Trader Vic's logo to prove I'd actually dined there. But I have nothing... no proof of the dinner date with my deceased father. I race back to the garage and open the passenger door to my car, unsure of what scrap of evidence I might find. There was no valet, ergo no valet ticket. Nothing. As I go to shut the door, something shiny on the floor near the running board catches my eye. I stoop to pick it up and catch a whiff of my dad's aftershave. The shiny item is an Illinois state quarter.

I reenter my house, locking the door behind me. My throat tightens. My chest aches and I cannot hold back the tears. It's like I've lost him all over again. Or have I? Was this evening merely a figment of my imagination? Maybe I will wake up in a few minutes from this wonderful dream turned nightmare.

At this very moment my cell phone rings. I run to my purse and retrieve it. It's Wynn. "Hi," I answer doing my best not to sound as if I've been crying.

"Hi, Gorgeous. How did your evening go?"

What do I say? Great! I had dinner with Dad. "It was fine." Hoping that by keeping my responses short will help me hide the emotion in my voice.

But Wynn can hear it. "What's wrong? You sound like you're upset."

I can't tell him even though I desperately want to. He'd probably believe me...but what if he didn't? "I just got done watching *Father of the Bride*. You know how that gets to me." It's only a little white lie.

Wynn laughs. "Yes, it does. You shouldn't watch sad movies when I'm not there to hold you. What did you have for dinner?"

Oh great. Now I'll have to lie again. "I just ran out and picked up some Chinese food. What about you?" Ok, fairly close to the truth. I'm definitely getting better at this.

"Mike and I finished the setup at the clinic and then he dragged me to a barbeque place. It wasn't half bad!"

Mike is one of Wynn's co-workers. "He dragged you? Really? You expect me to believe that you had to be taken against your will to a barbeque place?"

Wynn laughs. "Not buying that, huh? Well Mike said it's where he likes to eat when he's in town so I just wanted to make him happy. At least I didn't eat any of their rolls."

"So that you could have apple cobbler ala mode for dessert." I don't even make it a question. I am sure that's what Wynn did.

"It was peach, and of course, you are right. You know me well. What's your schedule tomorrow?"

"I'm teaching water aerobics and having lunch with Melissa."

"Great! Because we got so much done at this account today, I'll be able to be home tomorrow night in time to throw something on the grill for dinner. How does that sound?"

It sounds like something normal. Just what the doctor ordered. "That's perfect. I love you, Wynn."

"Sleep well, Sweetheart."

Maybe that's all I need: a good night's sleep.

CHAPTER SEVEN

The alarm on my clock radio is blaring. Startled, I sit up in bed and then reach over to turn it off. It's 6:30. My first water aerobics class for the day begins in an hour. Picking up my cell phone off the night stand, I check the weather radar as I do every morning to make sure no summer storms have cropped up overnight. All is clear, a normal day.

Normal. I nod, trying to convince myself that last night's dinner with my dead father was a dream. Do I feel relieved that I am not crazy after all? Or do I feel sad that I won't be having any more "visits" with Dad? Hmm…I guess a little of both.

I head to the kitchen and make some coffee. Looking around, I see everything is in order, although I still can't remember what I ate for dinner last night. The dream seems to have overpowered my memory. Just the smell of the brewing coffee is enough to make me more alert.

Have my dreams ever included eating with dead people? I interrupt the drip of the coffee to pour a little into one of my favorite mugs that Brock gave me. The dream just felt so real, so authentic, the kind that leaves you with a feeling, not just an image. And that dream left me with a sense of calm and joy.

I sip the hot coffee and freeze. The last "scene" of my dream had me finding an Illinois state quarter in my car! Just to prove that it was a dream, I look at the island in my kitchen where I usually put my purse. No quarter. I go out to my car and open the passenger door…no quarter. I make a loop around my family room…no quarter.

Glancing at the clock perched on the mantle, I realize I need to get my swimsuit on and I head back to the bathroom. Making one final sweeping glance of the bathroom counters, I note there is no coin. Relief washes over me. It was just a dream. Maybe if I'm lucky, I'll get to dream it again soon.

July mornings in Texas tend to be warm and somewhat humid and today is no exception. As I approach the entrance to our neighborhood pool, I notice several of my class members are already waiting outside the locked gate. We've arrived before the lifeguard.

I took my first water aerobics class while on vacation in Hawaii when I was pregnant with Chase. Having competed in swimming as a child, I loved the water and the instructor reignited that passion. It was several years later that a friend of mine invited me to join a class at our country club. At first, I had declined. Why would I pay to do water aerobics when I was perfectly happy doing my own workouts in my pool? Reluctantly, I agreed. My fellow classmates were so much fun and I quickly realized this was something far more than just a workout. This was about camaraderie and friendships.

Halfway through that summer our instructor, Darcy, pulled me aside after class. "Margo, I need to tell you something, but I am going to ask you not to share it with anyone just yet."

Darcy was a woman in her late twenties who had been an age group coach for several years for our country club swim team. She was loved by swimmers and parents and always had a positive outlook on life. But now she looked concerned.

"Sure. Your secret's safe with me," I replied.

"Good. My husband has accepted a job on the East Coast and we are moving in a few weeks."

"Oh no! Are you going with him right away?"

"Well, that's what I want to talk to you about. The only thing keeping me here is this class. I feel I committed to teach it and need to see it through. Unless..."

I looked at her, confused. "Unless?"

"Unless you'd consider taking it over for me."

"I'd love to...that is if it's okay with the Club, but I don't have any certification."

Darcy smiled, visibly relieved. "The only certification I have is one I got at the Park District. The Club didn't require it. I just wanted some extra training. I'm sure they'll approve you. Would you be able to start in a week or so?"

My smile could easily have served as my answer. "Of course."

I finished out that summer for Darcy and have been teaching there and at our neighborhood pool every summer since. The class members in both places have given me far more joy than I could ever give back to them, but I try.

"Good morning, ladies," I say as I unlock the gate to the pool. I'm always amazed that there are this many women willing to roll out of bed and get in the water first thing in the morning.

"Morning, Margo," they chime. Each and every one of these fabulous ladies has a smile on her face. As I stand on the pool deck waiting for the clock to tick to seven- thirty, I think back to several summers ago when we were going through some issues with my mom. These women comprise a priceless pool of advice and support...neither could I have done without that summer.

Forty-five minutes later, class is over and I am heading to my car to drive to my second class at our country club. When I arrive in the parking lot, there are quite a few cars. Swim practice has started in the main pool. Several young swimmers run past me, their goggles swinging in one hand and towel in the other. My class is in the smaller, adults only pool. I walk down the steps to the adult pool and set out our water weights and noodles. Hearing the happy chatter from the main pool deck above me, I reflect fondly on the fun-filled days when Brock and Chase were swimmers on the team. Those days passed too quickly and soon Brock was the head coach with Chase working for him as an age group coach. I had been afraid that Chase wouldn't like working for his brother, but he did.

It's not long before my first class member comes down the steps.

"Good morning, Norma," I greet her.

"Good morning, Margo," she replies as she places her towel and purse on one of the chaises. "How are you this morning?"

"I'm great! And you?

"Well, I'm moving a little slow, but I'm happy to be here."

Norma is almost always the first member to arrive and the first one in the pool, no matter how "refreshing" the water temperature may be. She always has a smile on her face... always. And over the years she has had several health challenges, both herself and with family members. But she's smiled through them all. She is also the oldest member in our class... she's in her early eighties and she is admired by every woman, young and old.

For several minutes, it's just Norma and me in the deep end of the pool waiting for the others to arrive. "Where is everybody this morning?" she asks.

"I'm sure they'll be here." Unlike my neighborhood class, this one typically arrives late...almost as if the start time is just a suggestion.

"Ah, there's Fran and Dorothy now," Norma points out.

About fifteen minutes into class, I instruct everyone to grab their noodles and automatically, I look towards the steps. Sure enough, Joanne is making her way down the stairs. "Hi everyone!" she calls. "Sorry I'm late, but the phone rang just as I was heading out the door."

We all love Joanne. Her exuberant and caring personality is infectious even if she habitually is our last arriving class member. I always think she should have been an actress; she's great at making an entrance.

When class is over, I put away the weights and noodles and head to my car. I am meeting my sister for lunch at one of our favorite places so I need to get home and showered. I carefully place my towel on my car seat since I am still wet and get in. Almost, as if on cue, my phone rings. It's Wynn.

"Good morning, Gorgeous. How did your classes go? Did you sleep well?"

"Good morning, Handsome. Both classes were well attended. And I slept fairly well but had wild dreams. How about you?'

"Eh, you know I don't sleep particularly well on the road, especially when you are not there next to me. I'll be glad when your classes are over for the summer so you can join me again."

"Me too. I missed you last night."

"How wild were your dreams? Anything I need to know about?" he says suggestively.

"Not wild in that kind of way."

"Oh, too bad. Well, anyway, I should be home late afternoon."

"Yay! I'm having lunch with Melissa at noon. Have a safe trip back."

"Have a nice lunch. Love you."

"Love you too." I disconnect the call from my steering wheel. On the drive back home, I debate on whether or not to tell Melissa about my "wild" dream.

• • •

Melissa and I do not live far from each other. However, we do live in different suburbs and our children went to different school districts. We shop at different grocery stores and as close as we are, geographically, we really don't have a chance to see each other very often...or not as often as I'd like. A few minutes after noon, she pulls up in front of my house. I lock the front door behind me and get into her SUV.

"Hi!" she greets me.

"Hello. How are you doing?"

"I'm fine," she says as she pulls away. "Is Tommy Bahama still okay with you?"

"Sounds great. I love that crab salad."

"As do I!"

It's not uncommon for us to order the same thing at a restaurant without even discussing it in advance. We've done that for years. Melissa is about four years younger than I am. During our childhood, she always wanted to look older. Now she's happy when someone who doesn't know us assumes she's the younger sister.

Fortunately, the restaurant has plenty of ceiling fans in their covered patio section so we are able to eat outside. In another month, it will be too hot and sticky to enjoy their terrace.

We both order iced tea and our salads arrive quickly. "Umm...so good," Melissa says.

I nod. "I have a question to ask you. I hope you won't think it's weird."

She shrugs. "What is it?"

"Have you had any vivid dreams about Dad?"

She tilts her head, contemplating my question as she stabs another bite of salad. "Not in a while. I had a few right after he died, but that's been a long time ago. Why? Have you?"

I take a deep breath. "Yes. Last night, I dreamt I had dinner with him."

Melissa laughs. "Really? Where did you eat?"

"Trader Vic's."

"Isn't that closed?"

I nod. "It has been since before Brock went to SMU."

"That's odd. What did you do yesterday?"

"I put flowers on his grave because I usually do around Father's Day. Then I went to NorthPark to pick up a new swimsuit."

"Well, so that's what got your brain thinking about him. Not sure about Trader Vic's though." Melissa seemed nonplussed by my dream.

"Yeah. That makes sense." It just didn't feel like it made sense.

We have a delightful lunch together, including a stop at the cupcake vending machine across the street from Tommy Bahama. It's such a novel gizmo: order a cupcake on a touch screen, swipe your credit card and voilà, after you raise the lid on the side of the wall, what you ordered magically appears. As I retrieve my cupcake, I hear something hit the sidewalk.

"Oops, it looks like you dropped something," Melissa says.

I look down. Spinning, at the base of my feet is an Illinois quarter.

CHAPTER EIGHT

After waving my sister good-bye, I unlock my front door and realize I am still clutching the Illinois state quarter in my left hand. *It's just a coincidence. Dinner with Dad was just a dream. Get a grip!* But just in case, I decide to head upstairs to Brock's room and see if his Illinois quarter is in the state coin holder my father had given him decades ago. He keeps it on his bookshelf. It's easy to find and as I gently open the trifold holder, I see the coin occupying the slot in the state of Illinois. It's interesting that there are a few states' slots available. Dad must have died before all the coins had been minted.

I need to figure out where to put this extra quarter. It needs to live in a safe place so I can monitor its "travels" and thus insure my sanity. I definitely can't leave it in Brock's room. I'm rarely in it except to change the sheets and towels. Ah! I'll put it in my drawer next to my toothpaste. That way I'll see it several times a day.

As I'm heading downstairs, I hear our garage door go up.

Wynn must be home early. I scoot into our master bathroom and deposit the quarter into my toothpaste drawer. "Hi Wynn!" I call as I head into the kitchen. But instead of Wynn standing there, it's Brock.

"Hi, Mom. Sorry I didn't let you know I was stopping by." He crosses the room and gives me a hug.

"What a nice surprise, Sweetie. What brings you to town?" Brock has a business degree in Sports Management and worked for years in football operations for his alma mater, Oklahoma State. But he finally got frustrated at the lack of career progression and went to work in sales for a California winery. He quickly rose to the top of the organization and became their chief operating officer, but missed Texas and the sports world. Last year, he moved to Tulsa where he started his own liquor distribution company.

"Well, I had an interview this morning."

"Oh, are you expanding your distribution business to Texas?" A mother can only hope her children will move back… not home, but nearby.

"Is Dad home?"

"No, he should be any minute," I answer glancing at the clock. At that very moment, Wynn walks in through the door to the garage.

"Well, hello, Son!" he greets Brock with a hug. "What brings you here?" Wynn walks over and gives me a kiss.

"He was just about to answer that question for me."

Brock takes a deep breath. "I had an interview this morning and lunch with the Rangers' organization."

Wynn smiles and nods. "They'd be a great organization to sell liquor to."

"No, Dad. The interview was for a position in baseball operations...Director of Baseball Operations to be exact!"

"What?" Wynn and I chorus at the same time.

"How did you get that interview? I'm guessing it wasn't through LinkedIn," I joke. Wynn is always telling the boys they need to be on LinkedIn to further their careers.

"Not this time. Remember the offensive coordinator who left OSU and went to work at another school?"

"The one who initially helped get you your internship?"

"Yes. Well, his son-in-law works for the Cardinals and has a friend at the Rangers who was looking for a new operations director. He looked me up and saw all of my operations experience at OSU and they gave me a call."

"Wow!" Wynn says. "That's incredible."

"How did the interview go?"

Brock is beaming. "This was the final stage where I met with the big boys, including Jon Daniels. They offered me the job!"

Wynn and I literally jump up and down. "Oh my gosh, that's fantastic!" I say as I hug Brock again. "You've always loved baseball."

When Brock was in high school, he started collecting baseball cards. I remember driving him countless times to the local baseball card shops where he would spend his hard-earned babysitting money to rip open pack after pack of cards, looking for the valuable ones. Sometimes he hit gold, but most of the time he didn't. However, being the entrepreneur that he is,

Brock studied the cards and players and ended up writing a column for *Beckett Baseball Magazine* while still in high school. He admired Jon Daniels then and I had been surprised when Brock had ended up working in football instead.

"That's just tremendous! Is it too soon to ask about tickets?" Wynn kids.

"I'm sure I'll have access to some tickets, Dad."

"When do you start?" I ask.

"Well, that's the interesting part of this. They want me ASAP, but I've got to figure out what I'm going to do with my company."

"Such problems to have, huh?" Wynn says.

"I don't really want to get rid of it. I just need to find someone I can trust to run it."

The three of us are silent for a minute. Then I realize Brock is looking at Wynn and me for a response.

"Do you mean us? Dad's still working and Tulsa isn't exactly around the corner," I say. Surely, he can't expect for us to take over his business.

"I've got great sales people in Oklahoma, but I want to move the operations down here. I was thinking maybe you could help manage the financial side of things, Mom, just until I can hire someone I can trust."

I smile. "Of course. I'd be happy to and I think I know the perfect person to do that for you. She's one of my closest friends."

"Let's celebrate!" Wynn interjects. "Or are you heading back to Tulsa?"

Brock looks at his watch. "Actually, I'm heading to Love Field in a few minutes to pick up Meredith. If you don't mind, we will spend a few days here while she and I are house hunting."

"Perfect. I'll make dinner reservations so we can all celebrate your new job!" says Wynn.

"And your return to Texas," I add.

Brock fills a glass with ice water from our refrigerator and takes a few gulps before setting the glass down at his place on our kitchen table, something he's done since he was in college. "Her flight arrives in about an hour so I'm going to head out. Will we have time to come back here before dinner or should we meet you at the restaurant?"

"Why don't we meet at the restaurant to save some time," Wynn suggests. "I'll text you when I get our reservation."

"Sounds like a plan," Brock says as he heads to his car. The grin has never left his face.

When the door closes, I look at Wynn. "Did that just happen? Did our son who always dreamed of being a GM of the Texas Rangers, just get a job with that organization?"

"I was about to ask you the same thing. Well if we're dreaming, I don't want to wake up!"

I freeze. There's that dream thing again! And I look up wondering if my dad just witnessed Brock's accomplishment. He would have been so proud of his grandson.

CHAPTER NINE

The next month seemed to fly by. Brock and Meredith were kind enough to include me in their house-hunting expedition which was a lot of fun. They found a lovely, large home on a good-sized lot near Southlake. The schools are good and the drive for Brock is only about half an hour. They'll be farther from us than I'd like, but much closer than they are now. They will close and move in the end of September. In the meantime, they are renting a house in the same area.

I've always considered August to be a "transitional" month. Back when the boys were in school, we celebrated the last few days of summer and were busy buying back-to-school clothes and supplies. Since the nest has been empty, August marks the end of my water aerobics classes, usually around Wynn's and my wedding anniversary, which is when we try to take a trip to escape the oppressive Texas heat. Since I always loved going back to school when I was young, August is also the time I get back to my other "career" of writing novels. One thing ends and another begins, which I find helpful and lifting to my spirits.

Wynn and I returned last week from a trip to Napa, one of our favorite places. During our flight out, we tried counting how many times during our marriage we'd been to wine country and finally decided this was our tenth trip. Even after so many visits, we still manage to find wineries we hadn't heard of and the tastings rarely disappoint us. We've gotten to know several winery owners and always return to our favorites.

Ordinarily, I would be resuming the work to market my novels today. But instead, I have one more water aerobics class to teach. One day during the last week of classes earlier this month, an unexpected storm blew in and I had to cancel the Thursday late afternoon class at the country club. So I promised the ladies we would have one more class after I got back from our trip.

I'm heading to the club now, hoping that everyone read their reminder email. It's Tuesday, which means the club will be closed and it will be nice and quiet. I pull into the lot and see several cars that are parked closer to the tennis courts. The courts are open every day. There are no cars parked near the pool. I'm the first to arrive.

I unlock the gate and begin the process of taking the water weights and noodles from the storage closet down to the adult pool. When I finish putting them out by the side, I check my waterproof watch. I still have five minutes before class officially starts so I head back up to the main pool deck to see if Chase's name is still on the swim team record board.

Scanning the board, I see Chase's name several times. A few of his records have been broken in the five years since he swam.

His next to last season, he made it his mission to break every single one of his brother's records while Brock was a coach. It was the one and only time when Brock cheered for his brother to beat his records. Ever since, the boys still dispute who the better swimmer was…an argument I expect they will still have long after I am gone!

I turn and look out at the peaceful main pool where so many meets took place, so many friends were made both for the boys and for Wynn and me and where so many fond, fun memories will always be. I can almost hear the beep of the bull horn to start a race, the splash of the water and the instant cheering of the spectators. The pool deck during those meets was literally covered with towels and swimmers. For about five years, my friend Martha and I headed the volunteers. Our swim team had almost two hundred members and the meets lasted around four hours. We had timers, hospitality, ready bench and ribbon volunteers. I can almost smell the hamburgers and French fries cooking at the snack bar on the far side of the pool.

Lost in my reverie, I realize the time has gotten away from me. Ten minutes have gone by. I race to the top of the stairs to the adult pool and peer down…no one is there. Hmm… maybe no one is coming? But I'll wait another five or ten minutes before I give up on the last class of this season.

"Looks like I may be your only student this evening," a voice from behind startles me.

I whip around to see my dad in his swimsuit with his terry cloth, short sleeved cover-up and a towel. "Dad! What are you doing here?" What will happen if someone does show up? Will they see him too?

He smiles, his chocolate brown eyes crinkle at the corners. "Well I was hoping to take your class. It sure has been a while since I've been on this pool deck. Boy, did I love watching Brock and Chase race! It was almost as exciting as watching you. Almost..."

I'm instantly transported to my last race. I was seeded second in my best stroke, backstroke. Dad was about to start his shift as a timer when he found me in the bull pen, the place where swimmers stayed until their events. Dad, wearing his official white shorts and a white shirt, came up to me and squatted down, his Cronus stopwatch was dangling from its chain around his neck. He gave me his stern, but loving look. "You know what you've got to do."

I was so nervous that all I could do was nod.

Dad nodded back. "Go get 'em, Tiger!" And he walked away.

I won that last race. But I can honestly say that watching my boys win their races was far more gratifying, although, I never would have imagined that at that time.

As if reading my mind, Dad interjected, "You were very determined to beat that girl that day. I'm so glad you got to experience the feeling of watching your sons strive towards and reach their goals. It must have been odd though to watch Chase break Brock's records. But I thought you handled it well."

I chuckle. "That was definitely tougher than winning my last race. I was cheering for Chase, but feeling bad for Brock. But as Wynn and I always told the boys: records are meant to be broken. Chase was VERY determined to break Brock's records."

Dad smiles. "I wonder who he got that determination from."

"Hmm…me?" I turn away from Dad to see if any of my class members have shown up and see no one. "Looks like a private class for you this evening, Dad." This would be a good test. Can a ghost swim?

But when I turn around, Dad's gone. I run back to the stairs to the adult pool deck, but he's not there either. I yank open the door to the men's room and call for him, but it's empty. I'm staring once again at the record boards. Seeing Dad was just a daydream. I return to the adult pool to put away the noodles and water weights, hoping he'll pop up. But once again, I am alone.

After safely stowing the equipment in the closet next to the guard hut, I head back to my car. *I'm not seeing things, am I? Why do I keep seeing Dad? Shoot! I didn't get to ask him any of my questions. I better keep that list with me…and I better make an appointment to see a therapist…soon!*

As I battle rush hour traffic to return home, I waver back and forth between convincing myself I really did see my father and thinking it was just my "vivid" imagination. I am, after all, wide-awake. Soon I'll be pulling in to our garage and Wynn will be there and everything will be okay.

After parking my car in its spot next to Wynn's, I head inside.

Wynn is watching a baseball game. As usual, he is standing about four feet away from our sixty-five-inch TV. His back is to me so he hasn't acknowledged my return. More than likely, he hasn't even heard the door open. Wynn's all-consuming focus on almost all sports irritates me. There are only two sports he doesn't follow: professional basketball and soccer. "Hi, Sweetheart!" I call to him from the kitchen table.

"Hi, Margo," Wynn hurriedly pauses the game and turns to me. "You're done for the season! How many did you have at class tonight?"

That's right. I'd totally forgotten this was my last class. And what's the answer to his question? One person/ghost turned up? "No one showed. That's why I'm home a little early." I look at the clock. But I'm really not that early. I must have talked to Dad longer than I thought.

"That's a shame. Those ladies are so loyal, I'm surprised that at least a few didn't show up."

I shrug and put my bag into our laundry room. "Well, I didn't get to say it to the class, so I'll say to you what I always say at the end of the last class of the season: 'That's a wrap.'"

I wonder when I'll see my dad again, I think to myself.

CHAPTER TEN

The night Dad appeared at my water aerobics class, I couldn't sleep. For several days, I was on edge, expecting him to appear at any moment. Wynn kept asking what was bothering me to which I always replied, "Oh, nothing." But after three decades of marriage, he knew something was up.

Since I can't confide in my husband, or sister or friends, I made an appointment with my valued therapist, Dr. Pope. It's been almost fifteen years since I've seen him, but his waiting room hasn't changed. I flick on the switch under his name and take a seat in one of the upholstered green chairs. Today I'm the only one waiting.

Promptly at two o'clock, Dr. Pope enters the room. "Margo, it's wonderful seeing you again. Come on back."

I smile and follow him. Dr. Pope's office is spacious with windows overlooking a park filled with trees. He motions for me to take a seat on the couch opposite his chair. "Tell me, what brings you in today?" He has my file on his lap along with a ruled notepad.

I take a breath. "Well, I think I may be going crazy."

Dr. Pope laughs. "And what makes you think that?"

"Did you ever see the movie, 'The Sixth Sense'?"

"Yes, Bruce Willis starred in that. As I recall, he saw dead people."

I nod.

"You're seeing dead people?"

"Just one."

"Interesting. Who are you seeing?"

"My dad."

Dr. Pope flips through the notes he made in my file. "The last time I saw you, we concluded your grief counseling. You seemed to have gone through the different stages and had accepted your father's death."

"Yes. I had. And I still do. So, I'm not sure why he's appearing to me."

"Tell me a little bit about these appearances. Has there been more than one?"

"There have been three. The first time I saw him he was in Dillard's at NorthPark Mall buying a shirt. I approached him and he invited me to dinner that night."

"Uh huh. And how long ago did this happen?" Dr. Pope is making notes.

"That was in June."

"And did you go to dinner with him?"

"Yes. He wanted to go back to Trader Vic's for dinner. Dad took me there when we came down to look at SMU. I explained to him that, unfortunately, the restaurant was no longer there, but he insisted he'd made a reservation so they had to be open."

Dr. Pope looks perplexed. "What did you do?"

I look steadily into his eyes. "I met Dad there for dinner."

"At a restaurant that doesn't exist…"

"It did. At least for that night. The outside looks like a salon. But as soon as Dad opened the door, it transformed into Trader Vic's, complete with Tikis."

"Did you have dinner?"

I nod. "And drinks."

"And then…"

"He rode home with me. Wynn was out of town. I went inside, disabled the alarm, turned around and Dad was gone."

I pause, afraid of what Dr. Pope will say about all of this. "You said there have been other times?"

"One other time. A few days ago, I went to the pool where I teach water aerobics to hold a make-up class. None of the class members showed up and just as I was about to leave, there was Dad."

My therapist's eyebrows raise. "And did he get in the pool and swim?"

"No. We talked and I went to the other pool deck to see if any of my class members had shown up and he was gone." A minute of silence hangs between us. "Do you think I'm crazy?"

Dr. Pope tilts his head and smiles warmly at me. "Do you?"

"I hope not. But I can't explain any of this. To my knowledge, Jesus is the only who died and reappeared."

"Are you having any difficulties in other areas of your life? Are you able to live your life as you always have?"

"Yes."

"Are you seeing or hearing anything else unusual?"

"No. Just Dad."

"Does he appear to you as he did during the last say...month of his life? Or does he look like you remember he looked when he was healthy?"

"He looks healthy."

"Hmm. What do you two talk about?"

"Heaven, the boys, events from my childhood..."

Dr. Pope takes a deep breath. "I don't think you're crazy, Margo. However, this is a very unusual occurrence, and one that deserves some attention. How's your marriage?"

"It's great! Wynn and I are doing fine."

"Were there any significant events leading up to the first time you saw your father?"

"Chase got married."

"Ah, and how did you feel about that?"

"Oh, I am happy for him. Libby, his wife, is an amazing young woman."

"You said you are happy *for him*. Are *you* happy?"

I start to give my standard answer of yes, but I can't hide the truth from Dr. Pope. "I was a little depressed. The boys don't really need me anymore."

Dr. Pope lowers his head and looks over the top of his glasses at me. "You really think that? It may feel that way now, but in a short amount of time they will need your wisdom and guidance, just as you needed that from your dad."

Oh, now I'm understanding this. "I get it. This is just my mind's way of comforting me."

"You may be reliving in your mind scenes with your dad. It's soothing. But you're not crazy. You just need to enjoy these moments. Look for his message to you. Really listen to what he is saying the next time this happens."

"So, you think this will happen again?"

Once again, he nods. "May or may not. I think that there are probably a few things you need to work out with yourself and this is the tool your mind is choosing to use. It's harmless unless you let it interfere with your daily life. Again, go with this. Relish these episodes with your dad. I think before long they will stop. But not until you are ready to fully let go of him." Dr. Pope looks at his watch. "We're almost out of time today. Would you like to schedule another appointment to check back in?"

"Yes." We schedule a time next month and he walks me to the "exit" door that leads directly to the hallway.

"Take good care, Margo. Call me if you need me."

I leave feeling relieved that I'm not crazy. But I'd still like to know why I ate dinner in a restaurant that no longer exists!

CHAPTER ELEVEN

August slowly merged into September. I miss the ladies in my water aerobics classes. I miss Chase and Libby. And I miss seeing my dad. I did take some time to write down my questions in case he appears again. Maybe just the act of writing them down has prevented him from returning. But at least I'm prepared.

The marketing of my trilogy seems to be going well. I have a few speaking engagements at some local book clubs on my calendar, but the work on my new novel is going slowly. Honestly, I am a bit down in the dumps.

As if on cue, my cell phone rings. I know without looking that it's Chase. His ringtone is his alma mater's fight song. "Hi, Sweetie."

"Hi, Ma," Chase greets me in character as Riff from *West Side Story*. When he was playing Riff his senior year in high school, he decided to use method acting and would come downstairs in a white undershirt, blue jeans rolled up above his ankles and white Converse tennis shoes. "How ya doin'?"

My mood instantly brightens. "I'm doing well. How are you and Libby doing?"

"Libby? Oh, yeah that chick I married. We's doing good."

"You're doing WELL, I think you mean, Riff." I've always been a stickler for using "good" and "well" correctly.

Chase laughs, breaking character. "Libby and I are doing well. The show's keeping me busy. But I love it! I can't wait for you and dad to watch it. And Libby's liking her new job."

"That's great to hear."

"We're thinking of coming home in a few days. The show breaks for Labor Day weekend and Libby is a little homesick. Also, Brock said he might be able to get tickets for all of us to go see the Rangers play the Yankees."

My day is definitely getting better. "That would be awesome. You're welcome to stay here although I understand if you want to stay with Libby's folks."

"We haven't figured that out yet. Brock invited us to stay with them at their rental house, but that's pretty far from you and Libby's parents. Her sister and cousins may be in town too, so we may need to stay at our house."

"I'll put fresh sheets on the bed just in case. As long as we get to see you..."

"Of course, you'll get to see us. I think Brock got tickets for you and Dad too."

"Wow, that sounds fun! We can pick you up at the airport and you can have my car for the weekend."

"Thanks, Mom. You're the best."

"I can't wait to hear all the details of your TV show."

"And I can't wait to give you a big hug. I'll text you our itinerary. I've got to run. They're calling me for the next scene. It was good to hear your voice. Love you!"

"Love you more!" I punch the red circle on my iPhone to disconnect. My conversations with Chase are always lively. He has so much energy and exudes positivity. I am looking forward to seeing both Libby and him.

I hear the garage door go up and Wynn walks in. "Hi, Sweetheart," he says. "It's going to be a good weekend."

I smile and nod. "Yes, it is. Chase and Libby are going to be in town."

"How do you know?"

I tilt my head. "How do *you* know?"

"Brock just texted me that he has tickets for us to the Rangers game on Saturday night and Chase and Libby are joining us."

"I just got off the phone with Chase is how I know." I walk across the kitchen and give Wynn a big hug. "It should be a lot of fun."

Wynn gives me a kiss. "A whole lot of fun since we have box seats!"

"What? Brock could get us into a box this soon in his career there?"

"Impressive, huh? I guess our son is in the big leagues… pun intended. And you'll like this: food and drink come with the box. When do Chase and Libby arrive?"

"I'm not sure yet. He said he'd text me the itinerary. And

I'm not sure if they are staying here or at Libby's house. Will Brock get to sit in the box with us?"

"I'd imagine so. For sure Meredith will be."

"This makes me so happy."

"It's good to see the smile back on your face."

• • •

Last night we picked up Chase and Libby at the airport and brought them back to our house where they are spending the weekend. Fortunately for me, Sarah Andrews already had committed to hosting visiting cousins from out of town and had no available beds for Libby and Chase. When I talked to her yesterday, she said she could "just spit" she was so mad at missing the opportunity to have the newlyweds stay with them. But she is having all of us over for brunch on Sunday.

I'm making chili for lunch today, even though it's still warm outside. Chase requested it along with some homemade pumpkin bread. Brock has too many "game day" responsibilities to join us, but we will pick up Meredith on our way to the game.

"Hmm…that smells delicious," Chase says as he comes up behind me.

"It sure does," adds Libby.

"Why thank you! It needs to simmer a bit longer so let's sit down. I want to hear about your job, Libby, and about the TV show."

Wynn is standing about three feet away from our big screen TV studying the college football game that's on. His back is to us so he doesn't hear us talking.

Chase looks at his dad then back at me. "I see some things never change," he comments. "How long will it be before he starts yelling at the refs?"

"Aww, come on ref. You've got to call that penalty!" Wynn exclaims as if he heard Chase. But I'm sure he didn't.

I look at Chase and Libby. "There's your answer. Not long."

We make our way into the family room and sit down while Wynn remains standing. "Would you like to join us?" I ask him.

He turns, startled. "What? Oh, sure."

"Libby, how do you like living in California?" I ask.

She smiles and responds with her soft, southern voice. "Well, it's been an adjustment. I'm not in Texas anymore, that's for sure. But the weather is beautiful and I absolutely love the people I'm working with."

I sense that Libby is doing her best to look on the bright side of her new life.

"And her co-workers adore her," Chase adds, putting his hand on her leg.

"Tell me about the show," I prompt.

"Yeah, what's it like being in front of the camera? Is it similar to the show we saw being taped at CBS studios when we went to check out the UT Los Angeles program?" Wynn wants to know.

"Well, we don't shoot at that studio, nor do we shoot in front of a live audience. But otherwise, it's similar. Usually on Mondays we have a cold read of the script. The cast sits around a table with the writers who make changes as we go. Then on Tuesdays we block the scenes that are shot in the studio and on Wednesdays we travel to any outdoor sites and actually shoot those scenes. Thursdays and Fridays are for rehearsing and shooting."

"Do you have a trailer?" I ask.

Chase nods. "Oh yes. Sometimes Libby joins me for lunch. That's a cool thing. They feed you almost nonstop it seems. And I wait in my trailer until I'm called for my scenes."

"But not everyone has a trailer, right?" asks Wynn.

"No, Dad, just us stars, the cast members who are shown in the opening every week. There's a lounge area for the extras and one-liners. My trailer's nice. I have a TV and video games and a desk."

"It's really exciting to be on set. I've gotten to watch a few episodes being taped. The crew is really friendly," adds Libby.

"We need to get you and Dad out there while we're still taping."

"That would be so much fun. How much longer will that go on?"

"I think through the beginning of November. Then we will have a hiatus for the holidays and be back at it again the end of January."

"I can't wait." Wynn nods and turns his attention back to the game.

"The chili should be about ready."

"What can I do to help?" Libby asks.

"You can set the table for me if you don't mind." A wise friend of mine told me years ago to always accept the help of a girlfriend/fiancé/wife to make her feel like she's part of the family...and not a guest in our home.

• • •

At five o'clock, we leave for the big game at Globe Life Park in Arlington. To be truthful, it's just a regular season game, one of the last ones before the playoffs begin. But it's the first time Brock's been granted use of one of the team's boxes. He wants us to be there early so he can drop by and say hello. Brock gave us a special parking pass so we can park right next to the stadium. We definitely feel important.

As we pull into the VIP lot, the security guard sees the tag hanging from our rearview mirror and waves us in. Meredith leans forward to tell Wynn that Brock just texted her and he will meet us at our designated gate so he can escort us to the suite.

"This is so exciting. I've always wanted to watch a game from a box. Just make sure you watch what you say about the players," I warn Wynn.

Wynn rolls his eyes. "Now would I do that?"

"Dad, when have you *not* done that at a game?" Chase wants to know.

"Tough crowd," Wynn laments.

We exit the car and head to the gate. Brock is waiting for us. He is beaming.

"Welcome! Can I see your tickets?" he teases. He puts his arm around Meredith. "Follow me."

Brock leads us to a private elevator which carries us to the suites floor. The doors open onto a beautiful mezzanine, complete with floor to ceiling windows overlooking the ballpark.

"This is gorgeous," I say.

"Just wait until you see the box we have!"

The suite Brock ushers us to is amazing. It's large enough to hold fifteen people, with standing room for more. There's a server laying out appetizers on a beautiful granite counter and a bartender across the room ready to pour whatever we would like.

"I'm very impressed, Son," Wynn says. "This is top-notch."

Chase is nodding as he checks out the view from the seats. "Not too shabby, Bro. Nice big screens too."

Brock nods. "The chef will bring by dinner after the game begins. But until then, I ordered some munchies for you. I'd love to stay, but I need to get back to my office. I'll try to swing by during the seventh inning stretch."

"Are there fireworks after the game tonight?" I ask. "And if there are, will you be watching them?" I'm alluding to Brock's dislike for fireworks which most likely began when he was very young and loud noises startled him.

"Of course, and yes, I will."

Meredith smiles, aware of our inside joke. "It's taken some time and effort, but I think I've finally gotten him to at least tolerate a fireworks display."

I've never attended a baseball game that seemed to go so quickly. The food and drinks were amazing and most importantly, the Rangers shut out the Yankees. We all had a blast and Brock was able to join us for the fireworks following the game. As we were exiting the suite, I turned and looked back, hoping to see my dad. But if he was there, I couldn't see him. It was hard to imagine that he had as good of a seat for this event as we did. Maybe Dr. Pope's advice is working.

CHAPTER TWELVE

To most Americans, Labor Day signals the end of summer. Kids return to school. Family vacations are over until the holidays. And life, in general, returns to normal. But in Texas, summer isn't over. In fact, we usually have more 100-degree days ahead of us. And often, summer doesn't breathe its last gasp until well into October.

Now that the holiday weekend is over and Libby and Brock have flown back to LA, it's time for my life to return to normal… whatever that means now. I guess it means I have too much time on my hands. By noon I've finished all the laundry, changed the sheets on our bed and on the guest bed and have gone to the grocery store to replenish our refrigerator and pantry. Wynn is out of his office this afternoon, making some calls locally. I decide to get in our pool and work out.

I grab my towel, water weights and noodle and open the door to our pool deck. The thick air almost knocks me over. Oh yes, summer is very much still present. I plop my towel down on one of our chaises and place my weights and noodle on the coping stones next to the shallow end of our pool and quickly descend down the steps into the cool water. Actually, the water feels cool because the air is so hot. It won't be long before I start sweating! I must remember to work out right after I get up in the morning, while our pool is still in the shade and the air is not so hot.

Years ago, before I ever taught water aerobics classes, I had choreographed my workout to music from the seventies. Surprisingly, my classes didn't really like working out to music because they wanted to talk to each other. Then I got out of the habit of turning my music on when I worked out alone and I have since come to enjoy the sounds of nature along with the peace and quiet. I start my warm up series and have second thoughts about not having my music playing today. After the commotion of the weekend, the silence seems deafening.

As I move into the next cardio series, I realize I'm either too lazy to get out and go inside to turn on some music or too diligent about not interrupting my routine. Still wavering on what to do, I grab my noodle and kneel on it...a great core exercise, I slowly move my arms in a breaststroke motion and head towards the deep end. Once I reach the deeper water, I stand on my noodle, one foot behind the other as if I am slalom water skiing.

"Are you water skiing again?" The voice coming from our diving board startles me so much that I fall off the noodle. It's Dad. He laughs. "I didn't mean to cause you to lose your balance, Hon."

He's wearing the same swimsuit and matching short-sleeved shirt that he wore when I saw him at the country club pool. His legs are dangling from the board and his feet are partly submerged in the water. *Just relish this! Listen to what he has to say!* "Kind of reminds me of when you fell off our sunfish sailboat while I was still on it!"

Dad shakes his head at the memory. "You and the boat went a few yards before I could catch up to you. Unfortunately, my prescription sunglasses plunged to the bottom of the lake."

"For a brief moment I panicked. Not because neither of us can't swim, but I wasn't sure how you'd get back in the sunfish without turning it over!"

"Yes, that was not easy. Nor, I imagine, did I look particularly graceful doing so."

Now it's my turn to laugh. "At least Mom didn't see it happen or she would have been dialing 911."

"True. But I did have to tell her what happened to my sunglasses."

"And after that you always wore them attached to an elastic band."

"I tried to learn from my mishaps."

"Care to join me in the pool? You can use my noodle."

He smiles. "Maybe in a bit. It sure is nice to have a pool in your backyard, isn't it?"

His reference to his refusal to put one in our yard in Illinois isn't lost on me. "Why yes, it is! I had to get married to have one since my father wouldn't give me one."

Dad quietly slips into the pool without making a splash. I

realize I'm holding my breath, afraid that he might disintegrate in the chlorine water. He swims his version of breaststroke, heading to our shallow end. I am instantly transported to my days as a young child when I would hang on to his shoulders, riding on his back for a "piggy back" ride.

"Touché, dear," his voice snaps me back to the moment. "By the way, I enjoyed the ballgame the other night."

So, he was there. "I was hoping you got to see that. And I was also hoping you might make an appearance."

"It was Brock's night. I didn't want to take any attention away from him."

My list of questions for him pop into my mind. "I have a ton of questions for you, Dad. Would you mind answering a few for me?" I am now sitting on my noodle, totally unaware of the water temperature. Dad is now perched on the shelf we have in the deep end, which is hidden from the door out to the pool.

"Sure. What do you want to know?"

"What's Heaven like?"

"Well, that's a good question, a question that may be best answered by describing what it's not. It's not somewhere 'up there' as so many believe. There definitely is a sky-like aspect to it, though. Heaven is magnificent...that's the best word in our vocabulary to describe it. And each soul's view of Heaven is different."

"You mean I could be standing right next to you in Heaven and would see something other than what you see?"

Dad nods. "Exactly. I know that seems a bit confusing, but it's accurate. Remember when you and Wynn went to Bora Bora?

And you saw colors in the ocean you'd never seen before?"

Oh my gosh, he was with us? "Yes, the blues were so intense. They were almost indescribable."

"Yes. That's right. For example, Heaven is filled with many souls whom you love and who love you. Just as you can't 'see' love, I can't give you an accurate description of the feeling of being surrounded by souls whose love is radiating toward you. Dying is not something to fear."

"Did it hurt…when you died?"

Dad takes a deep breath. "Not one bit."

"But you stopped breathing. That has to hurt. Your lungs would be burning before you could pass out."

"Remember, I was in a coma. Your grandfather appeared to me and extended his hand and I took it. There was no pain… at least for me. Do you recall the chaplain telling you the only people in pain in that hospital room were you and your mom and sister?"

I nod, afraid that I'm going to start crying thinking about that awful day.

"He was correct. Now I have a question for you."

"What could that possibly be?"

"Why are you so depressed? I've never seen you this lost."

"It's just that…the boys are grown. They have wives who've replaced me…"

Dad holds up his hand. "Stop right there, young lady. No one and I mean no one has replaced you. You know that."

"It feels like they have. The boys don't need me."

"You fill a very important role in their lives now. You are a trusted advisor. They know they can rely on you to give them strength when they need to be strong for their wives and down the road for their families."

"I guess. It's just that I spent so many years baking cookies for them, taking them to swim practice, watching their plays, listening to their dreams."

"Well, okay. You don't need to take them to swim practice anymore. You're still going to watch Chase film his TV show, right?"

"Yes," I grudgingly answer.

"And you still bake cookies for them?"

"Yes, but I feel silly doing it."

"Don't. I'd love some of your cookies and I know they do too. And most importantly, you still listen to their dreams."

I nod. "Okay, you've made your point."

"You just aren't a daily participant anymore. And that means you did your job raising them. But you're not done. They still need your wise counsel. Now you have time to pursue your dreams...like that book you're trying to write."

I take a deep breath and look at the man who always knew how to make me feel better. At that moment the door from our house swings open.

CHAPTER THIRTEEN

Wynn steps out onto the deck. "Hi, Margo! How was your morning? I tried texting you to see if you wanted to meet me for lunch, but when you didn't answer, I figured you were in the pool."

Frantically, I look at the shelf, afraid Wynn will see Dad. But Dad is gone. Damn! I wasn't ready for our discussion to end. Why did my husband have to interrupt us? I put on my fake smile and exit the pool, glancing back one more time just to make sure Dad isn't hiding somewhere.

"Did you lose something?" Wynn wants to know.

Just my mind. "No, just wanted to make sure I didn't leave my noodle in the pool."

Wynn laughs. "It's right here on the side." He points to the pool deck just above where dad had been sitting. "I'm going to go in and tape the Orioles game. Maybe we can grab some lunch after you change."

I nod, fake smile still on my face. "It will just take me a minute." Wynn has already gone back inside to his spot: four feet from the TV.

• • •

My mind keeps wandering back to my conversation with Dad by the pool a few days ago. As I carefully apply my makeup in preparation for my speaking engagement with a book club at lunchtime today, part of me wishes that Wynn hadn't come home so soon so that I would have had more time with my father to listen, as Dr. Pope suggested, to his wisdom. After all, I still have quite a list of questions that he needs to answer. But there is another part of me that wishes that Wynn would have seen him too…that way I could verify that I am not crazy, that my father isn't just a figment of my imagination.

Without my "vivid imagination," I would not be talking to this book club today because I wouldn't have written a book. I also like working logic puzzles which makes me feel balanced…a good thing since I'm a Libra. The point I'm trying to make with myself is that my imagination is not conjuring up Dad. If I had the power to do that, why would I have waited until now to begin having in-person conversations with him? To be transparent, I actually have tried to "summon" him, similar to how Elizabeth Montgomery on "Bewitched" used to get her mother or Esmerelda to appear. My nose doesn't wiggle like hers did, but sometimes all she had to do was call their name and "poof" they would appear. I guess I'm not a witch.

I enter my closet and select the outfit my good friend and

volunteer publicist, Pat, suggested I wear today. The navy-blue flowy pants and sleeveless multicolored tunic top are perfect for a hot fall day. I grab a long, navy necklace to finish the artsy look I want to portray to the group. I inspect myself in the mirror and take a quick selfie for final approval by my friend. She quickly texts back the thumbs up sign along with her usual "knock 'em dead, Margo." What would I do without her?

Wynn has already loaded my wheeled carry-on containing my books into the trunk of my car and has offered to go with me to help get it inside, but I assure him it will be no problem. Over the past few years, I have spoken to dozens of groups and have figured out the best way to transport enough copies to sell without looking like I'm moving in! In addition to the carry-on, I keep a box with extra copies in my trunk…just in case I sell out. The club I'm speaking to at lunchtime usually has thirty members attend, a good-sized group.

Fortunately, this book club is meeting at a country club not far from our house. My college roommate and sorority sister, Linda, was elected president this year and had purposely not invited me to speak until now so that she would have the pleasure of introducing me. I have to laugh at that. I'm not famous and most likely never will be. But for some reason, I'm treated as if I am when I speak to groups and that "fame" seems to reflect onto whoever invited me to come speak. I feel a bit of added pressure today to make sure that Linda looks like a winner in front of her friends.

I pull up a few minutes early under the porte cochere at Royal Oaks Country Club in Dallas. A valet opens my door and kindly lifts my bag of books out of my trunk. While he does that, I grab the rest of my props and the claim tag for my car, then enter through the massive double doors.

"Margo! It's great seeing you!" Linda is waiting in the opulent foyer. She hugs me. "Thank you for agreeing to speak to our club."

Linda hasn't changed much in the over thirty years since we were at SMU. She's still a petite blonde whose hair is now cut stylishly short. Her blue eyes twinkle as much as they did during our college escapades. The forehead wrinkles that seem to accompany most women our age are barely noticeable on Linda, and despite her chic outfit, she still exudes the Midwest charm that makes her so lovable.

"No, thank *you* for inviting me. Your support means more than you'll ever know."

"Aww...of course." She lowers her voice. "And you know I would have done this last year, but I wanted to wait until I was president, you know, to get some of the glory for knowing a published author."

"Okay, that makes me feel like a fraud. I'm no Mary Higgins Clark."

Linda laughs. "Not yet, but maybe someday soon?"

Before I can respond, we are interrupted. "Is this Margo Parker, the author?"

"Why yes, Beth. This is Margo Parker, our speaker today... and my former college roommate. Margo, this is Beth Landry."

I shake her hand. "Nice to meet you, Beth. Thank you for coming today." Linda is beaming.

"I loved your first book so much that I read the other two in a week! I can't wait to ask you some questions."

I can tell by looking at my longtime friend that Beth is not her favorite person, but she has to tolerate her.

"Beth, you'll need to save those questions for after Margo's presentation. Right now, I need to get her to the head table so she can join us for some lunch."

Beth nods and follows us to a private room overlooking the golf course. There are four, round white-clothed tables set for eight each. Beautiful fall flower arrangements grace the center of the tables. Closest to the windows is a rectangular table set for four with a podium perched on top in the center. There are two women already sitting on one side of the podium. Linda introduces them as the vice president and treasurer of the book club. After I exchange pleasantries with them, Linda directs me to my seat on the other side of the podium. She sits down next to me.

I survey the room. All of the seats at the four tables are full and the staff is frantically setting up two additional tables for members who are patiently standing just inside the door. It occurs to me that I have probably not brought enough books.

A server places a tureen of gazpacho in front of me. "Wow! This is a great turnout! And the room is gorgeous."

Linda's eyes sparkle and she sits up a little straighter. "This is the largest group we've had in all the years I've been a member."

"Thanks for all your hard work in getting such a fantastic turnout."

"Well, I did want you to feel special and I did talk you up. But truthfully, they love your books. A few of our core members read the first one last month and the emails started flying about how good it was."

I finish the last spoonful of soup and the server magically appears to replace it with an amazing steak salad. "Again, I wouldn't be here if it weren't for you."

"My former roommate, the celebrity. It's got to be a fun feeling for you, Margo. I feel like a star just sitting next to you."

"Please, you're making me feel silly."

"Just relax and enjoy it."

I have two basic speeches I give to clubs. One is about self-publishing, but my main presentation is on my writing process: how I develop the plot and characters; what and when I want my readers to know and how I market my books. And of course, I always leave time for questions. It's the latter talk I give today.

At the beginning of every presentation, I ask for a show of hand of how many have actually read the book I am there to discuss. As a former CFO, I still enjoy numbers. About fifty percent of book clubs' attendees, on average, have actually read the book. The more serious book clubs average closer to eighty percent and the groups that use the books as a reason to get together and socialize average closer to twenty-five percent. These are my estimates anyway. When I ask for a show of hands today, there are only four women who don't raise their hands. I have taken a quick count of those present and have counted forty-two!

Knowing how many have read the book also colors how much I can give away about the plot and if I need to make any spoiler alerts. With over ninety percent of the members having read the book, I feel no need to worry! However, this must be a pretty serious club and I may have to field some tough questions.

I have two favorite parts to my presentations: finding out what my readers are curious about and encouraging those in the group who may be considering writing their own novel. The first few questions today are typical. Who's my favorite author? How many hours a day do I write? When will my next book be published? After about thirty minutes of answering a wide range of thoughtful questions, Linda stands to end the meeting.

"Wait! I have one more question," says an older woman standing in the back of the room whom I hadn't noticed before.

Linda takes her seat. "I'd be happy to answer it," I say.

"Do you attribute any of your curiousness about people to someone in your past whom you wish you had gotten to know but never had the opportunity to do so?"

This question takes me by surprise. I pause, unsure of what she's really asking. "That's an excellent question," I say, because it's true, but mostly to give myself time to come up with an answer. *Margaret…*

"Margo, are you okay?" I hear Linda whisper.

I look down at her realizing I must look like I've seen a ghost and nod that I'm fine. "Actually, the answer to your question is Margaret, my grandmother who died when my dad was a baby. I've always wondered what she might think of these stories."

The woman in the back of the room smiles. "And maybe about the one you still haven't written?"

"That one as well. Thank you for your question and thank you, Linda, for inviting me to speak here today."

The room erupts with applause as Linda finally takes her place behind the podium. "Thank you, Margo, for a very entertaining afternoon. If any of you would like to purchase autographed copies of any of the books in Margo's trilogy, she'll be up here for a few more minutes."

Within twenty minutes, I run out of books. Linda makes a list and collects money from those who want autographed copies which Linda will have available at their next meeting. It's at this moment I realize I did not get to meet the woman from the back of the room. I look up and she's gone.

CHAPTER FOURTEEN

Linda stands next to me just inside the front doors of the country club while we wait for the valet to pull our cars around. "I'm sorry about that last question you got. I've never seen that woman before. I'm not sure she's even a member of our club."

"No worries. I'm sorry if I seemed a little weirded out by her question. To be honest, I'm still not exactly sure what she was asking."

"Who's Margaret?" Linda asked, her blonde head tilted. "I know you pretty well and I've never heard you talk about her."

"She was my dad's mother. She died when he was little so I never got to know her. He didn't either."

"Oh! That makes sense. I remember you talking about your grandfather and great aunt."

"Yes. And for some reason her name popped into my head when that woman asked the question. I guess it's a good thing it did or I would have had to really think hard to come up with an answer."

My car appears in the circle drive.

"Is that your car?"

I turn to her and give her a hug. "It is. Thank you, Linda, for giving me such a great opportunity today. I've never left a speaking engagement without a few books leftover."

Linda smiles. "And more to be ordered! Thank *you* for making me look like a rock star in front of my peers. Now we all can say we knew you when we see your books made into movies."

"Yeah, keep talking. Maybe someday," I joke.

A staff member opens the double door for me as I pick up my empty carry-on. The valet pops my trunk and gently places it inside. I hand him his tip. "Thank you, Ma'am. Enjoy the rest of your day." I climb into my Lexus and he closes the door. For a quick second, I smell something similar to my dad's cologne. The valet must have been wearing it.

No, not the valet who's wearing it. I look over and Dad is sitting in the passenger seat. "Dad!"

"Nice presentation, Hon. You had those ladies in the palm of your hand. Looks like you should have brought more books." Dad is beaming.

"You were there? I didn't see you." I see another car is almost behind mine. It's probably Linda's and since I don't want to risk her seeing my passenger, I quickly pull through the porte cochere and head toward the exit.

He chuckles. "I've been at all your speaking engagements. Did you really think I would miss one?"

"I didn't know that dead people could just show up anywhere they want to…"

"And they can't. There are…some parameters."

"But I never saw you. Not all, but most of these events have been attended only by women."

"Were there any men there today?"

"No."

He smiles and looks at me without saying a word.

"Wait, the woman who asked me that last question, that was…you?"

"I thought you needed to be tested with a deeper question, one you are not accustomed to."

"But the other women saw you, heard you."

"Yes, I hope so. Otherwise, it would have looked like you were talking to yourself when you replied. I couldn't appear as myself or Linda would have recognized me. Then as Lucy used to say to Ricky, 'we'd have a whole lot of s'plainin' to do.'"

I laugh. "Who were you at some of the other events?"

"Ah, sometimes I was just a fly on the wall. I did think your response to my question today was very interesting."

Margaret. "Her name just popped into my head. I can't even explain why. I haven't thought about her, well, since Chase's wedding when I wore her ring." I didn't want to bring up my finding the transcript of her funeral in our safe deposit box.

"I believe it's your ring now."

"Semantics. Anyway, it's my turn to ask you some of the questions I didn't have a chance to the other day in the pool. I'm sorry Wynn showed up and we were interrupted."

"Fair enough. Shoot."

I slow as the light ahead of me has turned red. And I decide to take the back way home in order to give myself more time with Dad. "Well, since you've said you've been at all my events, how do you spend your days in Heaven?"

"Days are an earthly phenomenon, designed to progress God's teachings amongst his followers. There is no concept of time in Heaven."

"So, there's no day and night?"

"Not at regular intervals, but yes, we still experience lightness and darkness, only in a positive way. I know that sounds kind of cryptic, but you don't yet have the frame of reference in which to understand any other explanation."

"Hmm. Okay. I feel like you're trying to help me with my math homework and giving me the long answer albeit the correct one."

Dad nods, mulling it over. "Yes, that's pretty accurate."

"Then what do you ...do up there? How do you spend your time?"

"Remember, it's not 'up there.' I do all the things I loved here on Earth: boating, eating great food, watching sunsets..."

I take an audible breath and tears instantly fill my eyes. "I think of you every time I watch the sunset in Florida. Are you watching them with me?"

"Of course, I am! They're God's masterpieces, aren't they? Every one is different and magnificent." He puts his hand on my shoulder and I soak up the warmth. "I've also experienced some amazing new things. And before you ask me what those are, I have to say that they are not anything within your comprehension."

The light turns green and I slowly accelerate. "You're making me feel stupid, Daddy. Can't you at least try?"

"Sadly, no. I literally don't have the words to even begin to describe them. Next question."

"Okay, I guess. Here's a simple yes or no question. Did they replay your life for you once you got to Heaven?"

"No."

"That's it? No?"

He holds his palms up. "They don't. What's done is done."

"Now that makes sense. I like that. While I'd love to relive certain days of my life, there are also some I don't need to see again...like the day you died."

"I'm sorry you had to go through that, Hon."

"That leads me to another question. I'm still a little angry with God for taking you. In fact, you can tell him I said that next time you see Him. That was the ultimate 'life's not fair' moment."

Dad laughs. "He's very aware of that, Margo. I don't need to reiterate it with Him."

"Good. He should be. We needed you here. I did. Melissa did. Mom did. Your grandchildren did. Heck, the world needed you here as an example for all to follow. Why in the world did God have to take you when he did? We all were left behind with the impossible task of filling the gaps you left in our lives."

"I'm not sure I can answer that."

"You mean He won't allow you to answer it? Or you don't know? Or I wouldn't be able to comprehend the answer?" I'm starting to sound angry.

"Just because I'm a resident of the Kingdom doesn't mean I know the answers to everything. I have my theories, but I'm not certain."

"Can you at least share your theory?" I'm now driving very slowly, hoping to catch every red light because I'm less than a mile from our house. And I want to know the answer to this question.

"I had fulfilled my purpose on Earth and God needed me for something else. And I'm emphasizing the word 'my.' You and your sister needed me as a father. Your mother needed a husband. My grandchildren needed a grandfather. But all of you had me for a time in that role. God had other plans for me."

I don't say anything.

"I know it's not what you want to hear, Hon. But it's the closest thing to the truth I can share with you...at least today."

I nod, willing the tears not to splash onto my cheeks. "We're almost to my house, Dad. I can just drive around or go to a parking lot so we can talk longer."

The kind smile that I always picture in my mind when I think of my father creeps across his face. "Let's save this discussion for another day. You need to share how your presentation went with Wynn. He's waiting to hear all about it. But I do have one suggestion for you."

"What's that?"

"Consider writing our story as your next novel."

"Interesting. I'm not sure others will be as interested in it as we are, but I can give it a try."

"Oh, and you need to check your phone. You have some important messages." He leans over, kisses me on the cheek and he's gone.

CHAPTER FIFTEEN

My phone! Shit! I always turn off the ringer on my cell before I make a presentation because no matter what steps I take, it always seems to make some kind of noise whether it's an Apple notification or the Ring doorbell chime. Admittedly, I'm technically challenged so it's just easier for me to turn it off. Ordinarily the first thing I do after a speaking engagement is call my volunteer publicist, Pat, and give her an update. But today I was distracted.

As I turn down our street, I glance at the digital clock on my dash. It's almost four o'clock! Wow! Time flies. Wynn's probably tried calling me. Maybe that's the voicemail Dad was referring to. How will I explain getting all the way home without checking my phone? I hope he's not worried about me. Maybe I will luck out and he will still be out calling on customers and has been too busy to contact me.

I pull into our driveway and grab my phone out of the side pocket of my purse and turn it on. The little apple seems to take forever to appear, but when it does my screen is filled with missed call and text notifications. Shit again! I press the garage door opener button on my rearview mirror, hoping that Wynn's car will not occupy its spot in our garage. It's there.

I maneuver my car next to his and shut off the engine. Wynn enters the garage from our house and motions me to pop my trunk so he can remove my carry-on. I press the button and exit my car.

"How did it go, Miss Author? I've been trying to reach you but your phone went directly to voicemail." He smiles and reaches for my bag. "Oh wait! This feels empty?" He shakes it. "Yes, definitely no books in here. I guess you were a success!"

I give him a hug. "Yes, I guess you could say that. And I have orders for another dozen of the complete trilogy!"

"That's my girl!"

"I'm sorry I missed your call. I just now remembered I'd turned my phone off before I spoke and forgot to turn it back on." All true.

We walk inside. "No problem. Um, Chase has been trying to get in touch with you."

I stop in my tracks and look at my phone. There are several missed calls from Chase, a text and a voicemail. "Is he okay? Did something happen?" I was unreachable for close to four hours and in that time my child needed me.

"He's fine, Margo. Let's go sit down."

"If he's fine, why do I need to sit down?"

"Just take a few minutes and go through your messages,"

Wynn says as we plop down on our leather couch. He puts his hand on my leg.

I'm too busy scrolling through messages to notice he's smiling. "I've never had this many missed calls and texts." Chase's text comes after two missed calls and a voicemail. The text reads: "Mom, text me when you're available to talk. It's kind of urgent, but all good." His voicemail says the same thing. "Do you know what he wants?" I ask Wynn.

Wynn shrugs. "Maybe?"

"I'm available now." I text Chase.

Instantly my phone erupts into the University of Texas fight song. I never bothered to change it after he graduated. "Hi, Sweetie! I'm so sorry I wasn't available when you called earlier. I was giving a presentation to Linda's book club down at Royal Oaks Country Club."

"Oh no worries, Mom. Dad let me know you were busy this afternoon. How'd it go?"

So, Wynn does know what Chase is calling about. "It went extremely well. There were over forty women there. I sold all of the books I had and have orders for more."

"That's fabulous. I'm proud of you."

I smile. "Thank you. Now what can I do for you?"

I hear Chase take a deep breath. "I need you to accept the next FaceTime call you get."

"Uh, okay? Would you like to give me a little more information?"

"No, not really. It will be from a number that's not in your phone. I didn't want you to think it was spam and not answer."

"Good thinking. I wouldn't have answered. Do you know when this call will be coming in?"

"Sometime today. Hopefully in the next few hours, but I can't promise that. Do you and Dad have any plans for dinner?"

"We might run out to get something to eat, but we don't have to."

"Okay. I think sticking around where it's quiet might be a good idea."

"Oh my gosh! Did you meet George Clooney and he's agreed to call me?" That would be worth hanging around for!

"Um, no. It's actually way better than that. I've got to run. Talk to you later. Love you, Ma!"

Ma, his Riff term for me. "Love you more."

"Riff" ends the call.

I stare at my phone, waiting for it to ring. "What's this all about?"

Wynn stands up. "You'll find out soon. Now how about a glass of something to celebrate a great afternoon?"

"Sure!" I answer while going through the other texts I missed on my phone. One is from Linda thanking me again and letting me know that several book club members want me to speak to their organizations. They want to get on my calendar soon. Several are from Wynn wanting to know when I'll be home. And the last one is from Brock: "Text me when you have time to talk."

Great! Both boys needed me while I was too busy playing author! I text back: "Am waiting for a FaceTime call. Not sure when it will happen, but don't want it to interrupt our conversation. Can we talk later this evening?"

"Of course. No rush," is his reply.

I get up from my spot on the couch. Wynn is searching our wine fridge. "What sounds good? I'm thinking one of our favorites to celebrate your success at the book club. Brion? Oakville Ranch? Switchback Ridge?" He's calling out names of our favorite Napa Valley wineries. "It's cooling off a little outside. Maybe we can sit by the pool? Maybe you'd rather have some bubbles? Or maybe that Avril Taylor rosé?"

"Surprise me! I'll grab some cheese and crackers and head outside."

"Don't forget to take your phone with you," he replies.

It seems like Wynn is taking a long time to bring out the wine. He must have gotten distracted by a game on TV or needed to return some work emails. Just as I decide to check on him and get a glass of water, my cell rings. It's a FaceTime alert. And as Chase said, it's a number I don't recognize.

"Wynn!" I shout. "It's the call!" He probably can't hear me from inside, but I need to answer before it goes to voicemail. I swipe the screen to answer. "Hello?" I smile waiting for the person calling to appear.

"Hi, Margo?"

Now I know I've gone crazy. The woman facing me looks an awful lot like Samantha Barrett.

"Yes, speaking." Maybe it's just someone Chase has met who looks like her and this is a prank.

"I'm Samantha Barrett. Your son, Chase, gave me your number."

Oh. My. God. Samantha Barrett is at the top of my list of favorite actresses. I take a deep breath. "Ms. Barrett, it's a pleasure meeting you. I have told Chase many times that if he ever got to meet you, he'd better introduce me too! Obviously, I'm a huge fan of yours. Loved you in your last movie." I'm so flustered that at this moment, I can't recall the title.

She laughs her unique laugh. "Well, thank you. You have a wonderful son, as I'm sure you've been told many times. I met him this week because I'm making a guest appearance on his show and he told me all about you."

"Gosh! This is just an honor. Thank you for your kind words about Chase."

"You're welcome. As a mother I know that's the best thing you can hear...a compliment about your child. But hopefully today, I may be able to 'one-up' that for you. Chase shared your trilogy with me. I've read all three of your novels and would like to discuss the possibility of turning them into a TV series."

I am almost speechless. First, I conjure up my dad and now my favorite actress who wants to make my dream come true. There is no question...I'm dreaming. Well, I might as well roll with it. "Of course! I'd love to discuss this with you."

Samantha flashes her movie star smile. "I was hoping you'd say that. Unfortunately, I've still got another week of shooting out here in LA or I'd come home to Texas and we could meet at my house."

Shoot. That would have been fun!

"Instead, and I know this is last minute so if you already have other plans, I understand. I'll send my jet to Love Field and fly you and your husband out here. Is there any chance you could be here this Saturday? I don't want to rush our discussions and I am available this weekend."

It's Wednesday. That gives me tomorrow to figure out what to wear to meet one of my idols and squeeze in my appointment with Dr. Pope. "Of course, I can be there this weekend. Just let me know the details."

"Excellent! I can't wait to meet you! Chase has told me so much about you. And by the way, he will be included in this series."

"As the lead character," I state, rather than ask, risking pushing the envelope. Definitely dreaming...

"I can't think of anyone better for the role, can you?"

I laugh nervously. "Not in a million years, Ms. Barrett."

"Great. We're already on the same page. Chase gave me your email so I'll send you the flight details. Oh, and Margo, please call me Sam."

"Sam. I can't wait. See you soon."

"Bye!"

"Bye!" I press the end circle. I can't believe Wynn missed this.

But of course, he didn't. He somehow snuck around and videoed the whole conversation without me knowing it. "Congratulations, Mrs. Parker. Looks like your dream is about to come true."

"Except this is a dream, right, Wynn? Any moment I'll wake up. I just fell asleep waiting for you to bring me a glass of wine."

Wynn walks to the door. "Be right back." He comes out with a bottle of Dom Perignon in an ice bucket and two champagne flutes. "You're not dreaming, Sweetheart. I have the proof recorded right here on my cell phone. He carefully pops the cork, creating the desired "whisper" which does not allow too many bubbles to escape and pours a glass for each of us.

As if on cue, the Ring doorbell chime on my phone alerts me there is someone at our door. I look at Wynn. "Is this a re-creation of the party you gave me that Halloween when I published my first book? Is the whole neighborhood about to invade our house?"

Wynn frowns. "Unfortunately, I just found out about this a few hours ago. Let me see who it is. It's probably just a delivery."

I patiently wait, mesmerized by the bubbles in my Waterford flute. When Wynn reappears, he is followed by Brock and Meredith. I immediately stand up to give them a hug. "Hi you two! What a pleasant surprise...and perfect timing in helping me celebrate."

"Let's get Chase on the phone," Wynn suggests, "so he can be part of the celebration."

"I've got it, Dad."

Brock FaceTimes Chase and puts him on speaker. "Congratulations, Mrs. Parker! You're part of the big leagues now," he says. "Libby and I can't wait to see you and Dad this weekend."

"Let's raise our glasses and toast Mom's dream coming true!" says Wynn.

"Hear, hear," adds Brock. "To our favorite author!"

I notice that Meredith is videoing the event on her phone. "Thank you, all! I couldn't have done it without you, especially you, Chase."

Chase has tears streaming down his face. "It was our dream, Mom. You did the hard work."

Now I'm crying. "Each one of you contributed to making this day come true for me. Meredith, you can stop videoing. Grab a glass of bubbles!"

My sweet daughter-in-law tilts her head and smiles. "Well, that may not be a good idea."

Brock steps forward. "We have our own news, today. Next March, you'll be grandparents!"

I'm stunned, and judging by the look on Wynn's face, he didn't have any knowledge of this. The day I thought couldn't have gotten any better, just did. "This news is the icing on the cake. Congratulations, you two!" We literally have a group hug with Chase on the phone in the middle of us all.

CHAPTER SIXTEEN

It's Thursday. The driver is picking us up tomorrow morning, which means I need to be packed and ready to go when I go to bed tonight...that is, if I can sleep. As I pull out of our garage, I speed dial Pat using my Bluetooth so my hands are free to drive to consult with her on what I should wear to meet Ms. Barrett... since I have no clue.

Pat picks up after the second ring. "Hey there! How are you doing today?" she greets me.

"You are not going to believe this."

"Believe what?"

"Wynn and I are flying out tomorrow on a private jet to meet Samantha Barrett in LA. She is interested in making my trilogy into a movie or TV series."

"Get out! When did this all happen?"

"Yesterday. She's a guest star on Chase's TV show and he gave her a copy of my book."

"Wait, you said private jet as in *her* private jet?"

"I think so."

"Oh my gosh! That's terrific!"

"Yes, except I have no idea what to wear. I need your help. Should I wear one of the outfits I wear when I speak to a book club?"

"Um...no. That look is a little too fancy. Where are you meeting her?"

"On the set of Chase's TV show. We will watch them tape it tomorrow afternoon. Then Saturday, Chase and I meet with her at her production office in Santa Monica."

"Okay. That's two different looks. Ms. Barrett will most likely be wearing jeans, either blue or white, when you meet her unless she's already in whatever she's wearing on the show which could be anything. So, let's say, she'll be casual. You're flying on a private jet. You want to look chic on the jet, but not overly so when you meet her for the first time. How do you feel about wearing your black jeans on the plane with some kind of short-sleeve blousy print shirt, tucked into the front and not the back and that solid off-white collarless jacket you have that zips up the front?"

I picture the outfit in my mind. "That sounds fine if you think it's okay that I wear denim."

"Well, it's black denim and everyone in California is very casual, right? You could go with white jeans..."

"You know I don't feel confident in my white jeans. Besides it's after Labor Day..."

"Which doesn't matter in California. Women wear white all year long there."

"Okay. And what do I wear to meet her the next day?"

"Again, it's the weekend, it's California and I think she'll be in something comfortable maybe even jeans. But this is an important meeting and I want you to be a little more, not a lot, dressed up. Do you have a stylish pair of black pants you could wear with a print shell and that cobalt blue blazer you have? The one with the angled buttons and the three-quarter length sleeves?"

I'm nodding. "Yes. That's a great idea. I'd feel confident wearing that."

"And that's what's important."

"What would I do without you?"

"Truthfully, I don't know," Pat jokes. "Maybe next time you can arrange for me to go along!"

I laugh as I pull into the parking lot of Dr. Pope's building. "Thank you, tons! I'd love to talk longer, but as you can imagine, I'm on a tight schedule today trying to get everything done." I don't want to share with her that I'm seeing my therapist.

"Have fun! You'll be great. And if you can, send me some pictures of you and Samantha!"

"I will. I'll call you on Monday."

"Can't wait. Bye."

I disconnect the call, turn off my car and enter Dr. Pope's waiting room with five minutes to spare. Today there are two other women occupying seats apart from each other. Two of the other therapist's switches are flipped. I raise Dr. Pope's and take a seat in the corner. As usual, Dr. Pope opens the door to the waiting room on time and ushers me back to his office.

His warm smile and caring eyes always put me at ease. I sit down on the couch. "So, tell me, any more visits with Dad?"

"Yes, two."

"Tell me about them. How did they make you feel?"

"I cherish every moment I have with Dad. Truthfully, I don't want these 'episodes' to end. The first time he showed up at my pool and actually swam with me. Wynn came home earlier than I had expected and as soon as he came out on the pool deck, Dad was gone."

"I see. And the second time?"

"Was the very next day. I made a presentation to a book club and he showed up in my car afterwards. He said he was actually in the room, appearing as an older woman who asked me the most difficult question I've ever been asked."

"Which was?"

"He asked me if I attribute my curiosity to anyone I wish I had known from my past. I'd never really thought about it, but instantly the name Margaret popped into my head. She was my grandmother who died when my father was very young. I told the woman I wonder what Margaret would think of my books."

"And what was this woman's, I mean your dad's, response?"

"Dad admitted that he had morphed into the older woman. At the end of our conversation, he asked me to consider writing our story."

"And what would that be?"

"I'm not sure."

"I'll bet you do. You just need to slow down and think about it." Dr. Pope smiles.

"On another front, I got a call from Samantha Barrett. She is interested in producing my trilogy as either a movie or TV series." The instant that comes out of my mouth, I realize that I must sound delusional. Oh my! Maybe this was all a hallucination. I grab my phone and pull up the email with my itinerary. It's there. Not a hallucination, but I hand it to Dr. Pope anyway.

He reads it. I look at him to verify that he is reading the same email I did. "Wow! Congratulations! Flying out on a private jet to meet with one of my favorite comediennes. You look unsure."

"Is this part of my being crazy? Did I manufacture all of this?"

"First, we have established that you are not crazy. This is a legitimate email. Why is it so hard for you to believe that she would be interested in producing your trilogy?"

I contemplate my answer before speaking. "I've always wanted to be the best in whatever I did in life. I graduated at the top of my classes, won a lot of swimming races, etc. But, since I've gotten married and raised a family, all of my successes were via my boys. And I've never envisioned myself as brushing shoulders with the famous."

Dr. Pope leans forward in his chair and takes my hands. "You need to believe in yourself. Maybe that's why you are seeing your father. He was your cheerleader. You're not going crazy. You are a talented woman who needs to believe in herself. I think once you do, your visits from your father will become less frequent, but clearer in meaning."

On my way home, I firmly expect Dad to appear, reaffirming what Dr. Pope said. But instead, I am alone in the car, knowing it may be the last time for a few days that I will have time to contemplate what's going on in my life.

CHAPTER SEVENTEEN

Wynn and I barely slept last night. The last time we were this excited about an upcoming trip, we were heading "across the pond" to Italy for the first time. Our driver, limo not Uber, is picking us up in about fifteen minutes to take us to the private jet terminal at Love Field. Our suitcase and carry-on are packed. We are ready to go.

"If I'm dreaming all of this, it sure is the longest dream I've ever had," I say to Wynn as we watch out the front windows for our ride. Wynn is busy checking sports scores on his phone. I'm not sure he hears me because it takes a minute for him to respond.

"Well, I've never packed a suitcase and showered in a dream before, nor have we dreamt in tandem." Wynn laughs then reaches over and kisses me on top of the head. "It's real, Sweetheart."

I take a deep breath. "And the part about us becoming grandparents next year? That's real too?"

Wynn nods. "That's what I heard them say."

"Then we need to talk about that." I adopt a serious tone.

Wynn turns to face me. "What about?"

"About what the baby is going to call us."

"Last I knew, babies weren't born talking."

"I know that, silly. But Brock and Meredith will be referring to us in front of our grandchild and I will absolutely not tolerate being called 'Grandma' or even worse 'Granny.'"

"Yeah. You don't look old enough yet for those monikers."

"And I never will, Winston." I only use his birth name when I'm mad at him or want to get his attention.

"Gotcha! I'm not overly fond of 'Grandpa' now that you mention it. Maybe we can discuss it on the flight out."

A black Cadillac Escalade pulls up in front of our house. "This must be Max," I say, double checking the driver's name on the itinerary Sam provided me. Wynn carries the suitcases outside and I set the alarm. Max quickly gets out of the SUV and takes the cases from Wynn.

"Good morning! I'm Max and you must be the Parkers?" Max has short dark hair, is dressed in a black suit complete with starched white shirt and narrow black tie and looks to be about forty-five.

"Yes, that's correct," I say extending my hand. "It's nice to meet you."

"And you as well." He opens the back passenger door for me. Wynn walks around to the other side. "Fortunately, traffic is not too bad this morning," Max adds. "We should arrive at the plane in about thirty minutes." He puts our luggage in the back and slips into his seat behind the steering wheel. "Is the temperature okay in here?"

"Yes, it's fine," I answer.

"How about music? Maybe an up-tempo jazz playlist to get you going this morning?"

Wynn nods. "Sounds perfect."

We ride in relative silence to the airport. I notice the Escalade's windows are tinted and I feel as if Max may have chauffeured several local dignitaries in our area from time to time. I debate about asking him which celebrities he's met and then decide that might make me look like a teenager.

"Have you been a driver long?" Wynn asks. And I'm pretty sure I know what his next question will be.

"I've been doing this for about ten years now," Max replies.

"Who's been your favorite celebrity during that time?" Wynn just can't help himself. I try giving him a warning look like "really, do you have to ask that?" but Wynn doesn't notice. However, Max catches my expression in his rear-view mirror.

"It's okay, Mrs. Parker. I get asked that a lot." Wynn glances over at me, frowning. "Laura Bush was really kind and surprisingly talkative. She wanted to know all about my family. Owen Wilson was a real hoot. He's naturally funny and also super nice."

Wynn keeps up the banter and asks Max about his family while I reread the itinerary. Our plane is scheduled to depart at nine thirty and arrive at the Bob Hope International Airport in Burbank at eleven thirty. A driver will meet us there and take us to the Warner Brothers studio lot where we will have lunch with Chase at noon and then watch the taping of his show this afternoon.

After the show wraps for the day, Chase and Libby will take us to the hotel where we can freshen up before heading to dinner with the two of them. On Saturday afternoon at two o'clock, we have been invited to meet with Ms. Barrett at her production company's office on the CBS Studio lot. Dinner it lists as TBA and we fly out Sunday afternoon at four o'clock.

The one thing I didn't have time to finalize is retaining an entertainment attorney. I surveyed a few of our attorney friends, none of whom specialize in the entertainment field, to see if they could recommend someone trustworthy. As usual, lawyers tend to move at their own pace...slowly...and I am still waiting to hear from them.

Max turns into the Love Field entrance and drives us to the private jet area. There are several lobby terminals associated with different plane rental companies. Max goes past all of these and slows when he reaches a gate with a guard hut. He presses the button for his window and it quietly lowers. "Parker, Margo and Winston," he announces to the security agent while handing him an official looking document.

The official nods. "I'll need to see their IDs, please."

Wynn and I quickly produce our drivers' licenses. The guard peruses them and peers into the back of the vehicle. He nods and waves us through.

I look at Wynn with a grin on my face.

"If either of you would like to use the bathroom facilities

here, I can drop you off at the next terminal area. If you're fine, I'll just take you to the plane."

"I'm fine," I say. Wynn nods. Max drives out to where our plane is parked. He stops the car about twenty yards away from the stairs leading up to the jet's door.

"Looks like they're ready for you," he says. "We are a few minutes early. I'll get your bags and you can head on up the stairway as soon as someone is there to greet you." Wynn tries to hand Max a tip which he refuses. "Thank you, Sir, but I've been taken care of. Enjoy your flight and I'll be here to pick you up Sunday evening."

"Thank you, Max," I smile as he opens my door and helps me out.

Wynn comes around to my side of the car which is closest to the plane. "Wow," he says to me softly. "This is a Gulfstream G 200. Very nice. I did a little research on different private jets. I think you're going to like this, Mrs. Parker."

As we approach the plane, a uniformed man descends down its stairway. "Good morning, Mr. and Mrs. Parker," he says. "I'm Captain Garrison and I'll be your head pilot on your flight to Burbank today." We shake his hand. "Please, feel free to board. Wheels up will be in about ten minutes."

"Thank you," I say as I head up the flight of stairs. I step over the threshold and am greeted by a flight attendant.

"Good morning, Mrs. Parker, Mr. Parker. My name is Bonni and I'll be your flight attendant today. Please sit wherever you'd like."

The outside of the Gulfstream is white with several navy-blue stripes along its body and tail. I'm surprised as I enter the cabin that I don't have to duck. The floor is carpeted and the seats on either side of the aisle are raised a few inches from the aisle floor and are a rich ivory leather. There are two rows of single seats, one on each side of the aisle facing each other with a small table in between. Behind the second row on the left is a sofa which faces the aisle and has room for three passengers. Across from the couch are two rows of two seats each with a table in between. I turn and look at my husband. "Where do you want to sit?"

Wynn shrugs his shoulders. "You pick."

"Feel free to spread out. You're the only ones on the flight," chimes Bonni, a petite blonde with a radiant smile.

"I like to look forward while we takeoff and land. So how about here?" I say to Wynn pointing to the two leather seats next to each other opposite the couch. "And then if we want to play cards later, we can sit across from each other."

I sit down next to the window and Wynn takes his place next to me. He leans over and whispers. "We have this entire plane to ourselves! Wow, wow, wow!"

Bonni approaches us. "Can I get you a glass of champagne, a mimosa, or perhaps a Bloody Mary?"

"A mimosa would be great," I say smiling at her.

"Make that two," adds Wynn.

Bonni makes her way to the front of the jet where the galley is located and pulls out a bottle of Veuve Clicquot and two crystal champagne flutes. She adds a splash of orange juice and brings them back to us along with two white napkins with "SB" in navy script on them. The captain joins the co-captain in the cockpit and Bonni goes up front to close the door.

"I assume you both have flown many times before, but I am required by the FAA to give you the detailed safety monologue." Once she finishes, she checks to make sure we buckled our seatbelts. "Our actual flying time to Burbank is three hours and fifty minutes. I'll be back to serve you brunch when we reach our cruising altitude."

Heavenly aromas waft our way from the galley. Bonni takes a seat in the front row, facing the cockpit as the plane begins the short taxi to the runway.

As the jet gains speed, Wynn leans over and asks me if I've brought a book to give away. Giving books to flight attendants is one of my marketing strategies. We usually fly Southwest Airlines and because Wynn is an "A-List Preferred Member" he boards before I do. When he is able to secure a spot in the exit row, he typically strikes up a conversation with the flight attendant and asks them if they like to read. Then when I get to the seat he's saving for me, I hand them an autographed copy.

"Oh, yes! I almost forgot with all the excitement of flying in this incredible plane. It's in my carry-on." When we reach cruising altitude, Captain Garrison turns off the seatbelt sign and I move to the other side of the table in front of us to retrieve a copy while Bonni is busy preparing our brunch. I take my book back to my seat. "I hate to tell you this, but I'm not sure I'll be able to fly commercially again."

Wynn finishes his mimosa. "Me either. This beats being an A-Lister. I guess you better negotiate this level of travel into your contract."

"Good point." I laugh. "This is all just surreal. If we get there and Sam has changed her mind about making my trilogy into a series, I'll be disappointed, but I've sure enjoyed the ride."

"I don't think she will change her mind. You might not get everything you want in the deal, though. Have you given any thought to a dollar amount?"

I shake my head. "I'm afraid to. You know I've just appreciated so much that anyone outside my circle of friends has read my books...I can't fathom what I might be able to get."

"Just don't forget how much time it took to write and publish all three. And how much time you spend marketing them. Others will be profiting from your ideas."

"That's an excellent point. I'm hoping whoever my attorney is will give me some direction."

Bonni comes down the aisle and covers the table in front of us with a white, linen cloth and two silverware settings rolled into cloth napkins. She quickly returns with warm towels to wash our hands.

"Thank you, Bonni. This is amazing."

"You are most welcome," she replies before heading back to the galley to retrieve our brunch plates. Brunch consists of a delicious egg casserole topped with fresh avocado, fresh fruit salad and an array of rolls and bread. "Would you like another mimosa?"

Wynn nods. "That would be great."

"And I'll bring you some water too."

My seat is so wide that the book I'm giving Bonni is resting next to my leg without touching it. I've forgotten, for the moment, that I've put it there.

She returns with our beverages. "Is that a good book?" she asks, pointing to my novel. "I'm always looking for a good read!"

I beam. "I think it's good...but that's because I wrote it! I always give away a copy to flight attendants. This is for you!" I put down my fork and hand it to her.

"Oh my gosh! Thank you so much! Would you autograph it for me please?"

"Absolutely. How do you spell your name?"

"It's B-o-n-n-i."

"Good thing I asked," I say as I write her name inside the cover page.

"Yes, my mother was very creative with the spelling. Thank you so much, Mrs. Parker. I'll be sure to let my fellow flight attendants know about this."

"It's the first in the trilogy and the rest are available on Amazon, Kindle and Nook."

"I'll read them all! By the way, save room for dessert. It's a salted caramel Bananas Foster and it's delicious."

I look over at Wynn who looks very content. "Yeah, this even beats the service in first class on our way to Rome. Make sure this is part of your contract, Ms. Author."

I roll my eyes. "I'll do my best."

After Bonni removes our plates, she brings us each a huge oval bowl with the as promised, Bananas Foster, sans flame of course. I dip my spoon into one of the three scoops of vanilla ice cream in my dish along with a bite of banana. It's amazing. "This tops any bananas foster I've had in a restaurant."

"I know," Bonni smiles. "I think it's the touch of salt they add to the caramel. Coffee?"

Wynn nods. "Mmm…this is delicious! A cup of coffee would be wonderful. Is it too early for a splash of Bailey's in it?"

"Of course not," Bonni replies.

"Make that two then," I add. "I'll be too full for lunch with Chase."

"Oh, that's right. Well, it's probably a good thing. He eats like a bird. We'll be lucky to get a salad that isn't all weeds."

"Very true. Shall we play cards since we have a table? Or would you rather take a nap on the couch?"

"So many options. Hmm…let's play cards and if there's time before we land, we can snooze on the couch. I can't believe how smooth this ride has been. I thought it might be a little rough since this isn't as heavy as a commercial jet."

"While it's so smooth, I think I'll check out the lavatory," which is something I desperately avoid doing on commercial flights. I slide open the door and a pristine sink and a generous size bathroom greet me. My fear of plane lavatories has just eased.

When I return to my seat, Wynn is standing in the aisle stretching. "Did it meet your incredibly high expectations? Pun intended."

"Yes, it's quite nice."

"Then I'll go take a look."

We barely had much time after our card game to enjoy the couch before I could feel the plane begin its descent. "Good afternoon, Mr. and Mrs. Parker," Captain Garrison announces over the intercom. "As you may have noticed, we have begun our descent into the greater Burbank area. Winds are light out of the west and the temperature is seventy-two degrees. We should be on the ground in about fifteen minutes. I hope you've enjoyed your flight today."

Wynn stays on the couch and I move to his seat next to the window so I can look out. As the plane hovers over the runway, before making contact with the tarmac, I think about how much my life has changed in the past forty-eight hours and I smile.

CHAPTER EIGHTEEN

Within five minutes of landing, Bonni has the door to the jet open and we are making our way down the stairs. A navy limousine is on the tarmac waiting for us. "Have a great stay," Bonni calls after us. "We'll see you Sunday evening. And thanks for the book!"

I turn to wave to her. "You're welcome. Have a good weekend."

The southern California air is perfect. There's almost no humidity and the temperature is delightful. The chauffeur opens the door for me. Our luggage has already been loaded into the trunk. "Mr. and Mrs. Parker? I have been instructed to take you to Warner Brothers studios, lot twenty-six."

"Yes, that sounds right," I say as I unzip my purse to check my itinerary. The Bob Hope International Airport is very close to several of the big studios. We actually landed about ten minutes early and will have a few minutes to spare before we meet up with Chase.

As we approach the studio, our chauffeur slows to check in with the security guard at the main gate. I feel like a movie star;

onlookers heads are turning to see who is inside the tinted windows. It's a good thing they can't see or sadly, they'd be disappointed.

After reviewing our driver's paperwork, the guard raises the mechanical arm and waves us in. We wind our way through several streets with various facades before arriving at lot twenty-six. Our driver exits the limo and opens my door for me. "Ma'am, I have further instructions to take your luggage to your hotel, if that's okay with you."

I look at Wynn to see if he thinks that's okay. "Yes, that's fine," he verifies.

"Very well then. Your son's trailer is the third one down on the right. His name is on its door. Enjoy your afternoon."

"Thank you," I say as we head off to find Chase.

Wynn takes my hand. "Did you ever think when we were watching Chase in all those high school musicals that we'd be looking for him in his own trailer on the lot of Warner Brothers?"

"Yes, I kind of did, actually. He has the talent and the looks and most importantly, the drive to make it here. I do miss hearing him sing, though."

As we pass each trailer, we get closer to the doors of studio twenty-six. The first two trailers are marked with names I don't recognize. The third one I do: Chase Parker! My eyes fill with tears. "Take a picture of this, Wynn, before we knock."

Wynn is having the same reaction I am, but manages to wipe away a tear that is rolling down his cheek before he reaches in his pocket for his phone. He snaps the picture. "Got it!"

I mount the first step up to the door and knock. Chase throws it open. "Ma!!! You made it!" He wraps me in a bear hug and doesn't let go for several seconds. I step aside so he can greet his dad.

"Dad!" he hugs Wynn. "How was the flight?" Chase winks at me. "*I* haven't even flown on a private jet yet."

"Ah, but you have your own trailer! Impressive," Wynn says.

"This is really decked out," I comment, noting a large screen TV, kitchenette, desk, built-in chaise and mini bar. There's also a separate chair next to a counter with a large mirror surrounded by globe lights. Obviously, this is where Chase gets made up. "Do you spend a lot of time in here?"

"Some days more than others. It depends on how many lines I have in the scenes they are rehearsing that day. And don't worry, Mom, I have plenty of lines."

Chase remembers my comments when he was in shows that I felt he should have had more lines and a bigger role. "Good to know. That means I won't have to bother the director."

"So really, how was the private jet? Were there other passengers on it?"

Wynn lets me answer. "Oh, it was just us," I try saying as nonchalantly as I can.

"Sweet! Was it a tiny plane? Six-seater?"

"Try eleven," Wynn adds.

"Wow. Well, we are meeting Libby in about fifteen minutes for lunch with the cast and crew. I have to be back in hair and makeup in an hour."

"You mean they don't do your makeup here in your trailer?" I ask.

Chase shakes his head. "That's just for touch-ups. After

lunch, Libby will give you a brief tour of the set and then will sit with you while we do the run through and then the taping. Rehearsals have been going super well so I think we should finish around four this afternoon. Then Libby and I will drop you at your hotel so you can freshen up before dinner."

"Sounds fabulous. I'm very proud of you, Chase." I give him another hug.

"Thanks, Ma."

We follow Chase inside to a cavernous room where several long tables are set with chairs on each side, some of which are already occupied with people eating. Libby is standing to the left just past the doorway. "Hi, Margo, Wynn," she says as she gives us each a hug. "How was your flight? I can't wait to hear all about it!"

Just then, it seems as if a hush falls over the room. The door behind us opens and Samantha Barrett walks in followed by a group of people, her entourage, I assume. Her hair is pulled into a ponytail and she is wearing jeans with a black shirt tucked in in front, but not in back. She pulls off her sunglasses and sees Chase.

"Hi, Sweet Pea," she says to him. "Did your folks get in?"

Chase motions behind her. "They did and here they are! Mom, Dad, I'd like you to meet Sam."

"Did she say you could call her that?" I say under my breath. "I raised you to be a bit more polite than that. And technically you should introduce us to her."

Sam laughs her heartiest laugh. "Oh my, you must be Margo, Chase's sweet momma." She instantly sweeps me into her arms.

"Your son has better manners than anyone I've ever met, rest assured. You did a fabulous job with him."

Before Wynn can offer her his hand to shake, she hugs him as well. "I have really had a ball working with your son this week. What a charmer."

"That he is," agrees Wynn.

"And I adore his wife as well. You must be so proud of your family. Come on. Follow me and we'll get some food."

She was so classy she didn't even ask us if we liked her private jet. "Thank you for sending your private jet for us," I say to her quietly so the other cast members in the buffet line don't hear. "It was amazing."

"It is pretty nice. My sister just flew back to Austin on it so it was in the area. I hope they fed you."

"Oh, they did," said Wynn. "The dessert was incredible."

Sam smiles, "The Bananas Foster?"

"Yes."

"My favorite. Anyway, the food here is okay. They do a fairly good job considering they have a large group to feed in a short amount of time. Chase and I are in the first scene after lunch so he and I will have to duck out early to get our makeup on."

During lunch we meet several of Chase's costars and crew members. Chase is sitting on one side of me and Libby on the other. "Maybe someday soon you'll be here to watch them shooting the first episode of your book," he whispers in my ear.

"I guess I'll find out tomorrow?" I whisper back.

Chase nods giving me the feeling that he knows more than I think he does.

"Libby, how's your job going? Are you adjusting to LA life?"

"I just love the people I'm working with. But it's been a little tough to adapt to the...shallowness, for lack of a better word, out here. It's all about how you look. By the way, congratulations on your future grandchild."

Sam, who is sitting on the other side of Libby overhears her comment. "What? You're going to be grandparents? That's something to celebrate. Cheers!" she lifts her glass of iced tea.

Wynn is beaming. "Thank you. We are very excited."

"When? And I assume this is via your other daughter-in-law?"

"Yes," I answer. "Meredith is due sometime next March."

"Well then, you and I have a lot to accomplish," Sam says to me. She looks at her phone. "But that discussion will have to wait until tomorrow. Chase, we need to finish up."

Chase nods and pushes back his chair. I look up at him. "Is it still appropriate for me to say 'break a leg?'"

He leans down and kisses the top of my head. "Of course, Ma. It wouldn't be right if you didn't."

"Then break a leg."

Following lunch, Libby gives us a tour. We are allowed to actually walk onto the different sets as long as we don't touch anything. The camera and lighting people are now checking all their gear with stand-ins so we make our way to our seats to watch the show.

"This series is not filmed in front of a live studio audience," Libby explains. "I try to manage my schedule though, so I am out here on Fridays when they shoot most of that week's episode. I especially wanted to be here this week since Ms. Barrett is the guest star. I love her movies, and in real life, she doesn't disappoint."

"Do they have guest stars every week?"

"No, this is the first time. Did Chase tell you her part in the show?"

"Oh gosh, no. I hope it's a comedic role."

"Well, kind of. She plays his mom."

"Well, I can't think of anyone I'd rather have play that role than her!"

More of the crew starts to come onto the set and a woman sits down in the chair marked Director.

"Okay everybody. Quiet on the set. We are rolling film. Take one."

It's amazing how patient everyone has to be while filming a TV show. Several scenes are reworked and rewritten before the director is happy with the how the episode looks. It's a little after four thirty when the director announces "That's a wrap folks!"

Chase walks over to us. "Well, what did you think?"

"You were amazing," I say. "You looked like a real pro."

Sam walks up behind him. "I hope you don't mind me playing his mom."

"Uh no. That's quite an honor."

Sam smiles. "I'll have a car pick you up at your hotel tomorrow around one thirty? Will that give you enough time to spend with Chase and Libby? I was thinking we could meet at my office and then head out for drinks and dinner if that works for you."

"That sounds perfect. I can't wait!"

"Me either," she smiles as she heads out the door.

CHAPTER NINETEEN

We had a fabulous time at dinner last night with Chase and Libby at their favorite seafood restaurant which was within walking distance of their house. In California, distance from one place to another is not measured in miles, as it is in Texas, but in how many minutes it takes to get there. When they looked for somewhere to live prior to their wedding, Chase made a point of finding something that would be in a safe neighborhood, preferably gated, and would be a twenty-minute drive or less from the studio where he would be filming his series. Fortunately, they found a home to rent in Glendale that, in non-rush hour traffic, is only a fifteen-minute drive (or about six miles if you're from Texas.)

I am anxious about my meeting with Sam today and notice I am fiddling with my bracelet while I stand at the window of our hotel room watching the traffic move by below. Since it's Saturday, the cars speed by on the 101.

"What time are the kids picking us up?" Wynn calls from the bathroom.

"They said at noon. Our brunch reservation is at twelve thirty."

Wynn walks over to me. "You're fidgeting again," he points to my wrist then takes me in his arms. "You have nothing to be nervous about."

I turn away from my post at the window and stop playing with my bracelet. "I know. It's just that I'm so close to possibly seeing my dream for my trilogy come true. And it affects Chase too. I know he's wanted to play the lead since he read the first book. And…I've never had to have a serious conversation with a celebrity."

Wynn looks into my eyes. "That's what people may be saying about you some day."

"Oh please! I'd be thrilled just to see 'based on the book by Margo Parker' on the credits," I reply using air quotes to emphasize my point.

"Make sure that gets in the contract. By the way, have you heard from any entertainment agents?"

"Yes, I'm interviewing three of them via Zoom early next week. It's too bad we can't stay longer. Two of the three have offices in Beverly Hills."

"Hmm…I guess it might be a little awkward to ask Ms. Barrett if we could stay an extra day and have the plane fly us back on Monday?"

I nod. "Yeah, I don't think I know her quite well enough to ask that favor. Zoom should be fine. And all three come with glowing recommendations. It makes me a little nervous to enter into any kind of discussion without one of them present."

"Then just keep things general. I'm sure she's not going to expect to be hammering out details with you today."

"True." I look at my watch. "I'll finish getting ready so we can be downstairs in a few minutes."

Brunch is delicious. The produce in California is always amazingly fresh and is often very creatively prepared. I am surprised I have an appetite, but Chase and Libby keep the conversation lively.

After the server clears our dessert plates, Chase pulls out his phone to check his messages. "Ma, you and I will need to leave in a few minutes. Sam texted me and said her driver is on his way to pick us up. Dad, if you don't mind hanging with Libby while we are in the meeting, we can rendezvous for dinner."

Panicked, I look at Wynn. "I thought you were going with me!"

Before he can reply, Chase says, "Ma, you don't need Dad there. I'll be there to hold your hand. You're a big girl, now."

Libby laughs. "You're going to be fine, Margo. And I have a few sight-seeing places to take Wynn. I'll keep him out of trouble for you."

I take a deep breath and smile at my new daughter-in-law. "Thank you. That's what I'm most worried about." Wynn simply rolls his eyes.

"Go on you two. I'll pay the bill and Libby and I will be on our way to our afternoon tour."

"That's fine. I just want to stop in the ladies' room on my way out."

Chase stands up and holds my chair for me. "Good idea. I'll do the same...in the men's room of course, not the ladies' room!"

Libby giggles as we walk away.

As promised, there's a navy-blue stretch limo waiting for us outside the restaurant. Wynn is waiting when I emerge from the bathroom and snaps a quick pic of Chase and me getting inside the car. It's the same car that picked us up at the airport, but a different driver today.

Sam's production company office is located in Santa Monica which today is a half hour drive. Ordinarily I'd be worried we'd get stuck in traffic and be late. But since it's her driver that's in charge, I relax.

"Do you know what she has in mind?" I ask Chase.

"She and I have discussed a couple of options, but honestly, I don't know if she's made a decision on which way she wants to go."

I'm confused. "Do you mean if she wants to buy my trilogy at all?"

Chase laughs. "I'm not sure if she'll opt for producing the entire trilogy right away. She may even bring in some additional investors. I do feel confident that she's going to make you some kind of offer today. Are you ready for that?"

"Of course!" I pause. "And hell no, I'm not ready. Both. I have absolutely no experience in this area so I feel like I'm flying by the seat of my pants. I'd feel a thousand times better if I had an agent or attorney with me."

"Don't worry. Sam is not going to take advantage of you. She may even have some suggestions for an agent and attorney. Representation is an essential part of the biz out here and she knows what the entertainment world is like back home in Texas."

I'm back to fidgeting with my bracelet. "That's exactly how I feel...like Dorothy in the 'Wizard of Oz.' I'm not in Texas anymore. I'm a fish out of water."

"Okay, but I'm your experience. I do have an agent and have been through these contracts...just once...but more than you have."

"I totally forgot you have an agent. Will he be there today?"

"It's a she and no, she won't. It's too early in the process for her to be involved."

The limo slows to a stop. The driver gets out and opens my door. "Ms. Barrett is waiting for you. The concierge in the lobby will direct you to her office. Have a good afternoon."

"Thank you," I say smoothing out my slacks. "Do I look okay?" I whisper to Chase.

"Of course, you do. Let's do this, Mom. Break a leg!"

Sam meets us at the door to her offices. "Welcome! You're right on time. Follow me to the conference room." The conference room has floor to ceiling windows which overlook the Pacific Ocean. A very modern, rectangular table with rounded corners and eight chairs takes up the center of the room. A chandelier with lights that look like enormous dangling ice cubes illuminates the room. A large screen TV hangs effortlessly on the wall opposite the windows. The books comprising my trilogy lie on top of the buffet table closest to the door.

She takes a seat at one end of the table. There are two navy-blue folders on either side of her. "Have a seat. What would you like to drink?"

"Water would be great," I manage to say.

"Chase? Your usual?"

"Absolutely." It turns out that Chase's "usual" is an Arnold Palmer.

Sam texts her assistant who within a few minutes magically appears with our drinks and a basket of fresh fruit. "Anything else?" she asks.

"I think we're good for now. Another participant will be arriving soon."

Another? Maybe Chase was right about additional investors. "Your office is gorgeous."

"Why thank you. I seem to be spending more and more time here as projects keep popping up...like this one. First let me start by saying I am so thankful to have had the opportunity to read your trilogy."

Uh oh. Here it comes. She's going to let me down gently or wants me to totally rewrite it. "I am honored you took the time to read it."

"When I talked to you a few days ago, I had envisioned creating a TV series based on the trilogy. There's plenty of plot line to last for several seasons. It would be a piece of cake to sell it to Netflix, Amazon, HBO Max, Apple TV+, etc. for them to make into an original series. I've had time over the past few days to mull it over, and I think it might be a better idea to make your first novel into a movie and then see how it's received. If it's received like I think it will be, then we have movies two and three. Or we see then what kinds of offers we get from the TV media moguls. What are your thoughts? How do you, the author, envision your creation?"

I'm so blown away, that I can't speak. "I...I of course defer to your judgement and would be absolutely fine with whatever you think. Seeing it on the big screen would be nothing short of thrilling. However, having it be a popular TV series that's on all the time would be awesome too. What do you think, Chase?"

Chase grins from ear to ear. "Movie...definitely. A movie would be my first pick."

Samantha nods. "As I mentioned to you on the phone, Margo, I want Chase to play the lead male. He's an extremely talented and handsome young actor and is the right age. This film will be his introduction to the big screen and we might need a 'name' actress to play opposite him. That can all be worked out and I have a few ideas for that. What's going to sell this movie is you."

"Me?" I ask. She must have meant Chase.

"You. You and Chase. You'll be the first mother/son team on the red carpet, or at a minimum, on the talk show circuit. How's that sound?"

"It sounds like I'm in a dream that I never want to wake up from!" Tears fill my eyes and I swat them away with the back of my hand.

Sam smiles. Chase is beaming. "Perfect. I'm glad you're happy. A movie is a huge project and time is of the essence. There's a window of opportunity for something fresh and new to premier the end of February. In order to accomplish this in such a short time frame, I've decided I need to collaborate with a few of my female production company owners. I hope you don't mind, but I've asked one of them to join us this afternoon so she can meet you." She texts something on her iPad and her assistant opens the door.

Robin Reed enters the conference room. Chase and I immediately stand. "You must be Margo. I'm Robin." As if I didn't recognize her.

Robin not only has her own production company, but also runs one of the best-known book clubs, "Robin Reads", which is probably second in popularity only to Oprah's Book Club. I shake her hand as does Chase. "What an honor to meet you! I'm probably not supposed to say this, but I'm a huge fan."

"That's so kind of you to say, Margo. And Chase, I hear great things about your TV series. I can't wait to see it."

"Thank you. It's a lot of fun."

"Well, it's even more fun being a movie star," Robin grins. "So hang on to your boots, you're in for a hell of a ride."

Sam motions for us to take our seats. "Margo has generously agreed, in principle, to let us move forward in producing a movie based on her first novel. Chase shared that his mom is currently unrepresented so we need to change that ASAP. I have several agents who want to represent you, Margo, and are willing to meet with you tomorrow morning. We'd like to get a contract inked with you within the next week."

"Chase, we will need to begin production within the next month," Robin takes over. "I know the director and producer of your series and will talk to them about loaning you to us for the next few months."

I notice a cloud crossing Chase's eyes. He's unsure. "Is that a possibility? I have a signed contract."

"We'll get with your agent and smooth over any ruffled feathers," says Sam. "But most of the time TV producers are thrilled when their unknown lead is tapped to star in a movie. It will be excellent press for the show."

Robin nods. "Yes, that's true. They often accelerate the shooting schedule to get more episodes in the can before they lose their star. We may even be able to give them six weeks. Finding a co-star in this short of time will be trickier, but we have a few ideas about that as well." Robin winks at Sam.

"As I mentioned before Robin joined us, the marketing of this movie hinges on the author/star—mother/son relationship. The world is looking for something with a happy ending and they will eat this up. That being said, Margo, we are going to require you to make appearances on many talk shows during the month of February. Would you be comfortable doing that?"

My mouth hangs open several seconds before I can get the words out. "You will need to coach me on what to say and not say, but heck yes, I think that would be a blast!"

"I told you," Chase says to Sam. So, he did know what she had up her sleeve.

"Excellent," Sam says. "Chase, you will need to go over some industry terms and make suggestions to your mom for things like what she wants in the green room and what kind of accommodations are acceptable to her. All of those things will need to be in your contract, Margo."

I look at Chase as if she's speaking a foreign language. "Not to worry. I've got her back."

"I'm sure you have a lot of questions," Robin says to me. "Here's my card, please feel free to contact me anytime. I loved reading your trilogy and I'd really like to make it part of my book club if you agree to it and if I can get the other investors to allow it."

Sam tilts her head. "That might be a great thing promotion wise. The books are available now so we'd have a little time to get on lists before the movie premieres. Again, we will need to get with Margo's agent on that."

Robin Read's book club selection, movie premier, green rooms, talk show appearances...my head is spinning. I'll wake up any minute now.

Once again Sam types something on her iPad. Her assistant comes in with a bucket of Dom Perignon and four glasses. "It's time to celebrate our new discoveries," she says while carefully uncorking the champagne and pouring my glass first. After filling everyone else's she raises hers. "To Margo and Chase. Thank you for joining our team!"

"Cheers!" echoes Robin.

CHAPTER TWENTY

I wake up. Soft daylight is sneaking in around the heavy drapes. It takes a minute for me to focus my eyes and reorient myself. Wynn is sleeping soundly, curled up next to me. As the room grows a bit brighter, I see the picture on the wall, the one of Brock when he was six years old. I'm in my bedroom. The curtains are mine.

The fact that I've just had one of the best dreams in my life is not lost on me. I'm devastated that it's not real, but amazed I can dream in such detail. Carefully, so as not to waken my sweet husband, I crawl out of our very comfortable bed. I survey the room. No luggage as if we've just returned. I sneak into the kitchen to make some coffee. And there, just inside the door that goes to our garage, is all of our luggage... the luggage we took to California.

As I stand looking at our bags and wondering how much was a dream, I spy a leather folder on our kitchen table. It's white with navy-blue script 'SB Productions" on it. Silently, I approach the table as if the folder might evaporate, and gingerly open it.

"Good morning, Sweetheart." Wynn's voice startles me. "They're still there, I see."

"Oh, good morning. I didn't mean to wake you." I kiss his unshaven cheek. "What's still there?"

"The contracts with your agent and the production company."

"We're awake, right?"

Wynn chuckles. "Yes, you are not dreaming. Our son in going to star in a movie, the one you wrote. Remember...you said you'd be happy with 'based on the book...'"

"By Margo Parker," I finish for him as I break into a smile. "We really went to her house and had dinner, didn't we?'

Wynn nods. "And flew back to Dallas last night on her private Gulfstream. And you met your agent yesterday before we got on the plane."

"Right, right. It's just so unreal to me."

"Well, I hope it becomes real to you soon. You have quite a few decisions to make and other documents to sign, remember? Plus, we have a playoff baseball game to attend tonight."

I'd almost forgotten. Brock has tickets for us to attend the first game in the American League Divisional series tonight. We are picking up Meredith on our way to the stadium. "Yes! That's right! I've got a lot to get done before we leave to go to the game."

"Maybe I should apply to be your secretary?"

Wynn winks at me as I laugh. "I can't afford you until I get my first paycheck." I scoop coffee into our maker and fill the pot with water from our fridge dispenser. "I need to reread those agreements today and get my questions answered before I sign and return them to Sam."

"They probably need to go through your agent first?"

"Yes, yes. Oh shoot, I really need to go over this with Chase." I look at the clock on our oven and see that it's already eight. "Do you think he's up already?"

"My guess is he's probably in the gym. But it wouldn't hurt to text him."

I flip the switch on the coffee maker and grab my phone. Within a minute after I hit 'send' the UT Fight Song fills our kitchen signaling Chase is calling.

"Hi, Sweetie. That was fast."

"Hey, Ma. I wanted to get back to you before my day starts. My agent is scheduled to talk to the EP's this morning ...that stands for executive producers...before we have our weekly table reading. I'm prepared for my schedule to dramatically change."

This is definitely real. "I'll bet. I'm just a little overwhelmed... no a lot overwhelmed...about what I should do next."

"Do you feel comfortable with your agent?"

"I do. I like her a lot and she seems very level-headed."

"I thought the same thing. Then reread your contract one more time or better yet ask Michael to read it and give you his thoughts." Michael is a family friend who works for a high-powered downtown Dallas law firm.

"Good idea as long as he has time today."

"It probably won't take him long. Get that done first. Then read through the rest of what Sam gave you. Then ask your agent any questions you have on those documents."

"Okay. Sounds like a plan."

"Ma…take a deep breath. This is all going to work out and we will be phenomenal."

"Can you see my smile? We should have FaceTimed. Keep me posted on what your EPs say. I hope this doesn't get you into too much trouble."

"This is not high school, Ma. It will all work out."

"I have no doubts. We are seeing your brother and Meredith at the game tonight."

"Are your seats in the suite again?"

"Of course."

"Private jet and playoff tickets in the GM's suite…you are living right, Mom."

"That I am. See you soon, I hope."

"Okay. Love you."

"Love you more." Our call ends, but our connection doesn't. How lucky am I to get to work with my son?

I was fortunate to get to work with my dad twice. The first time was during summers in high school as a teller at the bank where he was CEO. And when the boys were still in school, I sat on a board of directors with him. Both opportunities gave me great insight into how well-respected he was in the community and by those who worked with and for him. Working with Chase will be in a much different setting, one in which he will have to coach me.

• • •

Wynn and I are on our way to pick up Meredith before heading to the game. Brock warned us to leave early as traffic would be bad. He always lives by the motto that to be on time is to be late and to be early is to be on time, something he got from his mother! Unsurprisingly, Meredith is always ready early, one of her many great traits that make her so compatible with our son.

As we pull into their circle drive, Meredith is locking the front door. Wynn steps out of the car and opens the backdoor for her. "Are you ready for a great game?" he greets her.

Meredith slides into the backseat and waits for Wynn to get behind the steering wheel before answering. "Actually, I'm a bit nervous for the team. Brock is so confident that they will sweep the Red Socks in this series, that I'm afraid he will be disappointed if they lose tonight."

Before I can add to the conversation, Wynn pipes in. "They've got their best pitcher in tonight and home field advantage. I'm not worried."

I turn to face Meredith. "More importantly, how have you been feeling?"

"I've been feeling much better this trimester. No wooziness or fatigue like I had the first trimester. But although my clothes still fit, the waist bands are getting a tad snug. I've put on a few pounds."

"As is expected," I answer. "Maybe you should go maternity clothes shopping?"

"Would probably be a good idea, pretty soon. I'm trying to hold off on that as long as I can. I'm sure I'll get sick of wearing them."

"Actually, it's a lot of fun to try them on with the fake tummy they give you. It might be a good idea to get a couple of outfits now. I remember having to safety pin my suit skirts when I was pregnant with Brock because one morning I got up and nothing fit anymore."

"Good point. Would you by chance, want to go with us?"

I always appreciate when my daughters-in-law include me. I still remember quite vividly the day Meredith asked me to go wedding dress shopping with her mom and her. You'd think she'd offered me the moon. "Why of course! I'd love to go shopping with you. Maybe your mom could come down and go too?'

"Oh definitely. She won't want to miss seeing me look like I'm nine months pregnant. Do you know what your schedule is going to be like in the next few weeks? Brock said you're about to be really busy."

"Not too busy for you and my future grandchild. Check with your mom on a day that's good for her and I'll make myself available." It's amazing that in just a few months I've gone from having very little to do to having a packed schedule. And to think I was worried what my purpose in life would now be!

Wynn has navigated the traffic well and he pulls up to the VIP gate. Our tag is dangling from the rearview mirror and the guard waves us through. Most of the executives get an additional parking pass on game days for their spouses and family members. We are directed to park in a spot in the second row. Tonight is a 'white out' for the Rangers, meaning we all wear our white jerseys. It's still hot and sticky out even though it's the third week in September. I'm thankful we will be in the air-conditioning.

When we get to our suite, a few of Brock's groomsmen and their wives are already there. One lives in Houston and the other in Austin. It's nice they could make it up for the game.

"Margo, Wynn, Meredith," Brock's college roommate, Zack, greets us with a hug. "It's great seeing you again."

Next in line with a hug is his other college roommate, Garrett. "What? No cookies, Margo? How will I survive this game?" Garrett is teasing me. Even after they graduated from college, I always baked cookies any time Brock was going to see them.

"I know. I'm sorry. We just got back last night from California and I'm lucky that we made it here. Next time! I'm so glad you could be here! I know that means a lot to Brock."

Meredith is already deep in conversation with Zack's wife who is due with their first child in December. The game won't start for another thirty minutes and the server has just arrived to deliver our appetizers and dinner. Wynn is standing in the front row of the suite to watch batting practice. Normal...attending a baseball game. That's what this is. Well, except that we never used to sit in a suite. Once, Wynn, Brock and I attended a World Series game in the Rangers' old stadium against the St. Louis Cardinals, my favorite team. We sat in seats in the lower deck that ended up being partially obstructed by a pole. Wynn was furious. The Cards won that game and ended up winning the Series, although the boys still complain the Rangers were "robbed."

"Hey, Mom." Brock enters the suite and gives me a hug. "I see Dad is focused on batting practice."

"Yes, he is. Shocker!"

"There's plenty of food, everyone," Brock announces. "Help yourselves when you get hungry, like I'm going to do now before I have to go work."

"Work? Is that what you call it?" Garrett teases. "I wish I had to 'work' by watching a baseball game and dining on excellent food."

Brock shrugs. "Not a bad gig...but you can have a drink or two or three. I can't...because I'm working."

Zack comes over to grab some food. "Hey, thanks for inviting us. This is just the coolest thing, getting to watch a playoff game from a suite. Almost as cool as this," he grabs Brock's lanyard. "Brock Parker, Assistant General Manager Baseball Operations."

A grin takes over Brock's face. "Thanks. I won't lie. It's a dream job." He takes a bite of a roast beef sandwich. I notice they are made with Hawaiian Rolls, Brock's favorite. He grabs a few of the cookies and walks over to his dad.

Wynn looks up at our son. "Ready for win number one of the series tonight?"

Brock nods. "I'm not concerned at all. This is just a warmup for the World Series. By the way, I'll be able to get you and Mom tickets to the away games if you want to go to Boston."

"Really? You mean I could get to see the iconic Fenway Park?" Wynn is beside himself. He's always wanted to see the famed "Green Monster."

"Sure. But you need to be available when we go up there in a few days, because we will clinch the pennant there."

Wynn beams. “Count us in.”

Brock nods. “Hey you all, I’ve got to run. Enjoy the game.” He gives Meredith a quick kiss on his way out.

As Brock and his dad had predicted, the Texas Rangers won five to four with a walk-off homer.

CHAPTER TWENTY-ONE

March 16, 1934

The angel who was kneeling on the paved road, carefully lifted Margaret's soul from her still body. She smiled at him. "Oh, thank God! Ike needs your help. He's still in the car. I'm not sure where it went."

"Ike will be fine. I'm here to guide you." His voice sounded like wind chimes delicately dangling in the breeze on a summer day.

"But I'm fine. Nothing hurts. Let's go get Ike," Margaret pleaded as she and the angel ascended above the earth.

"He's staying behind to take care of your little boy," the angel patiently explained.

"What? No! Where are we going? I need to be here for William. He needs his mother. Put me down!"

"Sorry, but life's not fair. You have to come with me," the angel's voice now sounded like a loud whisper.

Margaret continued arguing with the angel, insisting that he was wrong. This couldn't be happening to her. She and Ike had almost made it home, back to William, her sweet baby. And if she'd died in the car accident, where was the bright white light? Where were the loved ones already in Heaven who would greet her? Oh that's right, she thought, they are all still alive: her grandparents, parents, sisters, husband and son. All still on Earth. "Look," she tried once more to plead with the angel, "this is a big mistake. Please let me speak to whoever is in charge." Maybe the negotiating skills she'd learned at the University of Illinois' business school would work.

The angel, still holding Margaret, stopped in front of the proverbial pearly gates and set her down. He shrugged, rolled his eyes and disappeared.

Margaret was frantic. She must have hit her head. Any moment she would wake up and Ike would be pulling into their driveway, she reasoned. When she looked around all she could see were clouds. The sun was out. The pearly gates seemed to have evaporated.

"Margaret Bennett Stearns?" a voice behind her boomed.

Margaret turned to see another angel-like figure. "Yes, that's me."

The spirit was flipping through a very large book. "I'm afraid your heavenly escort confused you with someone else he was sent to retrieve which explains why you are so adamant that you shouldn't be here, well at least for a very long time."

Margaret sighed. At last, here was someone with some common sense and she hoped some power to get her home. Her negotiating skills had come in handy. "Good. I need to get back as soon as possible." She noticed the spirit was frowning, his nose still in the book. "By the way, how much longer do I have…on Earth?"

"Hush! I'm calculating…thinking. It appears you had about another fifty-five years…Earth years that is."

Margaret smiled. "You mean have, not had, correct?"

"No. I mean had. You died, Margaret Bennett Stearns."

Margaret put her hands on her hips. "I most certainly did not. Send me back. Work one of your miracles. I *am* in the place where those can be performed, right?"

The spirit looked up from his book and tilted his head. "Yes. But you don't seem to understand. Your soul's vessel, what you think of as your body, is gone."

"What do you mean it's gone? I'm standing right here in front of you. My hands are on my hips and I am frowning."

The angel sighed and produced a large hand mirror. "I hate it when we have to prove a being is wrong. And I'm sure you're not going to like this."

Margaret looked into the mirror and saw nothing. "What? Is this a trick? I don't see anything except a tiny glow."

"That's your soul. Your body is back on Earth."

"Then what are we waiting for? Take me back there."

The angel grabbed the mirror from Margaret. "I'm afraid it's too late. You've been pronounced dead and your vessel…I mean your body…well it's already been…prepared."

If Margaret still had a heart, she would have felt it drop. "What do you mean…prepared? We've only been up here a few minutes."

"It seems like that because here we're on Heaven time. Think of how fast a few days out of eternity would go by."

"Look, you don't understand. I have the most handsome, sweetest little boy in the world and Ike and I need to raise him…together. There must be someone up here who can fix this. Let me see Jesus!"

The spirit laughed. "I can't let you see Jesus until your soul is due here which is not for another fifty-five years."

"So, what am I supposed to do for that time? Just be left in limbo here, outside the pearly gates?" Margaret looked around and saw that no one else was waiting.

"I'll be right back."

Margaret cried. There was no light, no stunning colors, just the clouds and the sun. What had she done to deserve this?

The spirit materialized directly in front of her. "We have a few options, but a bit of a dilemma. Since God, in his infinite wisdom, gave man free choice, we can't guarantee that if we put your soul in another woman's body that Ike would marry her, thus insuring you could raise your son."

"You can do that? Just pick some person on Earth and replace that person's soul with mine?"

The spirit fidgeted. "Not exactly. That soul's days in that particular body would have had to expire. I'm sure this is hard for you to comprehend because it's outside of earthly understanding."

"Go on. You said we have a few options."

"The best we can do, and this may take twenty to thirty years, is to put your soul in William's firstborn daughter. You wouldn't get to raise William, but you would spend lots of time with him. He'd be raising you."

"That's the best you can do? What if he never has children or only has boys?"

"I'm afraid that is the best we can do. You need to know that we can't guarantee any of that except for the gender of William's firstborn. You'll be in a new body which means a new brain, new memory. You won't remember any of this if you accept this option," he warned her.

Margaret laughed to herself. She'd always had an excellent memory. She'd remember. "Fine. If that's the best you can do."

Thirty years later, after three miscarriages of boys, William's wife gave birth to a girl.

CHAPTER TWENTY-TWO

The last week of September was a whirlwind of travel and activities. The Texas Rangers did, in fact, sweep the Boston Red Sox at Fenway Park, clinching a spot in the ALCS. Wynn and I were there, but not in a suite. We couldn't complain about seats ten rows behind the visiting team's dugout. What I noticed about the iconic venue was that it seemed so small, especially compared to the relatively new Globe Life Park where the Rangers play. However, I appreciated the fact that an older facility is revered, not simply discarded and replaced with something modern as seems to be the trend in Dallas these days. While we watched both games, Wynn loved telling me about all the baseball greats who had played on this field.

The days are rapidly approaching my fifty-fifth birthday. With all of the new demands on my time by my agent and Sam's production company, I've barely had time to think about it. Nor have I had a visit from Dad in a while. Maybe Dr. Pope was right.

Last year, Wynn had asked me what I wanted to do to celebrate the "speed-limit" birthday and I'd requested no surprise parties, maybe just a trip to Hawaii like we did on my fiftieth or to Turks and Caicos some other time of the year. October is never a good time to go to the Caribbean due to hurricanes. Or we could go stay at a super luxurious hotel I'd had my eye on in Big Sur, but recent wildfires in that part of California nixed that idea.

I'm lost in thought while making coffee this morning when the Texas Fight Song fills my kitchen. It's Chase. "Hi, Sweetie. How's it going?"

"Hey, almost birthday girl! I've got some great news! I'll be home the week after your big day to shoot some local scenes! Or maybe you already knew that."

"I didn't! That's exciting! What did the EP's say about your TV schedule?" I'm proud of myself for rattling off a showbiz acronym like I'm an old pro. Old maybe...pro, hardly!

"Believe it or not, I'm going to be able to do both."

"Do tell. This should be interesting."

"They've accelerated our production schedule here on the show. Once shooting begins on your movie, I'll be able to work half-time on the series and half on the movie except when I have to be on location which should only be for about a week in October. The local scenes will be shot on the Warner Brothers lot so I'll be nice and close to my TV studio. My agent said it will be a little crazy, but she thinks I can handle it. It's actually been done before. Plus, a lot of filming will be done after the show wraps for this year in early November."

"Wow. I'm tired just listening to all of that. Do you have your script yet?"

"I'm to receive it on your birthday. How awesome is that?"

"I think that's definitely one of those God Winks. Anyway, do you know what day you're coming to town? Is Libby joining you? Are you staying here or at a hotel?"

"You still ask a ton of questions, Ma. I'm just waiting for you to ask me 'who all was there?'" Chase is referring to a question I consistently asked when the boys were in high school after they'd been to a party or an event.

I laugh. "Well maybe I should ask who all is going to be *here*?"

"Not sure about Libby. She may come out on the weekend. And I'm not sure where I'm staying yet. I'd like to stay at home. It all depends on where the locations will be. And to who all will be there...you will be. Sam wants you on the set."

This will be one of those mother-of-the-groom moments where I have to smile and stay quiet. At least I've had practice. "That will be amazing."

"I'm sure your agent will be contacting you any day with the details."

"I can't wait."

"By the way, what are you doing for your birthday?"

"Dad hasn't said yet. But I'll look forward to celebrating it with you when you arrive in town. Since it looks like the Rangers might be playing in the World Series, we may go somewhere before that begins."

"Oh yeah. You can't miss that. When does that start?"

"In a few weeks."

"Great! I may be in town for some of that. Libby will have to come out if that's the case. Hey, I've got to run. The PA just knocked on the door of my trailer. It's time for me to go to hair and makeup."

"Okay, Chase. Thanks for sharing the good news with me!"

"Love you!"

"Love you more!"

Wynn comes into the kitchen with a huge box wrapped in birthday paper. "Happy Birthday a little early!" He sets the present down next to our breakfast table and pours me a cup of coffee. He is wearing an impish grin on his face.

"What's this?" I ask.

"It's your birthday present a few days early. Go ahead and open it."

Wynn looks quite pleased with himself. "Ok." I begin to open the box that appears to have been professionally wrapped. After all these years, Wynn's wrapping style has not changed. Underneath gold tissue paper is a beautiful, navy and black Tumi wheeled carry-on bag with my monogram on it. "Sweetheart, you shouldn't have. This is the top of the line in travel bags!"

"I thought your luggage needed updating now that you will be traveling to all of your speaking engagements. They don't make suitcases in that same style, but I thought that all your pieces don't need to match." He opens the door into the garage and brings in two more Tumi bags. These are silver blue hard-sided with a wave-like pattern. One of each size. Both have my monogram on it. "I hope you like them."

"Like them? I love them!"

"And we've been needing some new luggage. Now you won't have to be embarrassed when we pull up to a fancy hotel."

I go over and kiss Wynn on the lips. "Thank you. This was so thoughtful and...generous. Tumi is very expensive."

"You deserve it. Now for the bad news. I wanted to take you back to Maui, but now's not a good time and if we wait to go when the whales are there next February or March, we've got your movie and..."

"And our grandchild. You're right, Wynn, we won't want to be away then."

"Yes, so let's initiate these bags with a quick trip to Florida. Can you be ready to leave in a few days?"

I smile. "That sounds perfect. And of course, I'll be ready."

"That's a good thing since I've already made dinner reservations for your birthday."

"Where?"

"That's a surprise."

• • •

We arrive the day before my birthday at our condo on the beach in Naples. Fortunately, no hurricanes are brewing in the Gulf, giving us a cloudless sunset, our favorite time of the day. Wynn hands me a glass of Cabernet as we sit on our lanai, hoping to see the green flash as the sun dips into the ocean. We've seen it only a handful of times during our marriage. Sometimes it is a flash and others a brief glow. For years, prior to our first sighting, we were skeptical. But when my parents had seen it, I became a believer. However, it was several more years before

Wynn and I witnessed it from this very spot. Since then, we've seen the green flash in the Bahamas, Hawaii and Bora Bora.

"Cheers!" I raise my glass to Wynn.

"Cheers! I'm glad you agreed to come here."

"Like you had to twist my arm?"

"No, but you've been really busy."

"Yes, that's why this is such a nice respite."

Over the years it's been interesting to note that sometimes the sun sets quickly and other times it seems to hover over the water. Tonight, it sets slowly. Disappointingly, there is no green flash.

I wake up the next morning refreshed and immensely glad we have a few days to ourselves.

"Happy Birthday, Sweetheart!" Wynn kisses me before we get out of bed.

"Thank you!"

"I thought we'd go out for breakfast and then maybe you can work out in the pool. I have a few errands to do."

"That sounds perfect."

Breakfast at our favorite bayside restaurant was amazing. Wynn drops me off at the condo and I put on my swimsuit, grab my towel, weights and noodle and head to the pool.

One bonus of being in Naples in October is that it is not "season" yet. The restaurants aren't as crowded and today the pool is empty. Maybe I can get my workout in before anyone comes down.

Since I have the pool to myself, I start by taking my noodle and using it as a kickboard, making my way down to the deep end. I inhale deeply the comforting scent of sea air. As I turn to complete my two laps, I realize I am not alone. An older man is descending the steps at the shallow end. Darn! I didn't get down here soon enough.

As I get closer to the shallow end, my disappointment evaporates.

"Happy Birthday, Hon," my dad says. "This water is still the perfect temperature."

"Daddy! Seeing you is the best gift I could receive today." He stands in the shallow end and I sit on my noodle. No one else is around. I wish I had my cell phone so I could try snapping a picture of him.

"It's good to be back here."

"You know I think of you when I'm here, especially at sunset."

He nods and smiles. "Yes, we watched many sunsets while enjoying a cocktail. Too bad there wasn't a green flash last night."

Of course, he had been watching too! *Just remember to listen and enjoy the moment.* "Well, if they happened too often, they wouldn't be special."

"That's true. Since we have some time alone right now, there's something I need to share with you."

A gentle breeze blows from behind Dad and I catch a whiff of his cologne. I get off my noodle and put it on the side of the pool and move closer to my father. "What's that?"

"It's time for me to explain why you've been able to see me and other family members haven't. I believe you even asked me about this early on and I wasn't able at the time to give you a complete answer."

I wait for him to continue.

"I've tried to prepare you for today and what I'm about to tell you. We needed time to reconnect, but I probably should have told you sooner."

"Is this bad news?" I feel my stomach drop.

"No, but it's most likely going to be a shock."

"Go on."

"You remember that my mother, Margaret, died in a car accident when I was only fifteen months old."

"Yes, we were never supposed to talk to Granddad about it because he felt responsible. She's buried in St. Louis."

"Correct. Your grandfather was not responsible, but he felt that way because he lived and she didn't. Because we didn't talk a lot about her, you may not be aware of traits you have in common with her. You both were business majors which is something in and of itself since most women didn't go to college back in her day, much less major in commerce, a man's field."

"I did read that about her in her obituary."

"You both are very determined."

"So, you've seen her? What's she like?"

Dad continues without directly answering my question.

"You both loved your sons immensely."

"Okay…"

Dad takes a deep breath. "Remember growing up I always told you that life isn't fair?"

"How could I forget? And it isn't. And I'm sorry, Daddy, but I've never really accepted that. I'm still mad at God for taking you when we needed you here…on Earth." I'm trying desperately not to cry.

"That's the other thing you have in common with Margaret. Only she was mad at God for taking her from me…not me from her."

"Good for her. I like this woman whom I've never met."

Dad puts his hand on my shoulder and looks into my eyes. "I didn't realize when I gave you her engagement ring that I was actually returning it to its owner."

My heart seems to stop. Dr. Pope's words are fading away. "What? I don't understand."

"You really don't remember," he says as a statement, not a question.

My heart is now beating hard and I feel like I can't breathe. "I guess not. What don't I remember?" I almost never forget things.

"Your deal with God. You weren't supposed to die."

"I didn't, Dad. I'm right here."

"The only way God could reunite us was to put your soul into my firstborn daughter," he paused to let that sink in. "It turns out, you're not only my daughter, you're my mother."

Nothing Dr. Pope has counseled me on has prepared me for this moment. I put up both of my hands in protest and take a step back, looking around to see if anyone has joined us in the pool area. We are still alone. "Ok. That's just crazy. How do you expect me to believe that?"

Dad grabs me gently by the hand and pulls me closer. "Because I've never lied to you."

And I know, without a doubt in my mind, that he never

would. Tears are threatening to spill onto my cheeks. "Why are you telling me this now?"

"Because you have a right to know who you are and what your soul purpose has been."

"Which is?" The tears are racing down my face and splashing delicately into the pool.

"To know your son."

"So, what you're telling me is that I'm Margaret. I have her soul," I whisper, struggling to get the words out. "You raised me, but I'm your mother."

"Correct. I know it's hard to comprehend."

"Why wouldn't I have remembered that on some level? A mother just doesn't forget her son. I would never, ever forget Brock and Chase."

"That was part of the deal. In fact, you argued with God about that. You said you'd remember. But your soul is in a different vessel. Memory is a bodily function. You have Margo's brain, not Margaret's."

"If that's the case, then I lost you twice. Once when I died and then again when you died!" I'm feeling angry all of a sudden. "Why would God punish me that way?"

"He wouldn't and he didn't. He gave us forty years together. God listened to your plea to somehow get back to your son. You got to know me and what I was like on Earth. You didn't have to wait for me to die to see me again."

"Maybe you can clarify something for me. I dearly loved Granddad, your dad. But I never felt any romantic connection with him. Wouldn't I have? According to you, he was my husband."

"Again, that's part of the body...memory. But you did always feel a connection to him, didn't you? You felt sorry for him that he never remarried, that he blamed himself for the accident."

"That's true. He was such a kind and generous man. He didn't deserve feeling that way. He did an outstanding job raising you."

"And he hasn't seen you since, because you've been here. Dad didn't know you had Margaret's soul either until he died and you weren't in Heaven. But he's been watching."

"Wynn's my husband."

"Yes."

"And Granddad is okay with that."

"Yes. He likes Wynn very much. Remember? He met him before he died, before you two got engaged."

"That's right. He did. This is a lot for me to get my head around, Dad. Or do I call you son or William? Ugh, this is so confusing."

William looks at me with his chocolate brown eyes. "I'm sure it is. You need some time to accept and think about it. But remember, this has to do with your soul, the essence of who you are. Your body belongs to Margo, but your soul is Margaret's." He pauses for a moment, staring into my eyes. "Before I forget, I have a birthday gift for you. You know that picture of me in the frame on your dresser?"

I nod. "The black and white one of your mother holding you as a baby?"

"That's the one. When you get home, I want you to take it out of the frame and really look at it."

"Uh, okay."

"I think it will help clear this up, if not in your mind, in your heart." He looks up toward the automatic door that leads to the pool area. "Someone's coming. We will talk about this again. In the meantime, have a great day celebrating. I love you."

My back is to the doors. I turn to see who is intruding on my time with my dad and when I turn back around, he is gone.

CHAPTER TWENTY-THREE

Fortunately, it wasn't Wynn who was entering the pool area. I quickly swipe my tears away and continue with my workout, ignoring the person who intruded on what was undoubtedly the most important conversation I'd ever had with my dad… son…William. Ah! This is so baffling.

I truthfully had never once considered that I was Margaret or more accurately housed her spirit. Wasn't I, me? Hadn't I always been just Margo? This is absolutely ludicrous. While I believe in Heaven and hell, I don't believe in reincarnation. And wasn't that what Dad was describing? Or was it? How can I be fifty-five years old and not really know who am I? Or who I thought I was?

A plethora of thoughts are cluttering my brain, or should I say Margo's brain? I've lost count of how many repetitions I've done with the weight I'm holding in my right hand. I'm sure it's time to switch. Anger mixed with confusion and a strange sense of elation seem to envelope me all at once. If what Dad said is true, (and he, at least, must believe it), then how cool is it that I have had more than one role in his life? How many people have done that? I'm betting not many, or at least not many who would admit it. Because at the end of the day no one will believe me, including Dr. Pope.

I make my way to deeper water wondering if Dad will reappear now that the intruder has made his way out of the pool area and down to the beach. Two large seagulls fly in and perch by the side of the pool. They don't seem to notice I'm here. Or maybe they do and just don't care. For many years when I've been alone in the pool and birds have flown in, I've always wondered if it's my dad and granddad or maybe granddad and my grandmother. Now I know. It must have been Granddad and Dad. Margaret's evidently been with me every day my entire life. I glance at these birds again and swim a little closer to them. They tilt their heads and stare at me. Maybe it is Dad.

Accepting who my soul is, should I decide to go down that road, will take some time and lots of thought. The logical side of my brain keeps telling me that this can't possibly have happened. But the creative side is leaning heavily on my spirit, nudging it to convince the logical side to buy into this story. Because I really like this story.

Story! That's what Dad had said to me when he appeared after my last speaking engagement. "Why don't you write *our* story?" At the time I blew it off because it didn't make any sense. I didn't understand what our story was. Now I get it. On the one hand it would make an interesting read, but on the other hand, my family and friends would think I've gone off the deep end.

Which is literally where I am now. In the deep end of the pool.

I've probably done way more reps of each exercise than I usually do. Wynn will be back soon. I'm not sure if I should spend any more time on my birthday pondering this event because if I do, I might go back to the idea after I first saw my father at Dillard's that day...that I've lost it. I've gone crazy. And fifty-five is too young to be crazy.

The door to the pool area once again slides open and my sister walks out. Wait! Melissa? Am I seeing things? I didn't know she was going to be here. "Happy Birthday, Sis!" she calls from the edge of the upper deck before making her way down to the pool. "Surprise!"

"Oh my gosh! Thanks for coming! I had no idea you'd be here."

"Well how do I say no to your husband especially when he offers to throw us in a spa for half a day?" Melissa seems to be eyeing me suspiciously. "Looks like you could use that spa day. You look like you've seen a ghost!"

She has no idea. At least now I know why she hasn't seen Dad too. Ha! She's lucky she had a normal relationship with our father, William. She doesn't have to spend the rest of her life struggling with the idea she may be his mother as well. "I just need to get my tan back," I recover. "When are we going to the spa?"

Melissa sits on the coping stone next to me in the pool. "This afternoon so we can get a mani/pedi before dinner tonight. We both have massages scheduled first. I think our appointment is at two."

"Hey, Melissa!" Wynn walks up and gives her a hug. "I'm sorry your hubby couldn't join you, but I really appreciate your coming."

"How could I say no?"

"Have you told the birthday girl about the spa?"

"I have," she nods. "Our appointment is at two?"

"That's right, at the Ritz Carlton."

"Then I'm going to get my suit on so we can walk the beach and get some sun before then," Melissa stands. "I'll be back down in a few."

"Aren't you full of surprises?" I say to Wynn as I towel off.

"Actually, it was all Melissa's idea. I just helped her execute the plan. But the spa is my idea."

I slip on my cover-up and give Wynn a hug. "This is perfect. Melissa and I don't get to spend much time here together. The spa will be a treat!"

• • •

When Melissa and I return later this afternoon, Wynn informs us that we need to be ready to leave for dinner by six o'clock which only gives us an hour to get ready. It also means that we wouldn't be watching the sunset from the condo. Surely Wynn thought of that. I wonder where he is taking us to dinner? It must be some place where we can see the ocean. Maybe it's the Turtle Club which literally has tables on the beach. Or maybe it's back to the Ritz Carlton. I debate the other options while I'm putting on my makeup.

I look at my reflection in the mirror, trying to see my grandmother's face, but only mine is staring back. No, I remind myself, it's only her soul that I have, not her body. If I buy into this crazy theory my dearly departed father has imposed on me, then what does that mean? Am I really any different than before because of this piece of information? After all, I've lived my entire fifty-five years of life with this soul. I'm comfortable with it. From everything I've read and heard, my grandmother was a lovely person who died way too young. I've always been proud of my dad, but aren't most daughters? Just because I was proud of his many accomplishments, including his volunteer charity work, doesn't mean I'm his mother.

"Why are you shaking your head?" Wynn interrupts my thoughts.

I pause, eyeliner in hand. "I'm just trying to figure out where we are going for dinner."

Wynn kisses the back of my neck. "You think too much. Just relax. It's a place you love."

Okay, then that leaves out the Turtle Club and the Ritz. They are fine restaurants, but they don't hold any special place in my heart. Wynn slips into his cobalt blue sports coat and heads into the living room. He returns immediately.

"Your sister's ready!" he whispers surprisedly.

"What?" Usually, I'm waiting on her. I guess I've been too lost in thought. "I just need to put on my lipstick. I'll be right out."

We take the front elevator down to the parking garage and get into our rental car. Wynn drives past two restaurants that I especially like, but neither offers a gulf view. We get to the first stoplight and I expect Wynn will go straight. But instead, he turns right. Hmm, I hope he hasn't forgotten how to get to the other restaurant I'm thinking of. When he makes a right at the second light, I have a feeling of where we are going.

"Do you know where we are headed now?" he asks me.

I am grinning ear to ear. "The Edgewater Beach Hotel?"

"Yep!" Melissa answers from the back seat. "We're returning to one of our childhood haunts."

For a minute I think I'm going to cry. The four of us -my parents, sister and I- spent many Christmas vacations at this resort. When Melissa was a baby, my parents rented a one-bedroom unit that had a full kitchen. It was on the first floor so that Mom could sit outside on the patio while Melissa napped and Dad and I could swim in the pool which was steps away. As we got older, we stayed in rooms on upper floors. And during our teenage years, my parents rented an efficiency unit with a connecting hotel room for Melissa and me. She and I felt like adults having our own room separate from theirs and looking back, I'm sure my parents must have enjoyed the privacy. Since then, the hotel has been totally renovated and is all suites. They now have two pools, the one Dad, Melissa and I used to swim in and a new one which took the place of a putting green.

"This is perfect!" I turn to look at my sister. "Thank you for thinking of this. I'm so glad you're here. We have a lot of memories at this hotel."

Melissa smiles. "Like when we had our 'sand' bakery? And had pretend shows in the pool?"

"And that one New Year's Eve when you insisted your bed was actually spinning?"

My sister pretends she's mad at me for saying that. "Do you

really want to go there, Margo? Shall we talk about New Year's Eve escapades?"

"If that's the case, then I better head to the Ritz," Wynn chimes in.

"Umm, stop. Both of you! This is my birthday and therefore you aren't going to make fun of me!"

"Some people never grow up," Melissa jokes as Wynn pulls up the steep drive to the front of the hotel. Two uniformed valets open our doors. Melissa takes my arm and waits for the doorman to open the door. "Excuse me, can you tell us the best way to get to the pool? And do they still have that cute little chickee bar there?"

"Why yes, Ma'am, they do. You can take the elevators down to that level. Or you can go through the restaurant and down the stairway."

Melissa looks at me for a decision. "I vote for the stairway if you can handle it in your heels."

"Piece of cake," I say. The restaurant is on the second floor of the hotel. The hotel is horseshoe shaped with the ends facing the beach and the restaurant in the "U." There are graceful curved stairways on either side of the outdoor balcony of the restaurant. My sister and I carefully descend them.

The sun is still shining brightly although it has started its initial descent for the day. Wynn follows Melissa and me as we head to the pool. I walk over to the original pool and picture me on Dad's back, just like the "rides" he gave Brock and Chase at the condo pool. Two generations grew up spending the holidays with my dad in Naples.

Several couples are standing near the chickee bar next to the pool. One of the women turns as we approach. It's one of my best friends. "Kathy, what are you doing here? I didn't know you and Randy were going to be in Naples!" Kathy and Randy have actually stayed at this hotel before.

Melissa and Wynn give me a funny look. Kathy and Randy are quiet for a minute. "Surprise!" They are joined by our friends, Nancy and Scott who come towards us from their "hiding spots" at the tiki bar. I realize that my dearest friends have come all the way from Texas to help me celebrate. Melissa has once again surprised me and made my birthday memorable. They toast me right before the sun drops into the ocean and we all witness the green flash.

CHAPTER TWENTY-FOUR

The party was just what I needed. Getting to spend time with my sister and friends in a place where I spent holidays growing up, my normal childhood. My childhood, not Margaret's. How had my life gone from mundane to extraordinary so quickly? I am so blessed to have such dear friends and a sister who would take time out of their busy lives to travel to Florida for a party for me. And, of course, it goes without saying (though it should be said frequently) how blessed I am to have such a thoughtful, loving husband.

Today I'm back home and back to my new normal. I have a conference call with my agent and Sam at noon, an appointment with a wardrobe stylist at two, then Wynn and I head to the ballpark to cheer on the Rangers in the first game of the World Series. And sometime, I need to get to the grocery store and do the laundry...tasks from my "old" normal life. I probably should schedule another appointment with Dr. Pope if I can find the time.

I zip through my chores and power up my laptop for my Zoom conference call. I check myself on my camera to make sure I look okay before entering the meeting and note that I need to get my hair done. Other than that, I look presentable. I click on the Zoom meeting link and am instantly "seated" with Sam and my agent, Donna. I recognize Sam's conference room. She's wearing a black t-shirt. Donna appears to be seated at her desk in her office.

"Hi, Margo. A belated happy birthday to you," Donna greets me.

Sam looks startled. Her already large eyes grow bigger. "When was your birthday?"

"Two days ago. We celebrated in Florida."

"Well, happy birthday a few days late. Where in Florida?"

"Naples."

"Oh, I love Naples!"

She's been there? How many other celebrities have I missed seeing? "We do too. I've been going there since I was very young."

"So that's why you have a few scenes in your book in Naples. Great town. Great food and incredible sunsets. Donna, have you been there?"

Donna shakes her head. "No, but it sounds like I need to add it to my travel list."

Sam nods. "A definite must."

Donna, who is in her early thirties, is a petite redhead with a heart-shaped face and long eyelashes. You'd never think by looking at her that she's a shark, but she is! I'm glad she has my back in all these dealings which are new to me. I can tell she's done with the small talk and is ready to get down to business. As they say: time is money.

"Margo, this morning I'd like to nail down the details of your PR tour. I wanted Chase and his agent to join us, but neither was available. I guess Chase is shooting his last few episodes of his show and I don't know what his agent's excuse is. Anyway, let's start with your itinerary and then we can move to the details of each stop. I'm sure Chase's film schedule will allow him to mirror his mother's schedule?" This last question is directed at Sam.

"Absolutely. As Margo knows, his character is not in every scene, which gives us some flexibility."

"Great." Donna checks her list before looking up. "I'm proposing we begin with local interviews to give Margo a chance to adjust to the studio interview process. The local stations will eat this up. We can do a 'tease' when Chase is in town to shoot local scenes, then follow up with an interview about a week before the movie releases." She pauses, waiting for a response from us.

Sam has slipped on a pair of readers and appears to be scanning a document in front of her. "Hmm...do you think a tease might diminish the impact of the promo tour? Especially since it will only be a few months away?"

Donna shakes her head. "Nope, because it's a local, human interest type story now, not part of a press tour."

I don't say anything because I have no idea which would be better.

"Okay. I'll go with that," agrees Sam. "We are scheduled to begin shooting next week. The location scouts are already in town doing their front work."

"That doesn't give me a whole lot of time, but it's still doable," says Donna. "I show that WFAA is the main Dallas TV station. Would you agree, Margo?"

"Yes, that's what we watch anyway."

"Since the scenes won't be in Ft. Worth, I think we can skip their station. I'll also contact *The Dallas Morning News* to see if they want to run an article. And I have a source at *D Magazine* who would probably love to do a whole story. Their advance time is so long that they might want to take pictures when Chase is in town. With any luck, the story will run in their March issue which is released in February." Donna looks down and appears to be making notes. "Margo, we will need to add these to the list for your appointment with the stylist today. You'll need fall clothes for these interviews versus winter clothes for the remainder."

"Got it," I say.

"Next up will be the official press tour. We will start in New York. I've got you scheduled on *GMA*, *Live with Kelly and Ryan* and *The Today Show* with Hoda and Jenna. I might also add *Dr. Oz* since there's a medical theme to this movie. I haven't decided on that yet...still mulling it over."

Sam looks over the top of her readers. "I'd vote no on doing *Dr. Oz.* I don't quite see that as a fit."

Donna tilts her head side to side as she ponders Sam's remark. "You may be right. We have enough interviews on the West Coast to make up for that."

"You with us on all this?" Donna asks me.

"Oh, absolutely! I'm happy to do whatever interviews you

want me to." *Good job, Margo. Good job keeping yourself from not jumping up and down when you heard that you are going to be on your favorite talk show, Live with Kelly and Ryan. I can't wait to tell Chase. How will I handle not being star-struck on that show?*

"Good. Then we'll move on. You will fly to Dallas after your New York interviews and hit the local stations. Then back to LA where I have booked you on *The Kelly Clarkson Show* and *Entertainment Tonight. Jimmy Kimmel* is a maybe. The stylist you'll be working with this afternoon has all of these on her list. She'll be creating your 'persona', Margo, while keeping in mind the different TV markets you'll be airing in. That will end with the movie premiere on a date TBD in early March, right, Sam?"

"Yes. That sounds perfect. We might be able to get a billboard for them outside the studio. I'm working on that."

"Excellent. The other item on our agenda today is who will be part of your entourage, Margo. That will dictate the level of transportation we will require. Besides Chase, who else do you want to go with you?"

"Definitely Wynn. The rest depends on how many you will allow."

"Let's start with the whole list."

"My sister, Melissa, my 'volunteer' publicist, Pat, my personal hair stylist who also has a great eye for clothes, Brock and Meredith, if they're available. And of course, Chase's wife, Libby."

Sam looks at Donna and smiles. "Perfectly reasonable and plenty of space on the plane for additional folks Chase wants to include."

"Great! Then I will finalize the schedule, run it by Chase and his agent and get you both a copy sometime in the next few days, hopefully."

"You're going to have a great time with this, Margo!" Sam says.

I'm beaming. "I could only have imagined this in my wildest dreams. Thank you for making them come true."

Sam laughs her boisterous laugh. "My pleasure. Thank you for creating not only a great novel to produce, but also an amazing son."

"One more thing," Donna interjects. "I've added to your rider a few more items to have stocked in the green rooms and the plane. Coke Zero and almonds seemed a little on the minimalist side compared to most celebrities' wishes."

"That's fine. Thanks for looking out for me, Donna."

"It's what you pay me to do. Bye!"

"Bye!"

I click the "leave meeting" button. I can't wait to call Pat. who has given me so much good advice over the years, to see if she wants to travel with me…on a private plane!

The stylist arrives at our house promptly at two o'clock with a wheeled rack of clothes for me to try on. I won't lie, it's a lot of fun having someone else dressing you. The first fifteen minutes she shows me pictures of the outfits on a photo image of me. We review each picture to determine my "style", the image I want to portray and what the studio wants me to portray. After eliminating several looks, my stylist starts pulling different clothes off the rack. She arranges the collars, cuffs, etc. and then hands me various scarves and jewelry to accessorize the look. Last but not least are the shoes. I confess shoes are my weakness and the styles she brought were a lot of fun. Some of the clothes need altering and others simply don't fit. Two hours later we have identified an outfit for every interview and a few spares.

Just as she is heading out the door, I remembered that I would need something to wear to the movie premier. "Wait! What should I wear to the premier?" I call after her.

My stylist turns and looks back at me. "You'll be coming to LA to work with a designer on that after the first of the year."

How fun! I have an hour before we have to leave to head to the baseball game. I'd love to take a nap, but decide just to sit and relax for a few minutes. I haven't decided yet what to wear to the game. How ironic. I just spent the last two hours deciding what to wear for all my upcoming events and now I'm not sure what to wear tonight. I walk into my bedroom and open a dresser drawer in search of an outfit. Facing me, at eye level on top of the dresser, is the picture of Margaret holding my dad. I had forgotten all about Dad's "gift" to me. As I reach for the frame, the doorbell rings.

CHAPTER TWENTY-FIVE

I run to the door, still clutching the frame in my right hand. No one is there. I hear a truck pull away and find an Amazon box lying on the doorstep. I reach down and pull it inside. It's heavy, probably the author copies of my books I ordered several weeks ago. I place the box aside. It can wait. Selecting what I wear to the game tonight can wait. I've been home several days and have forgotten about taking this picture from its fragile glass frame.

My hands are shaking as I carefully slide the tabs on the back to an open position and lift the dilapidated cardboard back out of the way. An envelope falls onto the floor. As I stoop to scoop it up, the faint smell of honeysuckle wafts by. I turn over the envelope to see the front. "William" is written in a woman's script. The flap has not been sealed, but rather tucked in to the back. It's in remarkably good shape. I extract the cream-colored note hiding inside and, without unfolding it, I begin to read:

December 1932

Dearest Sweet William,

You stole my heart the day you were born. I could never have imagined the instantaneous joy you brought me the minute the doctor placed you in my arms. You are incredibly and indescribably beautiful...a gift from God. And I am grateful to Him for blessing your dad and me with you. You and I will always have an unbreakable bond. I wish you a life filled with as much happiness as you have brought us. My love for you

The sentence continues on the other side of the folded note. But I already know what the rest of it says. And I say it out loud. "Will shine brighter than the stars and will live long past when they quit twinkling." I know those words, because I wrote them in a journal to Brock when he was a baby. How could that be?

Tears splash down my cheeks and I carefully unfold the letter so they don't fall on Margaret's handwriting.

will shine brighter than the stars and will live long past when they quit twinkling.

Eternally yours.

Love,

Mother

I feel as if I've intruded on the most intimate communication a mother and son could have just like my journal to Brock. I remember filling its lined pages with thoughts of how his life was unfolding and the hopes I had for his future. I've never given it to him.

Gently, I place Margaret's letter back in its envelope and replace it behind their picture in its frame. Then I hesitantly walk to my nightstand and open the bottom drawer, hoping the journal is still there. I don't see it. Frantically I start removing items until at last, at the bottom of the drawer, I see the maroon leather binding. Without opening it, I clutch the book to my chest. I need to give this to Brock soon which means I'll have to explain to Chase why I didn't write one for him. Had I not been chasing him around the house when he was young and been busy taking Brock to and from school, I would have had the time. No, I'll write Chase's soon...so at least he'll have something personal from me. That will ease my conscience.

"What time are we leaving?" Wynn asks, startling me when he enters the bedroom.

I look at him blankly. "Leaving for what?"

"The game." He walks over to me and takes the journal from my hands. "What's this?"

I grab it back. "Oh nothing. It's just a journal I kept for Brock when he was little. I came across it when I was looking for something else. I meant to give it to him years ago."

"Why don't you put it in his room?" Wynn suggests, diverting his attention back to the ESPN scoreboard on his phone.

You mean the room he doesn't stay in anymore? I want to say. But instead, I place the leather book on top of my nightstand and head to my closet to get changed for the game.

• • •

I have to be honest. I've never really liked watching baseball games. They're too slow and too long for me. The atmosphere is fun for the first few innings. Then the boredom sets in and I secretly wish I could be working on my puzzle book.

Usually once or twice a year when the boys were growing up, Wynn and I would take them to a Rangers game. Wynn's favorite teams are the Orioles and the Mets so we'd often try to pick one of those games. Since the Mets are a National League team, they didn't always play the Rangers at home in Arlington.

In fact, our family has a lot of funny stories about those games. Chase likes to remind us that he missed several of the Opening Day games because his math grade was too low. At least, maybe, he learned a lesson about the importance of school. But he'll deny that to this day.

Once Brock got his driver's license, he took his brother to several games. Chase still likes to remind him about the night when an ad played on the jumbotron screen for a local news station advertising their new "4 Warn Weather" alert system. It was spring and there had been talk of potential storms that evening. But Brock viewed the ad as if it were in real time and insisted they leave the game. He realized there was no bad weather heading their way once they got to the car.

One of the last times the four of us went to a game, we watched the Yankees play. Maybe it was because the Yankees always draw a big crowd, but Wynn was able to only find four tickets together up in the nosebleed seats. Home plate looked like a postage stamp from our seats three rows from the top of the stadium. By the seventh inning stretch, the two Yankees fans behind us were very drunk and had gotten very obnoxious. The Rangers fan in the row in front of us was wearing a hat with antlers on it, a gimmick that caught on after a player had wiggled his hands by his ears one game to get the crowd to be loud. The antlered hat itself seemed to provoke the Yankee fan who began shouting obscenities. We did our best to ignore him for an inning. Then his buddy came back with more beer and they started shouting "five-five and nobody out." Finally, the Rangers fans sitting in front of us had had enough. One of them left to get security. Brock made me switch seats with him so that I wouldn't get caught in the fight that might ensue. Then Wynn switched seats with Brock. The security guard tried his best to subdue the Yankee fan, but when he took a swing at the guard, the fan was escorted out.

The Yankees ended up winning that game, but we had a great time talking about what happened on our way to the car. We were about halfway there when Brock grabbed my arm. "Look!" He pointed to two guys about fifty feet from us. One of whom was holding a white towel to his nose, spotted with blood. "It's that guy who was behind us."

Despite the apparent broken nose, the Yankee fan appeared to be laughing with his friend. "I'll bet he'll have a hell of a hangover tomorrow," Wynn commented.

We all laughed. "A great example of adults behaving badly," I added. To this day, I refuse to attend a Yankees game.

My favorite team has always been the St. Louis Cardinals…

until now. Where I grew up, you were either a Cardinals fan or a Cubs fan. During those days, Cubs fans were known as die-hards because their team rarely won. Plus, I had cousins who lived in St. Louis so it was an easy decision which team I cheered for. Now that Brock works for the Rangers, they of course are my favorite team (at least outwardly...inside I'll always be a Cards fan.)

Wynn, Brock and I attended a World Series game years ago between the Rangers and the Cards. Chase was in Orlando on a choir trip, wishing he could have gone with us. I proudly wore the Cardinals shirt my St. Louis cousin had sent me. Wynn and Brock gave me a hard time, but we received a lot of attention as a "house divided." The Cards ended up winning that game so it was a quiet ride back to our house. And it was even quieter the night they won the Series.

But tonight's a different story. Tonight is game six of the World Series. Once again, I get to watch my Cardinals play the home team...only this time I *must* cheer for the Rangers and leave my Cards' jersey at home. Brock was able to get tickets for Wynn and me to the first five games. We did not get to sit in the box then, but we did sit behind the Rangers dugout about five rows back. The Rangers split the home opener and headed to St. Louis. Wynn and I flew with Meredith and stayed at my cousins' house. Fortunately, my cousins are season ticket holders so they were able to go to the game too. The Cards won the first game in St. Louis, but lost the next two. The Rangers now lead in the series three to two. They could clinch it tonight.

This afternoon we are picking up Libby and Chase at the airport, then heading early to the game to watch batting practice.

Chase begins shooting his scenes of "our" movie on Monday. I've been invited to watch and I can't wait. They've blocked out the whole week to film, weather permitting. Late October weather can be hit or miss in Dallas. Chase and I have our first interview with the morning show on WFAA on Friday. Exciting times!

My cell rings. It's Brock. "Hi, Sweetie. Are you ready for the big game tonight?"

"You bet I am! I think tonight we will win the series! I thought I should give you a rundown of the events for this evening."

"Oh good."

"Do you think you and Dad and Chase and Libby could get to the stadium by five?"

"We are picking them up at DFW at four and plan on coming directly to the ballpark. As long as their plane is on time, I don't see why we wouldn't be able to make it by five."

"Great! There's a cocktail and heavy appetizers party in one of the private dining halls. I'm allowed five guests. Should be better food and some good people watching and Dad will still have time to watch batting practice either from your seats or from the party."

"That's good to hear. He's been counting on watching that."

"Don't forget the jerseys I gave you for Chase and Libby to wear. I wouldn't want them wearing that stupid red bird paraphernalia."

"Ok, let's not be calling my second favorite team names. They are, after all, the best team in the National League."

Brock snorts. "Yea, well, sadly they won't be able to say

best in the world. This time, the Rangers are going to prevail. No funny stuff."

I sigh. "They won fair and square."

"Debatable."

"You mean it would be bad form for me to wear my Cardinals shirt tonight?"

"Please tell me you won't."

"I won't," I laugh. "You're more important to me than my red birds are, as you and Dad like to call them."

"Okay. Good. Because they won't let you into any of the parties if you aren't appropriately dressed."

"Not to worry."

"When we win the game, there will be the requisite fireworks. I suggest you make your way to the dining hall where the cocktail party was. The World Series celebration will be held there. In fact, if we are ahead in the eighth inning, you can start heading that direction. The doors will be open."

He's sounds so positive that I decide not to ask him what the plan is if the Cardinals win and this goes to game seven. "Sounds like a plan."

"I'm sorry I couldn't get you in a box. Maybe next season."

"Oh, we are just excited to be at the game. The seats you got for us are amazing! Your brother will be thrilled."

"Meredith will come by and say hi. I will too, if I get a chance."

"How's she feeling?"

"Really well."

"That's great. We'll see you tonight. Good luck! Go Rangers!"

"Thanks, Mom."

• • •

Wynn and I pick up Chase and Libby at DFW and head directly to the ballpark. I hand them the Rangers jerseys Brock had given me for them to wear. I also give them their tickets. When we arrive at the parking lot, we are five minutes ahead of schedule, allowing Libby enough time to change into the shirt in the ladies' room.

The pregame party is very crowded and it's not long before we get separated from Chase and Libby. I spot Brock on the opposite side of the room talking to a group of people. Meredith, by his side, tugs on Brock's sleeve and points our direction. He lifts his chin to acknowledge us, but we are unable to cut across the room. Wynn keeps checking his watch, not wanting to miss batting practice. We finally make our way to an open spot by the floor-to-ceiling windows overlooking the field just as the Cardinals come out of their dugout. We juggle our drinks while we eat our appetizers standing up.

"At least it's a little quieter over here." I say to Wynn. "Remind me again why watching batting practice is so important to you."

"I really don't care that much about batting practice. It was the boys who liked it because it was their best chance to get autographs from the players."

"That's right! Brock would bring his baseball cards for them to sign."

Wynn nods. "And we'd bring some balls too."

I study my husband whose eyes haven't left the field. He

looks lost in a memory from the good old days. "Did you bring some balls tonight?"

"I might have." A grin crosses his face as he pulls two balls out of his pocket. "Where did Chase go? He and I need to get out there before the *winning* team takes the field."

I crane my neck and stand on my tiptoes to see around the group of people next to us. After scanning the crowd for a minute, I see Libby's blonde ponytail. "Over there," I point them out.

"I'll just text Chase. It'll be too difficult to maneuver our way over there."

Wynn types in three words on his phone and presses the send button.

I have balls.

That's what she said! LOL. So do I. Did you remember the Sharpie?

Of course, I did! Meet me behind the Rangers' dugout.

Will do. Libby's coming too. Bring Mom.

"Come on. Let's go down to the field," Wynn says pulling my arm.

I throw my drink and cocktail plate in the trash and follow my husband, noting the huge smile on his face. He will get to relive those glory days he spent with the boys at batting practice.

When we get to the interior walkway that circles the various restaurants and souvenir shops, I nudge Wynn. "Do you think maybe you should let the dads with uh, younger children have a chance at getting autographs first?"

Wynn stops dead in his tracks as if I have said the most absurd thing ever. "You didn't really mean that, right?"

I lift my palms to the sky. "Of course, I did."

He looks at me like I have three heads. "Not only is this the World Series. It's game six. Children have had their chance during all of the other home games. Tonight is for us die-hard fans."

"Oh, okay. Sorry."

As we make our way to the Rangers' dugout, I notice there are very few young children. Chase and Libby are already there. Before we get close enough, I see one of the players smile at Libby. She tosses him a ball and he signs it.

Wynn leans over. "See, that's how it's done. You get a pretty girl to get the player's attention and voilà!" He catches Chase's eye and gives him the thumbs up.

"Do you suppose Brock was able to get any of his baseball cards signed earlier?"

"I doubt that many of those players whose cards he has are still playing. Plus, he can get autographs anytime."

I cross my arms. "I was referring to the Cardinals."

Wynn shoots me a look of disgust. "Chirp chirp."

It turns out that Libby was the only one who was successful in obtaining an autograph. The Ranger was nice enough to date it as well.

When we arrive at our seats, Wynn takes out his binoculars. "There've got to be a lot of famous people here."

Chase rolls his eyes. "Dad, are you ever going to stop doing that?" He leans over to Libby. "He's seeing who is in the boxes."

Libby giggles. "Some day soon, people will be looking for your son, Wynn."

Wynn puts down his binoculars. "You're right about that."

At the end of the first inning the score is zero to zero. Meredith comes up to us, ball in hand. "Brock asked me to give this to you, Wynn." The ball is signed by Joey Gallo. "He didn't want you to feel left out." Meredith winks at me. Wynn's face lights up.

Wynn can say all he wants about watching batting practice just for the boys. It's also for the little boy that's still inside him!

"Tell Brock thanks," says Wynn, still grinning. "This guy is the star of the team."

The Cardinals are back up to bat at the top of the second. "I better get back to the box. I wish I could sit with you all. The crowd up there isn't nearly as fun."

"Ask my brother if I can switch with you for a few innings. That way you and Libby can get caught up."

"Great idea," says Meredith. "I'll be back in a bit."

At the top of the third, Meredith gives her lanyard to Chase and he goes to sit with his brother for a few innings. Neither team has scored yet. I'm happy to listen to my daughters-in-law talk. What a blessing they both are and the fact that they have become friends is icing on the cake.

While the Rangers' pitcher warms up, Wynn takes a minute to scan the box where Brock and Chase are sitting. "Ha! They're looking at me with their binoculars!" He waves.

My phone vibrates. It's a text from my St. Louis cousin who couldn't get tickets to this game. **GO CARDS!**

I give it a thumbs up and add: **Close game.**

Chase returns during the seventh inning stretch and Meredith reluctantly heads back to the suite. "Looks like this may go into extra innings, Mom." He's teasing me, because he knows that the longer the game, the more tortuous for me. Not to mention the fact that scoreless games are boring.

But a crack of the bat and the crowd standing snaps me back to what's happening on the field. Elvis Andrus has just hit a home run with the bases loaded. The Rangers are now ahead 4-0. The crowd erupts. Chase jumps up and down and high fives his dad.

"Looks like I spoke too soon," Chase says to me. "Be happy, Mom. This game will end sooner rather than later."

"If the Rangers are still ahead after the redbirds bat in the eighth, we are supposed to head back to where we had drinks before the game," Wynn tells Chase and Libby. "The celebration will be there."

"Don't count your chickens before they're hatched," I admonish Wynn.

"Oh, I'm shaking in my shoes," Wynn says.

Sure enough, an inning later the score is the same. It looks like my Cardinals will be shut out. But Brock will be elated. We head back to the dining area where a small crowd has already gathered.

But the Cardinals seem to rally in the ninth inning, scoring three runs off their first four batters. It's now 4-3 and the Cards still have two outs. Everyone in the room seems to be holding his breath.

"Are you worried?" I ask Wynn.

Wynn shakes his head. "Not in the least. They're exactly where they don't want to be...at the bottom of their batting order. It will be three more batters before they get back to the top.

The next "terrible batter" gets on base. Wynn and Chase exchange worried glances.

"If they can just get these next two out, we'll be fine," Chase says.

But the next batter gets a base hit. "Bottom of the order, huh?" I say.

Wynn is silent.

Brock and Meredith join us. I look at Brock. "We'll be okay," he says to me.

The final batter of the Cards batting order steps up to the plate. He doesn't swing at the first pitch, which is perfectly over the plate. Strike one. He swings and misses at the second. Strike two. The pitcher throws a fastball perfectly over the plate. The batter connects with the ball, popping it up. The shortstop catches it and the Rangers begin to celebrate.

"Ball game!" Wynn shouts to Brock.

The cheering is accented by the sounds of champagne corks popping. Brock hands each of us a World Champions t-shirt! And the party begins.

As I am hugging Brock, I notice a familiar face across the room. The man is zigzagging his way across the crowded room. My heart stops. It's Dad! I slowly pull away from Brock, pasting the smile on my face. Maybe this is a good thing. I won't be the only one who sees him!

I back away and suddenly Dad is right behind Brock. He's so close, I can smell his Obsession aftershave. Dad places his hands on Brock's shoulders and gives him a gentle squeeze. I can't hear what he's saying, but he's definitely whispering in Brock's ear. Frantically, I look at Wynn. He's talking to Chase and Libby, his back turned to Brock and me.

Just as Brock begins to turn, Meredith pulls on his arm and says something I can't hear. Brock nods and turns to face the now empty space behind him. He looks at me with a question on his face. "Did you just see who was behind me, Mom? He left before I could see who it was and talk to him."

Don't worry. You just missed seeing your dearly departed grandfather, one of your favorite people. Deciding not to upset my son during this joyful moment, I shake my head. "What did he say?"

"Huh. Ok. Just that he'd always been a huge Cardinals fan, but he was cheering for my team tonight and that he was proud of me. I thought he must have been someone I knew. His aftershave smelled familiar. Oh well. Would you mind taking Meredith home? She's feeling a little light-headed and tired. I may be here awhile longer."

"We'd be happy to do that. Besides, your brother has an early call time tomorrow. I'm sure he'll want to get his beauty rest!"

"What's this about needing to get my beauty rest?" Chase comes over.

"We're going to head out and take Meredith home. Since you have an early call time tomorrow, I thought you might want to turn in a little early, even if it's two hours later from your 'getting up' time in California."

"Good idea, Mom. Say, who was that man behind you, Brock? He looked a lot like Granddad!"

"Really? I don't know. He was gone when I turned around. Break a leg tomorrow!"

CHAPTER TWENTY-SIX

As it turned out, had we not needed to take Meredith home, we could have stayed longer at the party. And maybe then I could have looked for Dad. It's raining this morning and the shoot has been delayed until this afternoon when the weather is supposed to clear. That's the thing about Texas weather, if you don't like it, just wait a minute and it will change!

I'm fixing pancakes for Chase and Libby, even though they are not on Chase's "diet." I know he'll indulge me and eat at least one. The newlyweds are sitting at our breakfast table reading the newspaper while Wynn microwaves the bacon and syrup.

"Hmm...Mom that smells delicious. Your pancakes and bacon...perfect on a rainy morning. Thank you for going to the trouble to make my favorite breakfast," Chase says as I place his plate in front of him and Libby's in front of her. Wynn brings our plates to the table.

"It's my pleasure, Sweetie." I take my seat across from Chase. "What had they planned to shoot this morning?"

Chase reaches for his script and flips through his notes while he chews his first bite of pancake. "Mostly just some scenes of me going in and out of buildings around town. I don't have many lines. It should be easy to squeeze into the schedule once the weather clears. They took a lot of B roll shots last week."

Wynn looks up from the sports section. "What are 'B roll shots?'"

"Great question, Dad. That's when they show scenery for example. It's extra footage that they may or may not need to use in the film. They want the viewers to feel like what they are seeing really is taking place in Dallas even though almost all of the indoor scenes will be filmed in the studio in Burbank. Sometimes its easier and less expensive to shoot the actual building or park or whatever than to recreate it by building a set."

"Interesting," Wynn nods and goes back to checking the hockey scores.

"Libby, when are you going to see your folks?" I ask. "You are more than welcome to use our car."

"Oh, thanks. Mom actually wants to know if you'd like to join us for lunch today."

I'm about to answer when Chase cuts in. "No can do, Mom. We have a phone meeting with our agents at noon, our time, to go over the questions they are going to ask us when we are on *Good Morning Texas* later this week. Our call time for this afternoon is one-thirty. You plan to go, don't you?"

"Sorry, Libby. My boss just informed me that I can't go to lunch with you and your mom, at least not today." I frown at Chase.

"Don't look at me that way! The director will probably want to consult with you during the shoot," Chase says.

"Oh, yes, I'm so important." I roll my eyes. "I'm pretty sure authors don't have a say in anything."

Chase grins. "You never know. But one thing I do know, you'll learn a lot."

"Let's back up for a minute," Wynn interjects. "You get the questions in advance of an interview? Is that standard procedure?"

Chase's eyebrows shoot upwards. "Did you think all those celebrity interviews you've seen were just off the cuff responses?"

Wynn hangs his head sheepishly. "Well, yes, I guess I did."

"Very rare that would happen, especially on live TV. They, at a minimum, give you an outline of what will be discussed."

"Like how handsome your dad is?" Wynn can't help himself. Libby giggles.

"Something like that. Anyway, Dad, you are more than welcome to come with us...if you can promise you'll behave."

"You're no fun, you know that?" Wynn pretends he's exasperated with Chase. "I'll have to check with my secretary to see if I can fit it into my busy schedule." Wynn turns to me. "Am I available that day?"

I shake my head, feigning disgust. "I guess you can be."

As forecast, the sun broke through the clouds just before our noon phone meeting and the rain stopped. Chase and I arrive at the first shoot location about one-fifteen in downtown. We pull into the parking garage and head to one of the two motorhomes parked in the lot, their generators running.

"I take it this is for your hair and makeup?" I ask Chase.

Chase nods. "Because we are on location, they just have two RVs. One is for hair and makeup and the other is for craft service. Why don't you go get yourself something to eat and drink, Mom, while I get made up?"

"Good idea," I say nervously. I'm unsure if I should really be hanging out with the cast and crew.

Chase notices my hesitation. He takes my hands in his and looks me directly in the eyes. "Ma, if it weren't for you, none of these people would be here, right?"

"I guess."

"You guess?" Chase's blue eyes are piercing through mine.

"Well, when you put it that way, yes. They wouldn't be here without my story."

"Good. Now put on your self-confidence and introduce yourself to the crew and whoever else is in the other RV. I don't want you just standing around the parking garage."

A woman, wearing jeans and a solid black t-shirt and a tool belt filled with makeup brushes and aerosol bottles comes out of the makeup RV. "Oh hey," she says to us. "Are you Chase?"

"I am he."

"I'm Ginger. Your makeup artist. I'm ready whenever you are, but no rush."

"Great! Ginger, this is Margo Parker, the author of this movie."

Ginger shakes my hand. "Cool! I've never met the actual developer of a film. Nice to meet you, Mrs. Parker."

I'm pretty sure she may need to add some powder to my cheeks to tone down their redness. "Nice to meet you, Ginger."

"Wait, that means she's your mom," Ginger says to Chase. "That is wicked cool, a mother and son combo. You're welcome to come in the trailer and watch your son get made up. Or go next door and get something to eat and drink."

"I think I'll head next door," I answer, suddenly feeling a bit more confident. "See you soon."

Chase winks at me before following Ginger into the RV.

With a little remaining trepidation, I mount the few steps and open the door to the other RV. There are only two other women inside. "Hi, can we help you?" one says as she looks up from what appears to be a script.

"Hi, I'm Margo Parker."

"Oh, Chase's mom?"

"Yes."

The other woman looks up. "She's the author of the movie. I'm Tara, the on-site director." Tara offers me her hand. "Let me get your lanyard so you're official. This is Peggy, our script girl. She takes notes on each take so for example, if Chase is carrying a book in his right hand when the take ends, he's still carrying it in his right hand when we resume the next one."

I smile. "That's a very important and detailed job, Peggy. It's nice to meet you both."

Tara continues. "I apologize. Usually, our craft service is not this limited, but since we are only shooting for a few hours it's the best we can do. Why don't you get something to nibble on and a drink and I'll walk you to our first scene."

I grab a Coke Zero and a bag of pretzels and follow Tara and Peggy out of the RV. We walk out of the darkness of the parking garage and into the blinding Texas sun. The sidewalks and streets are now completely dry. There's no evidence of the barrage of rain we had earlier this morning. I follow Tara to a group of three directors' chairs. One has my name on it.

Tara motions for me to sit in my seat while she starts talking to the cameraman. I see her nod and head over to one of the crew who is holding a large screen that apparently is used to deflect some of the light. He tips it at a different angle. Tara steps back and nods.

It's now two o'clock. Chase comes up to me. "Does my lipstick look okay?" he jokes with me, but his lips do have a pink hue. "I told you there'd be a chair for you."

"Yes, your lipstick looks fine. Everyone here has been so nice."

Tara walks up to Chase and pulls him aside to give him some instructions. He walks to the revolving door and heads inside the glass office building. Then he walks out. Tara says something else to him that I can't hear. Chase repeats the same sequence.

This time Tara appears pleased and yells for quiet on the set. "Action," she says.

Chase again enters the building and then comes back out.

"And that's a take," Tara calls. "Good job, Chase. Next up."

Chase walks up to me. "Well, what did you think?'

"That's it? Pretty tough! Next time don't flub your lines!" I joke.

"I promise I won't since I don't have any today!"

Ginger approaches Chase with makeup brush in hand. "You need a little powder before the next scene." She gently taps the brush before swiping Chase's nose with it. "There, better."

For some reason Tara is not happy with the next scene. Finally, after the seventeenth take, she is satisfied. Movie filming is not always glamorous and exciting I am finding out. It can be quite long and boring. I'm making a mental list of excuses for why I can't make tomorrow's shoot. Or at least maybe I can miss part of it. At the top of my list is composing answers to the interview questions my agent gave me during our noon meeting. Yes, that's it! I really need to rehearse my answers in front of a mirror. I only have three days to prepare.

Watching a movie being filmed may be dull, but being interviewed about writing the movie is not! Bright and early Friday morning, Wynn drives us downtown to the Channel Eight studios at Victory Park. I'm wearing the chic, yet artsy, pantsuit approved by my stylist and agent. Chase is wearing dark wash denim jeans and a form-fitting long-sleeve black crew neck shirt. I would have made him wear a collared shirt, but it wasn't up to me.

Last night Chase and I rehearsed the interview with the help of Libby and Wynn. But somehow, it's different under the studio lights with cameramen and light technicians and the makeup artist who touched up my hair and is now applying powder to my nose. Chase gets his "shine" from me.

A crew member motions for us to sit in chairs next to each other at an angle from the interviewer who has yet to come on set. She's busy filming the segment prior to ours, so we must be quiet. As Chase approaches his chair, he notices a man's driving hat is on his seat. "Look," he whispers, pointing to the dark brown cap. It looks exactly like the hat my dad used to wear. When my sister and I were young we called it his burglar cap. I really don't remember why we thought a burglar would wear that style of hat. I realize it's a sign that Dad's here. Chase gently lifts it off his chair and sits down, holding it on his lap.

I'm wringing my hands and Chase reaches over to stop me. "You're going to be great," he mouths to me.

I give him my best smile and nod.

During the commercial break, the host comes over and shakes our hands before taking her seat. The same crew member takes the cap from Chase who almost reluctantly lets go. Then the five second count happens and we're on.

The actual interview took less than ten minutes and it felt like two. I am amazed how easy it was. Nothing to be nervous about! I could get used to this!

The crew member returns the hat to Chase who puts it on, checks his look in a mirror and decides to keep it.

CHAPTER TWENTY-SEVEN

Heaven, today.

William looks out over the water. The sun is shining brightly as it always does in his world, and he notices his favorite shade of "new" blue is present. New is how he thinks of it anyway. It's not a shade he ever experienced in his mortal life. She would like it. The gentle breeze smells like a combination of honeysuckle and lilacs and freshly mown grass, very similar to how a late spring day used to smell on Earth. It would be impossible to describe this incredible assault on the senses to anyone. He can't even understand it himself. All William knows is that he relishes this beauty and tranquility and he will be immensely grateful when his "task" is complete.

He sees an enormous yacht on the horizon which transforms almost instantly into an angel. The angel is suddenly in front of him.

"Do not let me startle you, William," the angel says. "I guess you knew I would show up sometime since you requested to speak to me."

"I appreciate your coming, Gabrielle. You most likely will not be surprised by my request."

"It's about your mother, isn't it?"

William nods.

"She's been a real challenge and quite frankly, has made my life, well I'd say hellish, but that would be an exaggeration and would be frowned on by my superiors. What is it now?"

William summons all of his tact and persuasiveness that he had as a mortal soul. Back in the day, he was known as a calm, wise and patient man. His character was never questioned and he was revered by many. When William asked others to jump, they usually said, "How high?" Heaven works differently, he's discovered during the time he's been here. Different in a good way. If mortals could actually live to the line in the Lord's Prayer: "Thy will be done on Earth as it is in Heaven" their lives would be vastly easier and more peaceful. How many times had he prayed those words himself and not actually given them much thought?

"She needs more time." William decides to go the simple, yet direct route.

"Why? Did she accept what you told her about her soul?"

"Not as yet. I do think I made some progress. I just don't feel her soul's purpose is quite complete. Do you?"

Gabrielle's white robes billow in the breeze reminding William of the days when he sold choir robes. "And just what have you deemed that purpose to be?"

William could never understand why Gabrielle spoke so formally. However, he was thankful that he didn't have to experience being an angel. Angels seemed to be tormented souls or maybe souls who still had some things to learn. Obviously, they weren't evil, but they definitely didn't seem joyful.

"She still needs time with her sons." William decided to make that his first reason.

"She's had three decades with them. That's more than she had with you."

Time for reason number two. "She's just now achieving her dreams."

"Which are?"

William is getting frustrated. Who is Gabrielle to judge? "Her book is being made into a movie starring her younger son. They are going to be traveling together to promote the movie which premieres early next year."

"What about her other son?"

William smiles. "He's about to attain two of his dreams also early next year. Margo needs to see that."

"How early?"

"Does it matter?"

"Are you arguing with me?"

"No, of course not. I'm just beseeching you to allow her to see these events come to fruition." There! William put his request into Gabrielle's vernacular.

"One moment, please." Poof! Gabrielle evaporates into the clouds suspended above the water. William isn't sure if he'd been successful or not. One thing he is confident of: God makes the judgement as to the timing of a soul's journey into his kingdom. William knows Margo well. He knows how passionate she is about her grown children. She will be an incredible grandmother. And her recent successes have made him proud. "Life's not fair." The phrase echoes in his heart. He wishes he hadn't harped so much on that when Margo was growing up.

The sun, which is illuminating the white clouds, seems to intensify. It's color changes to a golden yellow no mortal has seen. Its size grows exponentially. William feels the Lord's presence.

William lifts his soul closer to the Almighty.

"I have heard your plea, William."

"Thank you for your consideration, God."

"I think you've made some excellent points on her behalf."

William waits. "I will grant your request. But this will be the last one I can fulfill. To quote a phrase they use often on Earth, 'Come hell or highwater' she will be joining us soon. Your mission is still to get her to accept that ...to accept that life's not fair."

William knows he should be elated that the Lord has granted her more time. But he remembers how easy it is to get caught up with life as a mortal. He's sure her relationship with her sons and husband is paramount, topping any success as an author. That's probably why his request was granted.

The sun returns to its normal intensity and color. William decides to go back to his perch to watch the rest of her life play out.

CHAPTER TWENTY-EIGHT

It's been several weeks since the Texas Rangers won the World Series. Chase and Libby have returned to LA to resume filming the movie. Brock and Meredith took a much-needed vacation and have returned home. And I can't help thinking about how close my sons were to seeing their grandfather. There's no doubt in my mind that it was him. I wonder if either one of the boys has thought any more about it. There was so much commotion that night with the celebration that they've likely forgotten. And then the cap on Chase's seat at the interview. I had fully expected Chase to say something more about it on the way home from the interview, but he didn't. It's strange that neither son mentioned it to me. But I am glad Daddy got to cheer on both of his boys.

As I sit outside enjoying this unseasonably warm November day, I watch a hawk circling above, its graceful wings in sharp contrast with the azure blue sky. After the hawk's third circle, I wonder if it's trying to show off. It seems to be having a wonderful time catching the wind and soaring through the warm air, not a care in the world. The phrase, "I'm going to watch you like a hawk," enters my mind. Did my parents say it to me? Did I say it to the boys? I can't really remember. That species of bird must have incredible vision. I've watched one swoop down from high above and pick off a snake slithering innocently on the ground in our neighbor's yard.

Maybe it's Dad. He did say that sometimes he took the form of a bird. If it is him, I wish to heck he'd let me know whether I should tell my sister I've seen him or not. No, he'd say not. But is this really fair to Melissa? If she'd seen Dad, wouldn't I want her to tell me? Maybe she has! Maybe Dad told her not to tell me! Doubtful. I think she'd be acting weird if she had. Which begs the question: "Am I?" Am I acting strange around her?

Fortunately, or unfortunately, we haven't seen each other much since my birthday due to vacations and busy schedules. But she's due here in a few minutes and I need to make a decision on whether to tell her or not.

Throughout my life, I've found that half the battle of solving a puzzle is determining the best method to use to complete it. Maybe using my logic skills will help me decide. Let's look at this in reverse. If Melissa had been seeing Dad, would I want her to tell me? Of course! That way she could ask him questions for me and tell me how he is! Or no, I'd feel jealous. Why would he appear to her and not to me?

This has nothing to do with Melissa. Dad's words echo in my head. But she is his daughter too! *It's time for me to explain why you've been able to see me and other family members haven't. It turns out, you're not only my daughter, you're my mother.* No! That just can't be. There's no part of me that's going to buy that. And if that's true, why would he have appeared at the celebration a few weeks ago? Brock felt his hands on his shoulder and heard his voice. Maybe Dad's changed his mind? I need some kind of sign.

The door to our patio opens and Melissa steps out. I turn to face her. "Don't move." Her voice is low and ominous sounding. She freezes in her spot.

"Is it a snake?" I ask, holding perfectly still.

She slowly shakes her head. "Look very slowly towards your fence."

I rotate my shoulders as if I'm in slow motion. There, on our wrought iron fence, is the hawk. Now I have no doubt it's Dad. He's the sign I'm looking for. He wants me to tell Melissa. Maybe he's going to appear to her, to us, together!

But the hawk tilts his head and blinks. *I'll be watching you like a hawk.* No, he's here to make sure I don't tell my sister.

Melissa slowly creeps over to sit next to me on the couch. "I couldn't stand there forever," she whispers. "I feel like we're playing freeze tag!" The hawk doesn't move off his perch. "Maybe he thinks we're lunch?"

I laugh. "There have been several times when I've been in the deep end of the pool with just my head above the water wondering whether from far away the hawk could tell I'm not an animal, or snake as the case was one day."

"If he keeps the snake population down, then I love him."

She'd really love him if she knew who he was. I stare back at Dad, the hawk, and give him the "eagle" eye. *Your secret's safe with me, Daddy.* Daddy, not son or William. "I am not Margaret."

"You're not what?" Melissa asks.

Oh no! Did I say that out loud? "I'm not his lunch!"

With that, Dad takes off.

"That's a beautiful bird," Melissa says. "I'll bet he helps keep the rats and mice away too."

"Yep. Always good to have a hawk around unless you have small pets."

"How's Meredith? Did she and Brock get to go on their vacation?"

Melissa is referring to a brief scare the day after the Rangers' World Series celebration. Meredith was afraid she was miscarrying, but she'd just overdone it the day before. "She's fine and is showing now. They got back from their trip yesterday. How are the girls?"

"Both working hard. I wouldn't be surprised if there's a wedding in our household soon."

"Really? That would be great! When?"

"I'm guessing maybe next fall."

"We have a lot to look forward to next year."

"That we do!"

I'm comfortable with my decision to withhold my "Dad visits" from my sister at least for a little while longer. How crazy would I sound if I told her that I'm really her grandmother? I'm sure she would feel obligated to stage a psychiatric intervention for me. Yes, this is a secret I'll keep for a long, long time. I'll probably take it to my grave.

CHAPTER TWENTY-NINE

The holidays were a blur. We gathered together as a family at Melissa's house for Thanksgiving, sans Chase and Libby who had to stay in LA due to Chase's shoot schedule. Brock and Meredith joined us before heading to see Meredith's family the following day. We all got to feel the baby "kick" and my daughter-in-law was certainly glowing. She was definitely enjoying her second trimester.

We usually spend Christmas in Florida and I was disappointed that we couldn't this year. But it just didn't make sense for Chase and Libby to fly from coast-to-coast for the few days Chase had off. Plus, Libby wanted to spend time with her family here in town. I'm afraid that next year and for many years after we won't be able to spend Christmas there because it's easier for the little ones to be at home! Who knows, by then, Libby may be expecting.

Christmas is my favorite holiday. I decorate our home to the hilt and love hosting my annual party for my water aerobics class members. I love listening to the music, baking cookies, and the spirit of giving. But, the most important thing for me about Christmas is that our family spends it together. Brock, Meredith, Chase and Libby went to church with us Christmas Eve and dinner following. Libby's parents and siblings, who are also members of our church, joined us. The boys and their spouses came to our house for brunch and our gift exchange Christmas morning before heading to the girls' families. By Christmas afternoon, Wynn and I were ready to savor a glass of wine by the fireplace and rest!

Wynn and I had planned on heading to Florida in early January to escape the dreary winter weather, but Chase called requesting that I attend the final day of filming on our movie. The date was set for the second week in January. Part of me was ecstatic to go and the other part of me feared them potentially altering my story. I used to hate going to a movie when I'd read the book upon which it was based. Ninety-nine percent of the time, the book was far better. And I especially disliked it if they changed the ending. Which would be better? If they changed the ending and everyone said my book was better than the movie? Or if they changed the ending to something everyone liked better? I hope they didn't change the ending. After all, I wrote the story, they didn't.

While I was in LA, I tried on ball gowns for the premiere. The stylist actually had me select two: one for the movie premier and the other for the after-party. The first one is an off-the-shoulder cobalt blue gown which is very flattering to my figure. The second one is slightly more fun and casual. It's an ankle length skirt with more of a Bohemian top…something that is not usually my style, but is a lot of fun to wear.

Unfortunately, because they had not shot the ending, I still have yet to see the final film. Chase assures me that there were no *major* changes to my book. And what I saw during the last few days of filming followed my plot exactly! Now I'm hoping my book is as good as the movie! And how could the movie not be good when it stars my son?

It's almost the end of February. We've survived winter's worst weather and now the premiere is only ten days away. Chase is probably ready to send me to a foreign country since I ask him almost daily if he's seen a preview. He has not. Exasperation is starting to creep into his voice when I talk to him so I have resorted to texting.

Wynn and I are picking up Libby and Chase this evening at Love Field. My good friend and publicist, Pat, is also flying in tonight from Houston. Tomorrow, the five of us, plus my sister and my hair stylist, leave for the Big Apple! I wanted Brock and Meredith to come too, but she's only a month away from her due date and her OBGYN doesn't want her traveling. Sam's plane will be at Love Field tomorrow morning to, in her words, "pick us up." I'm not sure if she'll be joining us.

I had my "final fitting" for my wardrobe last week. Fortunately, I haven't gained any weight. The clothes, shoes and accessories are all hanging in my closet in a special wardrobe box. My stylist actually put an app on my phone with pictures of me in each outfit along with a detailed list of accessories to wear with each. A van is coming to pick up the clothing this afternoon to take them to the private hangar where Sam's plane will arrive.

We actually decided to go to New York City a few days early to see some Broadway shows. I think it will be a good thing for me to be busy so I'm not dwelling on how badly I might screw up these interviews. The local one Chase and I did was a piece of cake. I guess I'm just nervous about meeting my favorite talk show hosts.

A few minutes before five o'clock, Wynn comes downstairs from his home office. "What time are we leaving to pick up Chase?"

"I just checked and their flight is on time. I think we should leave in a few minutes. Pat's flight is also on schedule. How lucky are we that they are arriving within ten minutes of each other? I texted them that I'd meet them at baggage claim."

Wynn looks at his watch. "Let me freshen up and I'll be ready to go."

Rush hour traffic in the Dallas metroplex can be aggravating. Luckily for us, there has been an accident on Central Expressway just north of where we enter so traffic for us is lighter than normal. We make it to Love Field in about forty minutes. "Tomorrow we'll be heading to that private terminal," Wynn points to our right as we head up the street to the main terminal.

"Only tomorrow, you won't have to drive."

Wynn grins. "That's right. Are they sending two cars since we have seven people, plus bags?"

I shrug. "I didn't ask. Melissa said if there's not enough room, she could drive the overflow in her car."

"You have quite an entourage, Mrs. Parker," Wynn teases.

"Small, but mighty!"

Wynn finagles his way into a parking place at the first entrance to the main terminal. "Text me when they've got their bags and I'll pull up."

I nod and exit our SUV. The flights won't arrive at their respective gates for another five minutes. That gives me plenty of time to grab a Coke Zero at the Dunkin Donuts kiosk upstairs outside of security. During the "good old days," Love Field always had free donuts and coffee at each gate every morning. While I love donuts, especially the chocolate ones, I can no longer afford the calories.

Ten minutes later, my phone lights up. It's Chase. They have found my friend Pat and are heading in my direction! I make my way over to the double door exit and wait for them at the "arrivals" sign. I see my son first, weighted down by several carry-ons. Libby and Pat are deep in conversation, a few passengers behind him.

"Hi, Ma!" Chase promptly sets down the bags and envelopes me into one of his bear hugs. "Are you ready for our big adventure?"

I relish his embrace. "I can't believe it's here. No, I can't believe it's happening. I'm so thankful you're part of this journey or I'd be a nervous wreck."

"Aw, Ma, you're going to be great!"

When Chase lets me go, Libby and Pat give me a group hug. "Thank you for coming," I say to my dear friend.

"I wouldn't miss this for the world," Pat replies.

We head down the escalators to collect their bags which come up fairly quickly. I text Wynn who has spent his time waiting in the cell lot.

Wynn promptly pulls up to the curb and Chase loads the bags into the SUV. "Tomorrow someone will handle those for you, Chase," he says.

Chase shrugs. "I don't mind. I'm used to it."

"Well after this movie comes out, you'll probably never have to schlep your bags again," Pat says.

• • •

Despite a restless night, I wake up this morning feeling refreshed and ready to go. I shower and put on my "travel" outfit, the only one that didn't get packed with the rest of my wardrobe. Our flight leaves at eleven. The driver is arriving at ten...which seems like we're cutting it a little close, but I guess they won't leave without us. My sister said she'll be here around nine forty-five and my stylist is coming in just a few minutes to do my hair and makeup. I told him he didn't have to. It's not as if I'll be on TV today. But he insisted. I've known him for over twenty-five years. He's a gem!

Wynn makes me eat something for breakfast. "It's good to have a little something in your stomach. I know the food on the plane will be amazing, but I don't want you getting light-headed." He pours me a glass of orange juice and a mug of hot coffee. Chase, Libby and Pat join us at our breakfast table where my sweet husband has laid out a plate of danish and bagels.

The doorbell rings and I think it will be Joel, my stylist. But instead, it's my sister.

"You're early!" I greet her as she enters our kitchen.

She sticks her tongue out at me. "You didn't think I'd be late for this, did you?" She's referring to her perpetual tardiness throughout our childhood and a little bit into our adulthood as well.

"I'm just teasing you. Have something to eat. There will be food on the plane, but I don't know exactly what."

Just as I finish my last bite of bagel, the doorbell rings again. This time it's Joel. "Hey, I know I said I'm doing your hair and makeup, but maybe I should take a look at Chase's as well," he says as soon as he steps inside.

Joel has always adored Chase. "Sure. But not until you're done with me," I tease.

"Of course."

At five minutes to ten, a stretch limo pulls up in front of our house. My entourage and I are coiffed and beautiful and ready to set the Big Apple on its ear!

CHAPTER THIRTY

When we board the plane, I am once again greeted by Bonni, who was our flight attendant last year when Sam flew us to Burbank. She immediately takes our coats and hangs them in the closet. I recognize Captain Garrison standing just outside the cockpit wearing his full uniform, complete with cap.

"You have a larger group with you this time," he says to me, his blue eyes twinkling under his bushy eyebrows. "You'll have to fight each other for the best seats."

I smile up at him. "I probably should let the others have first dibs."

My sister is right behind me, followed by Chase and Libby. Pat and Joel are behind them and Wynn is bringing up the rear. I turn to Melissa. "You pick where you want to sit," I tell her.

"Hmm...this is gorgeous. I think I'll take one of these front seats. Maybe Pat can sit next to me and Joel can sit across the table from us. If that's okay with you, Chase."

Chase smiles at Bonni as he hands her Libby's coat. "That's fine, Aunt Melissa. We'll take the couch!"

Everyone gets situated and Bonni comes by with a tray of mimosas which have been poured into real crystal and placed on napkins with the SB initials in navy. "Would anyone like a glass?" she asks. "I also have orange juice and plain champagne. And I make a mean Bloody Mary."

"I'll have a Bloody Mary," my sister says as I accept a mimosa. Wynn and I are sitting in our "usual" seats across from the couch toward the back of the plane. This time I notice the burnished wood trim surrounding the windows. What a gorgeous aircraft.

When Bonni goes back down the aisle, I see Captain Garrison say something to her. She nods and closes the door to the plane. While she efficiently prepares Bloody Mary's for Melissa and Joel, our pilot comes to the front of the aisle. "In just a few minutes, folks, we will be taxiing to the runway. Our wheels up time is in twelve minutes, so if you need to use the restroom, now is a good time to do so. Today's estimated flight time is three hours and forty-five minutes. We'll be flying at an altitude of 26,000 feet. I plan on having you at the gate by sixteen hundred hours." He pauses and smiles. "For those of you who haven't met her before, our amazing flight attendant today is Bonni. She's here to take care of you. According to FAA regulations, she is required to go through her safety demonstration. Please give her your full attention. I hope you enjoy your flight." Captain Garrison continues walking down the aisle and hands me a navy-blue envelope. My name is written in white pen on the outside.

The note is from Sam.

Dear Margo,

I'm so sorry I couldn't make this trip. I hope to arrive in New York by Sunday afternoon. I'd like to meet with you and Chase for dinner Sunday evening. I'll keep you posted.

SB

Wynn has read the note over my shoulder. "That's too bad. It would have been a hoot flying up to NYC with her."

Maybe that's why she isn't joining us. She's too private of a person. I shrug. "All the people I need are right here in this plane. Although it's too bad Brock and Meredith couldn't join us."

I feel the plane slowly move. Bonni stands at the front of the aisle near Pat and Melissa. She goes through the normal safety demonstration. We clap for her when she finishes. "Why thank you. I don't usually get applause, just bored looks. I'll be serving drinks and appetizers after we reach our cruising altitude, followed by lunch in about an hour. Please let me know if there is anything I can do to make your flight more enjoyable." Bonni sits in one of the three open seats next to a window.

When the plane levels out, Bonni takes our drink orders and gives each of us a bottle of water. I'm anticipating warm nuts as our appetizer, but in addition to that she gives each of us bruschetta with goat cheese and tomatoes. For lunch, we have a choice of Crab Louie or steak sandwiches. Both are served with sweet potato fries. And of course, dessert involves ice cream. This time it's a sundae with your choice of fresh strawberries or hot fudge.

After lunch, Chase and Libby play spades with Wynn and me at our table. "This is incredible," Chase says.

"I know!" says Libby. "I could get used to this."

Chase puts his arm around her. "I plan on spoiling you as much as I can, my sweet wife."

Our flight proceeds uneventfully and we land on time, just as Captain Garrison promised. A limo picks us up at the airport and delivers us to the hotel we had booked on our own.

We spend all day Friday and Saturday touring NYC and taking in two Broadway musicals. By Sunday, we decide to relax in our rooms until it is time to check out and go to the hotel my agent has booked for us.

The Whitby Hotel is two blocks away from Central Park and the Museum of Modern Art. It is definitely a luxury hotel and the best part is that it is less than a mile from ABC Studios where our first interview is tomorrow morning, bright and early!

Melissa, Pat and Joel are taken to their rooms separately from the rest of us. I promise to text Melissa as soon as we get into our room.

A second staff member ushers the four of us to the top floor. Per the riders in our contracts, Chase and I always stay in suites when we travel to promote the film. Wynn and I have a lovely one-bedroom suite overlooking the park. It's decorated in burgundy and grey tones and has a large living area. Chase and Libby have the Whitby suite which has a huge outdoor terrace and an even larger living area than mine. Chase's rider requires a top-of-the-line suite, as it should. After all, he is about to become a movie star.

On the coffee table in our suite is a bottle of champagne and a bowl of fruit along with another navy-blue envelope. It's from Sam, welcoming us to our first press junket and apologizing for not being able to make it. However, she's made an early dinner reservation for all of us at one of her favorite restaurants in that area, Michael's New York. She promises to call Chase and me at eight this evening to answer any last-minute questions before our day of interviews tomorrow.

Dinner was fabulous and Chase and my call with Sam was brief, but very helpful and positive. As I'm brushing my teeth, Wynn comes up and kisses me on the crook of my neck. "Very impressive, Mrs. Parker. Not too many authors get this kind of royal treatment."

I finish and kiss him on the lips. "I'm so lucky."

"No, you're good. Well… maybe a little bit lucky to have Chase's connections."

"I've always said, it's better to be lucky than good. I just hope I'm good tomorrow."

Wynn looks at me in the bathroom mirror. "I'm sure you're nervous. Just try to remember to enjoy the moment."

I take his hand as I head to the bedroom. "Thanks for cheering me on. I couldn't do this without you."

He smiles. "What time should I set the alarm for?"

I pull up my agenda on my iPad. "The limo will pick up Chase and me at seven. Joel is doing my hair at six thirty. I need to shower before then, so let's say six? He said not to wash my hair. It's easier to style when it's a bit dirty. The official hair and makeup are at the studio from seven thirty to seven forty-five. Our interview is at eight fifteen. We finish at eight twenty-five and head to the *Kelly and Ryan* studio which is next door. We will have approximately thirty minutes for a wardrobe change and makeup refresh before we go on the air."

"When are you going to eat?" Wynn sounds stern.

"I hadn't even thought of that and it's not on the list. Maybe famous people don't eat?"

"Not this famous girl. You don't want to pass out on national TV, do you?"

Wynn is correct. I text Chase asking him when he plans to eat. After all, as his mom I should have thought of that. "Chase is eating a granola bar and yogurt in his room after Joel does his hair at six fifteen. He suggests I eat a little something before Joel shows up to our room. That means I need to get up by five thirty. Ugh."

Wynn looks at his watch. It's nine thirty. "Then I suggest we try to get some sleep. We don't want dark circles under those pretty brown eyes in the morning."

I walk over and gladly get into bed. "When are you and my entourage arriving?"

"I've ordered a car for us at seven. The VIP tickets give us access to a special room where there will be a light breakfast. We have seats reserved for us in the front row at both shows. Don't worry. I wouldn't miss this for the world!"

Wynn kisses me goodnight and surprisingly, I fall asleep quickly.

CHAPTER THIRTY-ONE

It's a lot different…getting up early to teach a water aerobics class from getting up early to be on TV. In the summer, I wake up, have a little bit of coffee, put on my suit, put on a pair of earrings and lipstick and I'm ready to go. This morning, Joel did my complete hair and makeup which someone else then "refreshed" and made sure my outfit looked perfect. With my water aerobics classes, I'm in control. Essentially, it's my show. Today, I'm along for the ride in a sense. However, the pressure is greater than in my classes. What if I come off boring? Or if I talk too much? Or there's a hair out of place?

All these thoughts are racing through my mind as I sit in the Green Room at *Good Morning America* with Chase, who maddingly looks perfectly relaxed.

"Ma," he says to me in his Riff voice. "What did your agent put in your rider to have on hand in the Green Room?"

I notice Chase is drinking a health drink. "Um, Coke Zero."

"Which you never drink in the mornings…what else?"

"I don't remember." I'm too nervous right now to eat or drink and I hadn't even noticed what's on the table. "How do we know that's not for someone else?"

"Because it's what you would have picked out." Chase walks back over to the table. "Cashews? Pretzels? Bananas? Hmm... and peanut clusters. That sounds like you, Ma."

"I think my agent added a few things. I guess I didn't think about what time of day I might be in a 'green room', which by the way, isn't even green. I should have asked for donuts and hazelnut coffee."

"Next time."

A woman with a headset on sticks her head inside the door. "You'll be on in two minutes." She quickly closes the door again.

I stand and go over to the mirror for one final check. Nothing in my teeth. Hair looks good. No smudges on my eye makeup. Chase gives me one of his bear hugs. "We're going to be great, Ma."

I look into his piercing blue eyes and relax. "Yes, yes, we are, Riff. We're going to knock them dead."

The production assistant, or PA as they say in the business, opens the door again and motions for us to follow her. "It's the commercial break right now. We need to get you into your seats, check your makeup and be ready in three minutes. Robin Roberts will be interviewing you."

Chase is seated in the chair closest to Robin Roberts who hasn't sat down yet. I'm next to Chase. A makeup woman powders Chase's nose then lifts my chin and inspects my face. She nods and walks away without doing anything. I guess being post-menopausal helps lessen the shine on my nose.

Robin seemingly appears out of nowhere. "Hi you all," she greets us with a smile as she takes her seat. "Welcome to *GMA*. I'm so glad I get to talk to you this morning."

"Thank you for having us," Chase replies.

"Yes, thank you. I've enjoyed watching you for many years." Was that the best I could come up with? My voice sounds strange. I sit up straighter and relax my shoulders.

"Why, thank you," Robin says to me.

"We're on in five, four, three, two, one." The light on the camera glows red.

"We have quite an unusual couple with us today. Margo and Chase Parker are a mother/son team who have produced a movie which is set to be released this Friday. The movie, *Lethal Impact* stars Chase and is based on a book written by Margo. Welcome, you two. Now Chase, some of our viewers may recognize you from your current TV series, *Hot Air,* which airs on this network. That show is your debut into the television world, correct?"

Thank God Chase gets to talk first. I just need to remember to smile and stay in the moment. That's what Sam advised last night.

Chase smiles and nods. "That is correct."

Robin continues, "What's it like going from a hit TV comedy to starring in a major motion picture, which I must add is not a comedy. This is a pretty dramatic part, right?"

"Yes, it is. It's been a bit of a whirlwind actually, but what a ride. TV and film are two different beasts, so to speak. And

I'm very fortunate to not only have two different mediums to perform in at the start of my career, but also two very different roles to play."

Good. He remembered to follow a 'not only' with a 'but also.' I always emphasized good grammar in our house.

"And what's this like for you, Margo?" *Oh no, it's my turn!* "What's it like to have your book made into a movie and have your son star in it?"

I give her my warmest smile. "As a writer, I'm embarrassed to say there aren't words to accurately describe the absolute joy I'm experiencing. Authors' books are like their children. You want them to succeed. Watching Chase become a character I developed is amazing...something I never would have imagined."

"And this may be just the vehicle that will propel him to super stardom. Let's take a look at a scene from *Lethal Impact*." The trailer runs. Chase is better than I ever imagined anyone in that role could be. He portrays his character perfectly.

The trailer ends. Robin looks at me. "Bet that makes you one proud mama."

"Absolutely," I reply.

"Chase, what did you think the first time you read your mom's book?"

"Well once I got over the fact that my mother wrote some sex scenes, I was really proud of her. I loved the story and told her I wanted to play the lead."

Robin laughs. "So, this has been a dream of both of yours for a long time?"

"Yes," we both answer simultaneously. I hope that wasn't an error on our parts.

"And Samantha Barrett and Robin Reed are the executive producers. What was it like when you got the call from them, Margo?"

"Unbelievable. I was afraid Chase was pranking me. But then I met with them and realized our dream was becoming a reality. They are intelligent women who are lovely to work with."

Robin nods. "*Lethal Impact* is also now a Robin Reads Book Club selection." She holds up a copy of my book. "The movie opens in theaters across the country this Friday. Thank you both for joining us this morning. We'll be right back."

"And we're off air," the crew member says. The red light blinks off.

"Great job, you two. You seemed very relaxed. Good interview. Margo, would you sign my copy for me?" Robin asks.

"Of course." I've autographed quite a few copies over the years, but never one to a person who is this famous. "I'm honored."

Immediately after I sign my name to Robin Roberts' copy, Chase and I are whisked away by a crew member and return to the Green Room where our driver is waiting.

"I thought we could walk to the *Kelly and Ryan* studio," I whisper to Chase as we trail the chauffeur down the narrow hallway. He opens double metal doors and bright sunlight douses us. Chase shrugs as he whips out his sunglasses and puts them on. He truly looks like a movie star.

"I delivered your wardrobe earlier," the driver says as he holds open the door to the limo. "The entrance is at the far end of the block. I'll be able to drop you off right in front of the cast entry door."

I soon realize that what looks close on my Google Maps is further than I had thought. City blocks are pretty long and given our extremely tight time frame, taking a car makes sense.

As we pull up in front of the *Live Kelly and Ryan* studio sign, Chase leans over in the backseat and says quietly, "This is what you've dreamed of, Mom. This is your moment to shine."

I'm about to correct his last sentence saying it's his moment to shine, when our driver opens up my door. For years, Wynn has been offering to get me tickets to watch this show being taped. He knows I am a huge fan of Kelly Ripa and in more recent years, of Ryan Seacrest as well.

A page meets us at the entrance and escorts us to their guest dressing rooms where our wardrobe boxes are waiting. We each have our own room. "Go ahead and change. There's a restroom across the hall," the page instructs, "I'll be back to take you to hair and makeup in about ten minutes."

For a minute, I freeze. What if this isn't the correct outfit my stylist and I chose for today? But then I remember all of my "East Coast" wardrobe is in this box, meaning my outfit for tomorrow's interview will be in here as well. This morning I wore pants with an "artsy" top. For this show, I am wearing a slightly edgy pantsuit. I'm glad my stylist talked me out of wearing a dress. I don't need my legs to show on national TV.

It feels as if I'm changing and waiting for a doctor to enter the exam room. I rush to put on my second outfit of the day, but not so hastily as to forget to reapply my deodorant. After

I finish putting on the jumpsuit and shoes, I switch out my earrings, necklace and bracelet. This has probably taken me all of five minutes which gives me time to inspect my hair and makeup in the mirror. Hmmm…the hair looks pretty good, but I definitely need more lipstick.

There's a knock on the door before it swings open. "We're ready for you, Mrs. Parker. I'll be touching up your hair and makeup," the petite brunette says as she motions for me to follow her down the hall. I notice the door to Chase's dressing room is open and he is nowhere in sight. "Your hair looks really good."

"Thanks," I say.

"I'll probably add just a bit more volume to it and give it a spritz. Have a seat," she says as we arrive in a larger room with four chairs that look like they came from my hair salon. I half expect Joel to come strolling in to "fix" my hair himself. Chase occupies one of the other chairs. His eyes are closed as his makeup artist applies more powder to his nose and forehead and a dab of concealer to a blemish on his chin.

I look at the large, digital clock in the corner of the room. The green numbers read 9:10 and a small, red light blinks above indicating, I imagine, that the show is on air. Usually, Kelly and Ryan's opening lasts fifteen to twenty minutes without any commercial breaks. Ever since I found out Chase and I were going to be on the show, I've studied the timing of the guests, how they walk onto the stage and greet the hosts, etc. I actually made Chase rehearse this part with me before we left home. He did his best not to laugh.

From across the room, I hear my son. He says something to his makeup girl and another quickly walks over. He's holding court. Not a surprise. They remove the cape which was protecting his clothes and he walks over to me.

My stylist has finished puffing up my hair and is now applying lip liner and lipstick so I can't talk. "You look like a movie star, Mom," he says.

The woman finishes and hands me a mirror. "What do you think?" she asks.

I stare at the woman who's staring back at me from the mirror. "I think you're a magician. I've never looked this glamorous!"

She laughs, extracting the mirror from my hand. "Thank you!" Checking the digital clock, she looks back at me. "We have about three minutes before Joe comes to get you two."

I start to wonder if I looked okay on *GMA*, but am able to distract my negative thoughts by taking in the room. "Is this where Kelly and Ryan are made up every day?"

She nods. "Yes. Kelly is usually in this very chair. I'm her stylist."

Wow! How lucky am I?

The door opens. "We have two minutes to air. I need Margo and Chase Parker to follow me," the man says very matter-of-factly as he looks around the room.

"That's us," replies Chase.

Once we get into the hallway, Joe checks his clipboard. "They want Margo to lead followed by Chase."

Oh gosh! I was hoping Chase would make his entrance first, but we did practice both ways. This must mean I'll be sitting closest to Kelly. We follow Joe to the opposite side of the stage where Kelly and Ryan enter each morning and wait in the wings. The hosts are seated in their director's chairs waiting for the commercial break to end.

"In five, four, three, two, one," the crew member counts down and the red camera light comes on.

"We're back!" says Ryan. "Usually, a mother is focused on helping her children, from a young age, achieve their dreams."

"That's right," adds Kelly. "We take them to practices and games and rehearsals. But this morning we are fortunate to have a mother and son who helped each other reach their dreams in a most unusual way. You might know her from her best-selling book, *Lethal Impact*, which is now a Robin Reads Book Club selection."

"And you will recognize her son from the new hit TV comedy, *Hot Air.*" Ryan says.

"Please welcome, Margo and Chase Parker," Kelly introduces us.

I'm already smiling as Chase gives me a gentle nudge. The audience is standing, clapping as we walk by. I feel like I'm walking in slow motion. I see Wynn, Libby, Melissa, Pat and Joel in the front row and relax. I can do this.

I hug Kelly and then cross to Ryan as Chase embraces Kelly. We sit in our respective chairs. I am at an angle to the hosts as is Chase, just like we've seen on TV a million times. A small table is between Kelly and me with a "Live" mug filled with water for me in case I need it. I wonder if they'll give the mug to me after the show.

"So, Chase," Ryan says after the audience sits down. "What's it like to be starring in the movie based on your mom's novel? And tell us how this all came about."

I turn and watch my son. I've never been prouder of him. "Well, my mom wrote *Lethal Impact* a long time ago when my older brother was little. Then I came along and, as she puts it, I 'kept her running' so she had to put it down. Several years ago, my dad encouraged her to finish her novel. I read it and told her how much I loved it and that I wanted to star in the movie version."

"And what did she say?" Ryan prompts.

"She laughed and said maybe I'd be old enough once she found someone to produce it."

"And tell us how that happened, Margo. Did your agent find someone or...?" Kelly asks me.

"I didn't have an agent then. Chase happened to mention it to Samantha Barrett when she was on set with him and she called me."

"Samantha Barrett? She just called you? Out of the blue?" Kelly asks.

"Well, I gave Mom the heads up to answer her phone since she wouldn't recognize the caller," Chase interrupts.

"But you didn't tell her who would be calling?" Kelly continues.

"Nope. I didn't want to ruin the surprise."

I just keep smiling, soaking this all in.

"We have a short clip of the movie. Let's take a look," interrupts Ryan.

The trailer runs and the lights come back on. "This is your first film? Really?" Kelly wants to know.

Chase nods.

"You're amazing in that part. I read the book, Margo, and I have to say that I've already started the second book in the trilogy. It's a page-turner," says Kelly.

"Thanks, I'm honored you took the time to read it."

"Now, is it true, Margo, that you're a long-time fan of *All My Children*? And by long-time, I mean from the beginning." Ryan asks.

If it's possible for me to widen my smile, I do. "Yes. When I was in elementary school the show was in black and white and was only on for half an hour. My sister, who's here with me today, and I would come home from school for lunch and watch it. Our mother started watching *All My Children* because an actress who'd been on another soap Mom watched was starring in it. And I watched *AMC* until the end."

"I heard you indirectly caused the NHL to go on strike?" Kelly intervenes.

"Oh yeah," Chase says. "I'll never forget that day. I came home from school and my mom was crying. I thought someone had died. Nope, she had just watched the final episode of *All My Children*. My brother and dad and I gave her a hard time which was the wrong thing to do. She was seriously upset."

Kelly looks compassionate and reaches out to put her hand on my arm. "And what did you say to them?"

I laugh. "I said, 'What if you found out there was no more hockey? That it was gone, the entire NHL, forever.' And they just laughed at me. They said that would never happen. And within a short time after that, the players went on strike and there was no hockey for most of that season."

"She still loves telling that story," adds Chase as he rolls his eyes.

"Good for you!" Kelly says. "And good for you that you pursued your dream while helping your son pursue his."

The audience claps.

"Here at *Kelly and Ryan*, we love to help people see their dreams come true," says Ryan.

"That's right," adds Kelly. "Margo, we have a few people here who would love for you to autograph their books." Kelly is holding up a copy of *Lethal Impact*. The *All My Children* theme song starts playing.

"Ladies and Gentlemen, Margo and Chase, please welcome Susan Lucci, Cameron Mathison and Jill Larson!"

Oh. My. God. I must be dreaming. Any minute the alarm on my cell phone is going to chime. I must look stunned because Kelly has come to my side and has her arm around me. "Are you okay?" she whispers as I watch three of my favorite *AMC* characters enter the stage.

All I can do is nod, as tears race down my cheeks. Each of them has one of my books tucked under their arms. They come up and shake Chase's hand and give me a hug.

"*Lethal Impact* opens Friday in movie theaters across the country! We'll be right back," says Ryan over the audience cheers.

During the commercial break, we find out that the *All My Children* actors are here to promote a prime-time return during the next segment.

Joe approaches Chase and me while we are talking to the cast members. "They will circle back and meet you in the Green Room once they are finished so you can autograph their books."

"Really?" I ask.

"Really," Joe says and motions for us to follow him.

I grab a Coke Zero when we get to the Green Room and watch the next segment. As promised- when it concludes- Susan, Cameron and Jill join Chase and me.

"I'm speechless," I say to them. "I watched you for so many years, I feel like I know you. I'm so excited you'll be back on TV again!"

The three were very kind. We chatted until the show ended and Kelly and Ryan came in. I was so glad when our "entourage" joined us and got to meet them too. We were able to get a few pictures taken with them before we had to leave. I couldn't have had a better day if I'd written it myself!

CHAPTER THIRTY-TWO

As soon as Chase and I were done with our interview on *The Today Show with Hoda and Jenna*, our chauffeur drove all of us to the airport where we boarded the private jet and headed back to Dallas. Jenna led the interview since we are from Texas and she shares that connection with us. The two had been very warm and friendly. I found it a bit uncomfortable to be treated like a celebrity by actual celebrities. Chase, of course, took it all in stride. He needs to get used to it, where as I will fade away after the movie premiers.

The plane touched down and taxied to the private hangar just before five. I was grateful that we had a driver waiting to take us home since we would be in the thick of rush hour traffic.

Now we have a day of local interviews. Then less than twenty-four hours after that, we fly to Los Angeles where Chase and I have two full days of interviews ahead of *Lethal Impact's* debut. I am tired. While all of the attention and accompanying hoopla were fun, it's taxing to always be "up." Not that I'm complaining!

Our entourage is busy chatting with each other as the limo glides through the congested streets of Dallas. Wynn is holding my hand, observing the crew, too. "It's been a lot of fun so far and we're only half-way through," he whispers in my ear.

I nod and stifle a yawn. "Would you see if there's a Coke Zero in that cooler?" I ask him.

Wynn leans forward and extracts the familiar black can with the red "Coke Zero" label.

"Did you really think they wouldn't stock your favorite?" he jokes.

I smile and take the ice-cold can. "I'm not used to expecting my every need to be met."

Wynn feigns a hurt look.

"You've taken very good care of me all of these years. I didn't mean that."

Almost an hour later, the driver pulls up in front of our house. The stretch limo is definitely turning the heads of those out for a walk on our street. Before exiting the car, the chauffeur turns to us and announces. "I'll be back here at two on Wednesday afternoon. Your flight leaves at three."

"Thank you," Chase says. "We look forward to seeing you then." Chase exits the limo and holds his hand out to his wife. The driver unloads our bags and takes them up to our front door. Pat is spending the night with us. My sister will go home, as will Joel.

"I'll see you at the salon tomorrow," Joel says. "I want to freshen up your hair before your local interview." That's code for he thinks my gray hair is showing!

"Thank you," I say to him. "I hope you get a good night's sleep."

My sister gives me a hug. "And I hope you sleep well, too," she says to me. "I could get used to flying on private jets."

It seemed like we were home for twenty minutes, not forty-eight hours. My phone has been ringing non-stop. When it rings again, my caller ID announces it is "Brock."

"Hey, Mom, how's the famous author doing?"

I sink down onto our family room leather sofa. "To be honest, I'm pooped. How's Meredith?"

Brock chuckles. "Meredith's doing well. She had an appointment today. The doctor's sticking with his original due date of April third, but Meredith insists baby Parker has dropped and is ready to be born."

"She's rarely wrong..."

"I know that!"

"But I do hope the baby can wait until at least next week when we're back in town. I don't want to miss this!"

"I feel pretty certain you won't miss out. You do sound tired."

"Yep, but not nearly as tired as you will be in a few weeks. So, you better rest up, Sweetie."

"I'm getting a lot of sleep. Unfortunately, Meredith is up several times a night to go to the bathroom."

"That's very normal. It prepares her for the long nights to come. But we'll hopefully be around to help out. How's work going?'

Brock pauses. "It's been busy. Lots of meetings ahead of Spring Training starting in a few days. Fortunately, I've been able to get out of going to Arizona."

"Oh, that's right. Remember when Dad and I took you and your brother out there for Spring Break?"

"How could I forget Chase hobbling around in that boot that he had for his high ankle sprain?"

"He did pretty well getting around with that. Remember Wile E. Coyote at the resort?"

Chase plops down on the sofa next to me. "Is that Brock?"

"Yes."

Chase grabs the phone from me. "Hey Bro!"

"Hey! You and Mom looked great on TV."

"We are just about to sit down and watch it. You weren't making fun of the boot I had to wear on Spring Break in Scottsdale, were you?"

"Me? Would I do that?"

"Yeah, you'd do that."

"Actually, what was funnier than watching you limp around in that boot was the father and his kids sitting next to us at breakfast at the hotel that first morning."

Chase starts laughing. "Oh, yeah, when the waitress walked up to him and asked what he wanted to drink and his little three-year-old kid said he'd already had too much the night before?"

I can hear Brock laughing over the phone. "That was hysterical. I'm really sad we can't be at the opening this weekend, but Meredith and I will be with you in spirit. Make sure they take lots of pics of you and Mom on the red carpet."

"I will. And you take good care of your wife and unborn baby."

"Will do. Safe travels, Chase."

"Thanks!"

• • •

Today feels like Groundhog Day. It's Wednesday. Joel arrives again and styles my now gray-free hair. My sister arrives early... again... and the driver is as punctual as he was last Friday when he picked us up. He stows our bag in the trunk and holds the door open for us. It's a dreary day in late February. March is just around the corner. I wonder if it will come in like a lion or like a lamb.

When we arrive at the now familiar private jet terminal at Love Field, we exit the limo and mount the steps to SB's plane. Once again Bonni is just inside the Gulf Stream's door waiting to cheerfully greet us and take our coats.

"You all looked great on the interviews," she says. "I'm sorry Captain Garrison and I weren't here to fly you home yesterday, but we had already been booked by another client."

I hand her my leather jacket and give her a hug. "Our flight was fine, but wasn't the same without you two!" I head on back to my usual seat.

After Captain Garrison comes back to greet us and Bonni goes through her safety presentation, she shuts the door to the aircraft and heads to an open seat. Before she sits down, she says, "Because our pilot is in a hurry to not miss his take-off slot, I will bring you drinks as soon as he indicates I'm free to move about the cabin. Shortly after that, I'll be serving you lunch since it's only one o'clock in LA."

Three hours later we pull up to the private terminal at the Bob Hope International Airport in Burbank. Our driver is standing next to his stretch limo several yards away, waiting for the ground crew to unload our luggage.

I give Bonni a hug goodbye. "Will you be working our flight back to Dallas?"

"We both will," Captain Garrison adds and then winks at me. "We're a package deal."

"Break a leg tomorrow night!" Bonni whispers in my ear. "You'll be great."

I step into the warm Southern California sunshine and carefully make my way down the jet's stairway. Like a mother duck, the rest of my group is behind me, led by Chase.

After our bags our loaded into the trunk of the limo, our chauffeur slides into his position behind the wheel. Without turning to face us, he presses his speaker button. "Ms. Barrett has requested that I take Mrs. Margo Parker and Mr. Chase Parker to the studio straightaway. She wants to meet with you briefly. I am to deliver the rest of you to your hotel."

I immediately look at Chase; my eyes are wide. "Do you think something's wrong?" I whisper to him.

Chase smiles. "Ma! Relax! She probably just wants to review some the logistics for tomorrow. Besides, we have to go right by the studio on the way to the hotel. Remember how close it is to this airport?"

I nod. "How could I forget the day you and I flew out here for the first day of your last semester in college? Your apartment was right across the street from the studios."

Chase also nods. "That seems like a lifetime ago."

It's not long before the limo begins turning onto the street where the studio is. "Chase, look!" Libby shouts.

"Stop the car," I command our driver. He obeys by pulling

into the nearest parking lot. Across the street is the largest billboard I've ever seen. And on that sign is the largest picture of Chase I've ever seen. *Lethal Impact* it says above his face. "In theaters March 3," it reads below.

Every one of us grabs our phones and snaps pictures. This is the moment we all realize that Chase has become a movie star.

CHAPTER THIRTY-THREE

Chase was right. Sam just wanted to go over the schedule for tomorrow and to let us know that she had set up a private dinner for us this evening at our hotel. She was very complimentary of the interviews we had completed so far and said there was a lot of "buzz" starting about this mother and son team. Many theaters around the country had already sold out of tickets for the Friday showings.

Robin phoned in to update me on book sales and see if I'd be available to go on a book tour. How can I say no? But what about my grandbaby's arrival? I explained as politely as I could about the upcoming event and she graciously said we would work around my new grandchild's future appearance!

When we get back in the limo to head to the hotel, I rest my head against the seat and close my eyes. "This all seems so unbelievable to me," I say to Chase.

"I'm sure it does. You went from unknown author to part of

a famous mother/son duo. To be honest, it's a little overwhelming for me too."

I open my eyes and look at my son. "I'm so glad to hear you say that. Now I don't feel as much like a fish out of water."

"You'll get used it. When I first did promos for *Hot Air* it seemed a bit unreal to me, almost like I was faking it. And truthfully, that's what a lot of acting is…faking it."

"Fake it 'til you make it?"

"Exactly. Wow, look at this," Chase points out the front of our hotel as our driver pulls up under the portico. "It's the Hotel Bel-Air, an iconic hotel."

"Or as your brother would say in his best Borat imitation, 'Very nice!'"

"Yeah. I really wish he could have been here."

The hotel doorman opens my door and I climb out of the car after thanking our chauffeur who has been immensely patient with us.

"Have you checked in, Ma'am?" the doorman inquires.

"I believe my husband has, Wynn Parker?"

"Ah yes. Mr. Parker is in our Grace Kelly Suite awaiting your arrival. I will show you the way." Then he looks at Chase. "And you sir, have you checked in?"

"No, but my wife has. Libby Parker?" Even though Chase and Libby have a home nearby, Chase's contract allows him to stay in a local hotel when he is making appearances.

A wave of recognition crossed the doorman's face. "Ah, yes. You are Chase Parker. You and your wife have the Premier Canyon Suite. Please, both of you follow me."

I thought our rooms in New York were amazing, but the Grace Kelly suite was incredible. Wynn was waiting for me on our private patio, a bucket with a bottle of champagne sat next to him.

"I see you waited for me," I say giving him a hug.

Wynn grins. "Pretty nice digs, huh?"

"I'd say."

"How did your meeting go? Any earth-shattering news?"

I shake my head as I put down my purse. "No, Chase was right. She just wanted to go over the chain of events for tomorrow."

"You look tired. How about a glass of bubbles and a dip in the pool?" Wynn points to our own private pool here on the patio.

"Great idea. I probably won't have time to get in tomorrow. Sam arranged for us to have dinner this evening here at Wolfgang Puck's restaurant. She said it would be nice and private and we wouldn't have to worry about autograph seekers. Isn't that a hoot?"

Wynn chuckles. "Not a problem I'd ever thought we would have, but hey, I'm sure we can handle it."

• • •

Wynn and I had a great time relaxing in our private pool, drinking the champagne Sam had sent us and I was able to take a quick power nap. The dinner that followed in a very secluded room in the restaurant had been delicious and a lot of fun. And, the next morning, Chase and I breezed through our interviews with four different morning shows like we were old pros.

After lunch, Wynn suggested I relax while he and my sister, along with Pat and Joel took a tour of Hollywood they had already booked, not knowing when Chase and I would finish. I eagerly accepted his suggestion and told them to have fun. Joel wasn't scheduled to do my hair until four, so I have a good three hours to sit by the pool and read.

I change into my suit, grab the paperback I'm reading along with my puzzle book and walk out onto my private patio, complete with two chaises. The sound of the small waterfall in the pool is mesmerizing and it takes me a few minutes to open the book.

"How does that one compare to yours?"

I literally jump at the sound of the man's voice coming from the chaise next to mine. "Dad, you startled me!" I feel guilty the moment I see him. How long has it been since I've even thought of him? I'm not sure if I'm relieved or disturbed that my therapy sessions haven't kept Dad away.

"Sorry, Hon. I didn't mean to make you jump. Nice suite. Grace Kelly was always one of my favorite stars. She was the definition of class. It's very fitting they would assign you to this room."

"It is lovely, just like she was."

"I wanted to catch up with you in NYC, but you were surrounded by people almost every minute of the day. By the way, you and Chase gave great interviews. Your fan base is growing, Mrs. Parker."

"I know. Robin updated me earlier today with the book club sales totals and I've sold over a million copies since she's promoted me." It was so awesome to be able to share this with my father who had always taken great pride in my accomplishments.

"A million copies? Did you ever think you'd sell that many books? It was just the push you needed, wasn't it?"

I nod. "To be honest, I was afraid about going on this tour with Chase. I felt I'd be in his shadow...you know, kind of like a tagalong. Here's Chase's mother. We have to pay attention to her even though all we want to do is talk to him. Poor thing."

"And that's not at all what happened."

"No. The interviewers were very fair. They treated us like we were a team."

"Because you are. He wouldn't be here without you... literally."

"Nor I without him. Not in this situation anyway."

"Mothers and sons make great combos."

Oh yeah, that's right. He thinks I'm his mother. "So do fathers and daughters." I'm not ready to give in to the idea of being Margaret. I look into his eyes and hope I haven't hurt his feelings. "I've thought about this a lot...about having Margaret's soul. And as much as I think it's a very romantic idea, I just can't buy into it, Daddy. There's no doubt in my mind that I'm your daughter."

My father looks down at his hands then back up at me. "You think too much with your head and not enough with your heart."

Ouch! That stings! "You're probably right. But I've always adored you and that comes from my heart."

Dad looks pensive. "There was something else you used to say to me when you were young."

"Which was…?"

"That you'd always be my little girl."

That's right. How could I have said that if I was really Margaret? I nod.

"And it took every ounce of self-control I had not to cry. I know I didn't tell you often enough, but I hope you remember that I told you it was a privilege to raise you."

"I do remember that."

"When I found out you have Margaret's soul, that statement took on an entirely new meaning. You should have been the one to raise me, not that I didn't learn a thing or two from you."

I tilt my head, trying my best to comprehend what he was telling me. "Like what?"

"How to be more patient for one thing."

I'm mid sip of my drink and I literally choke on it when I start laughing. "You mean like when you tried to teach me how to drive?" Dad took me out on a country road one time when I was fifteen. He became easily exasperated and I became frustrated to the point I was ready to cry. When Mom found out he was trying to teach me to use the brake with my left foot and the accelerator with my right, she promptly took over being my driving instructor.

"I was patient with you then. It's a more efficient way to drive."

I've recovered from choking. "Oh, okay. Then how did I teach you to be more patient?"

"When we attended board meetings together and I got a little overzealous."

"True. I just put my hand on your wrist and you seemed to settle down."

"Haven't you ever done that with Brock or Chase?"

A chill settles over me. I had. On numerous occasions. It was a maternal reaction. "Yes," I whisper.

"And speaking of maternal gestures, what about that night in your closet."

"The night in my closet?" Has he lost it?

"When you said 'Oh Ike, what are we going to do now?'"

I can't breathe. He'd just mentioned the memory I had buried so deep I thought I would never retrieve it. It was the first moment when I knew that my dad was probably going to die in the near future. Distraught, I entered my walk-in closet off the bedroom one night and without turning on the light, I sat down and wept. I said those very words out loud and instantly wondered why I had done that. Ike, my grandfather, had died the summer before Wynn and I were married. And I never called him Ike. But Margaret would have.

An awkward silence hangs between us in the California sunshine. "I do remember that. I was beyond upset at the thought of losing you."

"And in your heart, you searched your soul for an answer… Margaret's soul. You reached out to the only other man she loved, my father."

Before I can respond, I hear my cell phone ringing inside my suite. It might be Sam or Chase. "I've got to get that, Dad. I'll be right back." I race inside just in time to see the missed call showing "spam risk." Thoroughly annoyed by this unnecessary interruption, I head back to the pool. Of course, Dad is gone. But a yellowed envelope addressed to Ike Stearns sits on top of my puzzle book.

I gently slide the two-page letter out of the opened end of the envelope. It's a letter from Margaret's father to Ike dated over a month after she died.

April 25th, 1934

Dear Ike:

I am sending this letter to your home address as I assume that by now you have been able to leave the hospital as you indicated in your recent letter that you expected to be out of there in a short time.

We are all naturally anxious to know how your arm is progressing as that, of course, has been the one thing of which we have been afraid might result in an impairment of its usefulness, and we are certainly hoping that the doctors have been able to get it in such shape that eventually you will be able to use it as well as formerly.

Mother Bennett is not doing as well as was hoped for and believe that a good deal of her trouble can be attributed to her worry and fret over the burial of Margaret. She is very anxious to have Margaret brought home just as soon as you are able to travel, but does not, of course, wish you to undertake to make the trip until you are in physical shape to do so. Just as soon as you are, however, we would appreciate your letting us know so that all arrangements can be made for the funeral.

We desire, of course, to have the interment private, only the immediate members of the family who so desire and very intimate friends to be present.

We would certainly like, if it could be so arranged, to have Mr. and Mrs. Weber and Mr. and Mrs. Smith accompany you as we feel that in view of their close friendship with Margaret, she would desire to have them present.

We can take care of all of them, if necessary, between the Schuchardts and ourselves if they desire to stay over and naturally, we shall expect you to stay with us just as long as you can.

When we were in town, the question of bringing Margaret home was discussed with Mr. Weber, who volunteered to render every assistance in making the arrangements for you and ourselves at your end, and I sincerely hope that you will ask him to lend his assistance as he might feel hurt unless you did so.

He has certainly been a wonderful friend and has been of wonderful assistance in this emergency and he and his wife have certainly endeared themselves to Mrs. Bennett and myself. He is certainly a wonderful character and we feel it a privilege indeed to number him among our sincere friends.

Mr. Smith and his wife were also more than helpful and we never will be able to adequately express our appreciation of their help rendered when it was so greatly needed.

If it could be arranged for Reverend Northwood to officiate, we would be more than glad to have him do so. I would gladly take care of any expense that he would be put to by reason of making the trip to St. Louis. He is certainly a wonderful man and apparently thought a great deal of Margaret and we know is a sincere friend of yours, and believe that he would appreciate being requested to officiate even though he may not be able to do so. This, however, we will leave entirely in your hands.

With love from all,

Sincerely yours,

Dad Bennett

Oh, Daddy, what a lovely letter, I think to myself. Then realize I'm not sure if the "Daddy" I'm referring to is William or Dad Bennett. It's time I really consider accepting that I have Margaret's soul. And if that's the case, how sad that my husband was unable to attend my funeral and my parents patiently awaited the return of my body, Margaret's body, to bury. They must have been heartbroken. I notice that the two pages are held together with a straight pin. It was typed on my father's company letterhead. There...I just said it...my father...Dad Bennett. I carefully fold the letter and insert it back into its envelope and place it for safekeeping in my leather folder.

The doorbell to my suite rings. I stand to walk to the door and look out the peephole. It's Wynn. I swing open the door to let him in.

"Hi, Sweetheart. Sorry, but I forgot my key." Wynn kisses me on my head. "What have you been up to?"

I quickly turn, looking at the pair of now empty chaises by our small pool. "Oh, nothing. Just relaxing before our big night tonight." But, inside, my heart was in turmoil. I was anything but relaxed.

CHAPTER THIRTY-FOUR

There really is a red carpet. And I'm on it right now! It's not as extensive as the one at the Oscars, and the paparazzi is very scaled back. Nonetheless, when I exited the limo a few seconds ago, I could hear the clicks of the cameras going off. I am one of the first to arrive. Chase and Libby will be next to last. Samantha and Robin will bring up the rear…so to speak.

My smile is plastered on my face. Wynn, who looks drop-dead handsome in his tux, has his hand on my elbow. He's gently steering me slowly down the crimson path. About fifty feet away is a reporter. I think it says *ET* on her microphone. "Do we walk up to her? Or wait for her to flag us over?" Wynn whispers in my ear.

"Sam said to always wait." I'm so glad right now that Chase and I had that briefing with her. We are inching closer, taking our time, stopping to smile at the photographers lining the way. We are almost to the *ET* reporter when a cheer goes up from the crowd. Chase and Libby have arrived! Our son looks dazzling in a very trendy blue crushed velvet tux. He exits the limo first, helping Libby step out in her gorgeous, shimmering gold dress. Chase takes her hand in his and heads towards us.

It's at this moment that the *ET* woman flags me over. "You must be Margo Parker," she says.

"I am and this is my husband, Wynn." I make sure to keep smiling.

"You must be not only a proud husband tonight, but also a proud father," she says to Wynn.

"Oh, I am!"

"What's it like, Margo, to watch your son portray the hero of your novel, *Lethal Impact*?"

"It's a dream come true. I can't think of anyone else who could more accurately portray the hero than Chase."

"And speaking of him, here's Chase Parker now!"

Chase approaches us and gives me one of his big bear hugs. "Hi, Ma. You look fabulous!"

"And this must be your wife, Libby?"

Libby nods, but Chase answers. "That's right! I have both of my best girls with me tonight!"

Wynn and Libby casually drop back behind us. Had Sam not coached me, I would have stepped back with them. But I remember that we are the mother/son duo they want to interview, not just Chase, the star of the movie.

"To our knowledge, you are the first mother/son author/star to be on any red carpet. How does that feel?"

"I'm so proud of Chase tonight. And I am certainly blessed to be sharing this moment with him."

Chase has his arm around my shoulder and hugs me. "I'm the one who's proud. My mother set an incredible example for me. She showed me that it's never too late to pursue your dreams. She's worked just as hard as I have to get here. And without her writing this amazing novel, I wouldn't be here."

"That's so true," the *ET* reporter says. She turns to me. "Margo, was there a moment in Chase's formative years when you knew he would become an actor?"

"I have to pick just one?"

The reporter laughs. "The earliest one."

"It was probably when he played the Phantom in high school. I cried when Christine left him in the end. I felt so bad for him and had forgotten that it was really just Chase behind that mask."

Chase frowns. "I thought you said you cried during the entire performance."

"Well, I did. But those were tears of joy and pride."

"It's great to see the looks of joy and pride on both of your faces tonight. I, for one, can't wait to get in there and watch your film. Congrats to both of you!"

The host steps away and we zigzag down the red carpet taking interviews with three other TV hosts. We are almost to the theater entrance when another cheer goes up from the crowd that has gathered. Samantha and Robin have arrived.

Once inside the theater, several photographers take our pictures on the grand staircase. I've chosen a cobalt blue beaded gown and am wearing the diamond and sapphire dangling earrings Wynn gave me.

An usher escorts us to our seats. "I don't suppose we get popcorn." I whisper to Chase.

He sighs and rolls his eyes. "Not tonight. You'll have to go without."

Libby enters our row first, followed by Chase, me and then Wynn. I turn around and look up at the balcony where our "entourage" is sitting. The rest of the downstairs is packed. I'm wondering who all these people are, but Libby beats me to asking Chase about it.

"Most likely they're studio execs and their friends and investors," he responds.

The lights dim and Samantha, Robin and their entourage slip in to their seats in front of ours. Sam turns to me and whispers, "Are you nervous, Margo?"

I nod. "I have only seen the trailers."

"I think you'll be pleased. Don't you, Chase?"

Chase beams. "She'll be very happy."

I honestly don't think I've been this nervous since Chase played the Phantom in high school. What if this movie is a flop? And even worse, what if this hurts Chase's career? What if? Isn't that how I always come up with ideas for my novels? What if my dad is telling me the truth and I really am Margaret?

An hour and a half flies by. Chase's performance was outstanding. The audience applauds enthusiastically as the credits roll and I see "based on the novel by Margo Parker." There were several embellishments to my story, but overall, the film stayed true to my book, including the ending.

Robin turns to me. "Stand up and turn around," she says to Chase and me. Chase helps me to my feet and we turn to receive a standing ovation.

Wynn is on his feet applauding now. "You did it, Margo! Your novel made it to the big screen and so did our son."

Tears are streaming down my face. Never in my wildest dreams did I think this day would happen.

The ushers make their way down the aisle and escort Samantha and Robin and their group out of the building and to their waiting limo. A second set of ushers comes to get us. As we move into the aisle I look up and see our group waving wildly at us. Several rows behind them, I see my dad. He nods and holds his hands above his head, applauding.

The limos take us to Sam's house where tents have been erected in her yard that overlooks the ocean. Tiny white lights are strung everywhere in the trees and waitstaff wearing white jackets and black slacks are carrying silver trays holding crystal flutes of champagne. Sam was nice enough to include my sister and friends who somehow arrived before we did. They are waiting in the circular drive when we pull up.

"Wow!" Pat says as she gives me a hug. "I think I was the first of your friends to read *Lethal Impact* and I always knew it would make a great movie. Chase, you did an incredible job. I'm so proud of you!"

Pat used to live in our neighborhood when Chase and her daughter were young. I never attended an event without her approving my wardrobe selection and tonight was no exception.

Once the stylist and I narrowed down the choices, Pat selected this cobalt blue dress without hesitation.

Joel comes over and discreetly fixes my hair after congratulating me while Melissa is talking to Chase. She catches my eye and mouths, "Loved it!"

"What are we all waiting for?" asks Chase. "Come on! The party's started!"

A five-course sit-down dinner followed the cocktail hour. We all have assigned places and thankfully, Sam seats my group together with us. She and Robin are the consummate hosts, making their way to each table, including ours. We have our choice of sea bass, salmon or steak and, for dessert, the servers present us with an array of choices from bread pudding to chocolate lava cakes.

Following dinner, a live band provides music to dance to. While Libby and Chase are talking to another couple a few tables away, Sam comes over and plops down in Chase's empty seat. "So, have you heard the buzz?"

For a moment my heart sinks. I study her face for a hint if the "buzz" is good or bad news. But she remains stoic.

"No, I have not heard a word."

She nods as if she feels sorry for me. "Well, then I guess I'll have to be the proverbial messenger." She pauses before breaking into her trademark smile. "This is going to be a huge hit! The investors are already asking for options to make your other two novels into films. Sorry, no small screen for your books."

"You're kidding? Really?"

"Really," she nods.

"Oh, my heavens! Thank you for believing in me!" I hug her and she hugs me back.

"No, thank *you* for letting me produce your story and for having such a talented son. There's no looking back for that young man."

CHAPTER THIRTY-FIVE

It was way past our bedtime when Wynn and I finally got back to the Grace Kelly suite at the Hotel Bel-Air. In fact, it was already Friday morning. At some point during the evening, Chase and Libby left with some of the other cast members to continue their celebration. The sunlight peaking through the blinds wakens me. I roll over and look at the clock. It's already ten! Wynn is still fast asleep. Our brunch reservation isn't until eleven so I quietly slip out of bed, grab the robe off the chair in the corner and head out onto our private patio.

I fully expect to find my father sitting on the chaise he occupied yesterday, but it is empty. A cup of coffee is just what I need, I decide. So, I creep back into the living area of our suite and pop a hazelnut coffee pod into the Keurig. As soon as the hot, black liquid fills my mug, I head back outside and sit in the chair at the table for two next to the pool. The steam coming off the coffee circles upwards as I hold it in my hand. I take a deep breath. Yesterday was a ton of fun, a day I'd gladly live over again and again. But I'm glad the rat race has ended, at least for today. At least for me. Chase has more interviews and resumes his shoot schedule for *Hot Air* next week. After brunch today, he and Libby are heading back to their home.

"There you are!" Wynn's voice startles me. "I woke up and you were gone!"

"I haven't been up long. I hope my making a cup of coffee didn't wake you."

"No, I slept like a rock." Wynn sits in the chair opposite me. "Smells good," he says referring to my coffee.

"There's another hazelnut pod left. I'll go make you a cup."

He immediately stands. "I've got it. You just relax."

A few minutes later, Wynn returns with his mug filled with coffee and cream. "I got a text this morning from Brock."

"Is Meredith okay? Has she had the baby?"

"Calm down. She's fine, I think. He wants to know if we could attend a Spring Training game out in Arizona either Sunday or Monday."

"Sunday? We don't get home until tonight and then we have the party at Times Ten following the movie showing for our friends tomorrow night." So much for the rat race ending. "Besides, Meredith can't travel. If Brock has to be in Arizona, maybe we should stay in town. Just in case…"

"Her folks are coming to town this weekend for your party, remember? I expect they'd just stay on a few days. Who knows? They may even stay until the baby is born. I've already checked and Southwest has a flight out Sunday morning at ten, arriving into Phoenix at eleven. It's an afternoon game both days. We can make either one, or both. It's up to you."

I go into the bedroom to retrieve my phone in order to check my calendar. "I can do either one. But I have to be back home before Friday. I have my annual appointment with Dr. Davis." Dr. Davis is the surgical oncologist who removed half my thyroid years ago.

"We can be home Monday night, if you want…Tuesday at the latest. We could stay at the Phoenician and I'll put you in the spa Monday morning."

I can tell Wynn wants to go. I do too; I'm just ready to be home for a while. "The Phoenician, huh?"

Wynn nods. "I can't promise you'll run into George Clooney, though."

I laugh. "Okay," I respond a little reluctantly. "Book us on that Sunday morning flight."

"You got it."

"And Wynn?"

"Yes, Sweetheart?"

"Can we not plan anything after that? Please? Just in case the baby comes early?"

"Of course!"

"I'm looking forward to the next chapter in my life…of being a grandmother!"

Brunch with Libby, Chase and the rest of my "entourage" was fabulous. The food in California is always so fresh and delicious. We ate al fresco and soaked up the warm sunshine and exchanged stories about last night's party.

"Where did you two go?" I ask Chase and Libby.

Chase is busy chewing his breakfast burrito so Libby answers. "Sarah, the lead actress, took us all to a hidden nightclub, kind of like a speakeasy. She rented out the whole place. There was a live band. It was very cool."

Chase finishes his bite of burrito. "Yeah, Mom, it was that place that you and Dad were going to take me to when I was out here for school, but when you found out how much it cost, you decided to skip it."

"Oh, I remember that place. Our friends' daughter went there for free, I found out later. You had to commit to buying so much alcohol?"

"Yep. That wasn't a problem with the crowd Sarah had there last night. She invited the entire cast and crew. It was a blast! Great way to end the day."

"Speaking of parties, who all is going to your shindig tomorrow night?" Libby asks. "I know my parents will be there."

"I'll be there," my friend Pat chimes in. "And my husband is coming up for it too."

"Of course, we will be there as well," says my sister.

"My husband and I will swing by for a little bit. We have a birthday party to attend," adds Joel.

"I'm expecting about fifty," Wynn says.

"Fifty? Five-Oh?" I am astonished that many are coming.

"Do you think we don't have that many friends who want to celebrate? And by the way, I have arranged for you to have popcorn fresh off the popper before the party."

Ah, fresh, hot popcorn. One of my favorites. "You are my hero, Wynn."

"Hey! Hey, Dad, I'm the hero of this movie." Chase pretends to be offended.

"But I'm the hero of her life."

"Aww," says Libby. "Your daddy is so sweet, Chase."

Chase rolls his eyes, feigning disgust. "Well, at least I learned from the best."

After we finish our brunch, we say our goodbyes to Chase and Libby. "This was so much fun," I whisper to Chase as he gives me one last bear hug. "I've loved every moment we spent together. Always remember how proud I am of you. I'll always be president of your fan club." I'm trying hard not to cry as I let go of him.

Chase looks me in the eye. "I'm proud of you too, Ma. Have a safe trip home. Love you."

"Love you more," I reply. It's what I've always said to him.

• • •

Sam's jet is once again waiting for us at the Bob Hope International Airport. Captain Garrison is at the base of the stairs leading up to the entryway of the Gulfstream. "Welcome back," he greets us. "I noticed Chase and Libby are not on our manifest today. Was that a mistake?"

"No. They live here. And now that the movie hoopla is over, Chase has to get back to working on his TV series," I reply.

"Bonni and I have tickets to see *Lethal Impact* tonight. We can't wait! Congratulations!"

I head up the stairs, taking in the warm California air. Bonni welcomes me with her angelic smile. She takes my coat and hangs it in the closet. "Congratulations! I've heard a lot of people talking about when they're going to see your movie."

"Thank you." I drink in every detail of this magnificent jet knowing I'll probably never have the opportunity to fly on it again. Fearing I'll never get to see Bonni again, I hand her one of my cards. "Keep in touch. Let me know whenever you're in Dallas and we will get together."

"Oh, that's so kind of you. I promise I'll do that."

Prior to "wheels up", Captain Garrison informs us that due to a Pacific front, we will have some significant tail winds today, a good thing. Our flying time to Dallas Love Field will be just under three hours.

CHAPTER THIRTY-SIX

It's great being home, although I do miss staying in the Grace Kelly suite. And I miss seeing Chase and Libby. I would have time to breathe today if we weren't leaving tomorrow to head west once again. Instead of relaxing, I'm starting the third load of laundry this morning and as soon as it's dry, I'm packing the few items I'll need in Arizona. I want to be ready to leave tomorrow morning when we go to the screening and after-party tonight.

Fortunately, my contract allows me to keep the wardrobe purchased for my public appearances. Wynn has requested I wear the same dress tonight that I wore at the premiere. I feel that it's a bit dressy for a movie theater and our favorite wine bar, but he insists he's communicated with the invitees that tonight is a formal affair.

By four o'clock, I'm doing my hair and applying my makeup myself for this evening. Being a pseudo celebrity definitely had its perks when getting ready to go out. I miss Joel. Sighing, I look into my lighted magnifying mirror attached to our bathroom wall. Maybe in Arizona I won't have to put on as much makeup. And maybe I can let my naturally curly hair just dry on its own. After all, there's not much humidity in the desert so my curls won't frizz!

An hour later, I'm dressed and ready to go, standing in front of my full-length mirror for a final inspection. "Our driver's here," Wynn calls.

My head snaps in the direction of his voice. "What driver? Ha, ha, very funny!"

Wynn comes to our bedroom doorway. "Don't believe me? Come see for yourself."

I grab my purse, following him to the foyer. Looking out the window, I see a black, stretch-limo idling in front of our house. A uniformed driver is standing by the rear passenger door.

"Isn't that the driver who took us to the airport a few days ago?" I ask Wynn.

"One and the same." Wynn is grinning impishly. It's one of the traits that made me fall in love with him. "I may have said something to him last week. Besides, I don't want to drive home from this party."

I take Wynn's arm and kiss him on the cheek. "You're adorable. Thanks for taking such good care of me."

"Someone's got to do it."

Our driver takes us to the theater where my husband has arranged for a red carpet outside. The invitees are lining both sides of it and cheer when we pull up. "Really? This is a little embarrassing," I say to Wynn before we exit the limo.

"Hey, enjoy it. It may be the last time you get to be famous."

I had more fun watching *Lethal Impact* this time. I was more relaxed and could watch our friends' reactions. They all seemed to love it.

When the movie ends, Wynn and I head back to our limo. The chauffer heads to Times Ten Cellars, our favorite local wine bar, where Wynn has placed another red carpet. He has rented all three of their party rooms in the main building. There's a small version of the billboard of Chase hanging on one wall. Each table is set with one of my books as part of the center piece. And two bartenders are serving Avril Taylor wines.

"You've really outdone yourself," I say to Wynn as we walk in. "Thank you."

"Don't thank me. You did all the hard work." Wynn says something else I can't hear over the applause from our friends.

The party is a huge success and by ten, the last of our friends have left. Wynn and I are exhausted and we fall asleep in the limo on the ride home.

When the driver stops in front of our house, Wynn and I wake with a start. "Is he taking us to the airport tomorrow morning?" I whisper to Wynn.

Wynn shakes his head. "Nope. Sorry. Fairy tale ends tonight, Mrs. Parker. The clock is about to strike midnight."

• • •

The next morning, Wynn has already loaded our luggage into his company car and is waiting in the garage for me to set our house alarm. I punch in our code and close the door into the house behind me. Wynn has already pulled his car into our driveway and has the passenger door open for me.

He's wearing a driving cap. I freeze. It's the same cap my dad used to wear. "Where did you get that hat?"

"I found it on the top shelf in our coat closet the other day. I thought you needed to have a chauffeur at your service today."

There's never been a driving cap in our hall closet. Dad must have been there. "You are just so darned thoughtful, Wynn Parker."

Because it's Sunday, traffic to the airport is very light. We are able to get there in less than half an hour. "Weren't we just here?" I ask Wynn as he turns in to the entrance to Love Field.

"Yes," he stifles a yawn, still tired from last night.

"Wait! You missed the turn into the private terminal area."

He laughs. "Remember, Cinderella? Party's over. We are back to the parking garage and regular terminal where the working class boards."

I snap my fingers. "Oh, shoot. And here I thought I was living the dream."

"You are." Wynn pulls into a spot and removes our two carry-ons from the trunk of his car. We packed lightly since we are only staying two nights.

If I can't fly on a Gulfstream jet, Southwest Airlines is the next best thing. They have convenient flights. Love Field has great restaurants and is very clean. And best of all, the Southwest flight attendants are friendly and a lot of fun. Wynn boards before I do since he is a Southwest "A-Lister." By the time I get to the seat he's saved me, he's told our flight attendant all about our recent trips on the private jet. As I usually do, I give the flight attendant a copy of *Lethal Impact.* She asks me to autograph it for her. This copy has one of the new covers with the Robin Reads Book Club seal. She hasn't seen the movie yet and decides to read the book first. Always a good call, I think.

Our flight to Phoenix's Sky Harbor Airport is uneventful. When we exit the secured area, Brock is waiting for us.

"Hi, Mom and Dad! Glad you could come!" He gives us each a hug.

"We wouldn't miss it!" Wynn says.

Brock takes my carry-on and we follow him to his rental car. "How long will you be here?" I ask him.

"Just until Tuesday morning, when you leave. I can take you to the airport."

"Are you on our flight?" Wynn wants to know.

"Uh, no. Actually, I'm on the company jet. I tried to get you two on it with me, but it was already full."

Wynn laughs. "I have a company car and you have a company jet! I guess that's what happens when you are part of the big leagues!"

We climb into the SUV and Brock starts the engine to cool it off. "I'm glad you mentioned that, Dad."

Wynn is confused. "Mentioned what?"

"The big leagues. The buck stops with me now."

"What? I don't understand," I say.

The smile I used to love when Brock was a young boy inches from one cheek to the other. "Your driver today is the new general manager of the Texas Rangers Baseball Team."

I shriek. Wynn, who is riding shotgun, reaches over and hugs our son. "Wow! Congratulations!"

"This is amazing," I say. "When did this happen?"

"A few days ago," Brock replies. "I wanted to tell you when you were all out in Hollywood, but it was yours and Chase's time to shine. And besides, I really wanted to tell you in person. That's why I asked you to come out for a game."

"I'm so proud of you," Wynn says. "This is the job you always wanted."

Brock nods. "I'm so excited. Unfortunately, this is not the best time to become a new father."

"Don't worry. You'll have lots of help between Libby's mother and me. Things will be a breeze," I interject.

"Well, I am glad that you will be finished with promoting the film so that you will be around more to help."

"We're not going anywhere once we get home from here," I say.

The book tour Robin discussed with me gnaws at the back of my head.

. . .

Our time with Brock went too quickly. Of course, we sat in the Manager's Box for both games. The Rangers' wins were icing on the cake. Brock said the announcement of his new position would be in *The Dallas Morning News* on Wednesday.

As our plane touches down for a final time at Dallas Love Field, I reflect on my life. Is it really possible that just nine months ago I was sad and lost, wondering what my purpose was in life now that my sons were married and happy? I never imagined any of this would happen: Chase becoming a movie star; Brock becoming General Manager of his lifelong favorite baseball team; and my novel becoming a movie. And I never would have dreamt that my father would appear to me, helping me through this time in my life. I smile. I've seen it all now. If I die tomorrow, I'll die one happy mother.

CHAPTER THIRTY-SEVEN

Heaven, today

Gabrielle appeared to be pacing without touching any ground. An open, massive ledger hovered in front of him. He shook his head. The Almighty Father would be less than pleased with him if he were unsuccessful for a second time in bringing Margaret's soul to Him. Suddenly the gray doom surrounding him lightened. Bright white clouds against a brilliant blue background replaced the fog. He lifted his head to see the soul he had summoned, William.

William loved sunny days and brilliant colors; therefore, wherever he went, that environment always followed. "Good day, Angel Gabrielle," William smiled warmly. "You needed to see me?"

Relieved, yet exasperated with William's cheerfulness, Gabrielle nodded. "Yes, I do. Today is your last visit with your daughter…mother…" He sighed, frustrated at what to call this soul. "With Margaret. Her body expires today. If we can't get her here now, she may not make it *here* at all." This probably wasn't true, but Gabrielle didn't want to take any chances.

"What does that mean?" William laughed. "You can't possibly think God would let Margaret go *there*."

A booming laugh echoed behind them. It was God. He floated in front of them filling all the space around and between William and the angel. "Now, Gabrielle," God reprimanded, "I thought we'd discuss how important truth telling is. You must go back and relearn that behavior in order to correct your ways. You are dismissed for now."

Poof! Gabrielle seemed to evaporate.

"Your Heavenly Father, I am sorry that I have not prevailed in bringing Margaret home."

"Ah, William. It isn't because you haven't tried. Margaret isn't joining us easily because of how fiercely she loves her family. I am immensely pleased with her. Her soul has had the rare dual opportunity of being mother and daughter to you. Hence, her relationship with you is twice as strong as with any other soul. It's a union that, quite simply put, can never be broken. Margaret trusts you one hundred percent. Reassure her that being separated from her husband and sons is only temporary and will seem like a fleeting moment once she is here. She'll listen this time."

William nodded. God's indescribable majesty never ceased to amaze him. "Of course, Heavenly Father. I'll bring her back with me. But I can't guarantee she'll be happy about it."

God laughed again. "Well, she certainly wasn't the first time around. Fierce, feisty and determined are some of the words I would use to describe her. When Margaret thinks she is right about something, she digs in her heels. She expects life to be fair and when it isn't, she thinks she can fix it."

"Yes, if I had a nickel for every time I told Margo that life wasn't fair…"

"And the sooner she accepted that, the happier she'd be." God finished his sentence for him.

William smiled. "I forget you are all-knowing."

"It might be a good strategy today. It's the final thing separating her from you. She must accept that life, as she knows it, isn't fair."

"But the life where she's coming to is!" William exclaimed. "That's it! That's how I know she will come with me. She's heard that so many times in her life, she'll want to prove to me that she's accepted that life isn't fair. Thank you, Heavenly Father."

In the next moment, William is sitting on the couch in Margo's living room.

CHAPTER THIRTY-EIGHT

It's a typical March day in North Texas: cloudy, a bit on the cool side and windy. Wynn just left for a day trip to Oklahoma City. He'll be back in time for dinner tonight. Not only is the weather typical, my life is getting back to normal. Well, except for the call I received last night from my agent, Donna, with the box office results from the weekend. *Lethal Impact* was a huge hit and grossed more than they had anticipated. She said Sam and Robin want to exercise the options on my other two novels. This is great news, especially since Donna had been able to negotiate into my contract a percentage of the box office receipts. She is very level-headed and explained that for the next "go-around" she'd be asking for substantially more money.

But today, I don't have to worry about contracts or publicity or interviews. I can just finish the laundry and relax...and wait to see if Meredith calls me with any news of her having the baby. Smiling at the thought, I pour myself another cup of coffee in the mug which bears the logo of Brock's alma mater.

He gave me the mug for Mother's Day when he was in college and it's my favorite.

Appreciating the peacefulness, I decide to sip my hazelnut coffee and finish reading the paper at our breakfast table. I peruse the arts section and realize I'm restless. The stillness was great for about fifteen minutes, but I'm about to go crazy with the silence that seems to enshroud me.

I set my empty mug down on the kitchen counter and head into our living room where my piano is. The last time I played was before Christmas. It's time for me to get back to playing some non-holiday music. As I walk into the living room, I gasp out loud. Dad is sitting on the sofa that faces the windows overlooking our pool.

"Well, good morning," he says in his well-modulated voice.

"Good morning, Daddy. Would you like some coffee?" I've seen him often enough now that I practice what Dr. Pope suggested during these "encounters": just act like they are nothing out of the ordinary and enjoy the moment.

"I think I'll pass today." He's smiling and pats the sofa cushion. "Come sit next to me unless you'd like to play a few tunes."

I stay standing next to my Baldwin baby grand. "When was the last time I played for you?"

He tilts his head as he ponders the question. "The last time you played for me or the last time I heard you playing? They are two different occasions."

That's right. He can listen to my playing any time he wants. "The last time I played for you...when you were still alive."

"I seem to remember being over here a little early for

the family Christmas gathering and listening to you play 'O Holy Night.'"

"That's right. I asked you to sit in the family room so you wouldn't make me nervous sitting behind me."

Dad laughs. "I never quite understood why that should make you nervous. It's not as if I can play the piano. And I don't remember ever criticizing your playing ability."

"No, you never did. I remember when I was learning to play, you'd come home from work and I would be practicing. You'd take your time hanging up your coat in the hall closet and then you'd come up to me and tell me how nice my playing sounded."

"Because it did sound good. I always enjoyed listening to you practice. How about playing a little something for me now? Let's see if you've overcome your fear of me sitting in the same room while you play."

"That sounds like a challenge I need to accept. What would you like to hear?"

"How about that lullaby you play?"

"You mean the one by Billy Joel?"

Dad nods. "Yes, that's the one."

I love this song and I never play it without thinking of my dad. "I'm not sure that's a good choice."

"Because it makes you cry sometimes?"

He knows. I nod. "Yes, because it reminds me of you."

"Well now that I'm here, it won't be so sad for you to play, right?"

I pull out the piano bench and open the music. "Okay," I say, "but I'm not singing along. I need to focus on the keys."

"That's fine. When you're ready."

I make it through the song without any mistakes...or tears. Dad claps softly. Gently, I close the sheet music and scoot the bench back under the piano. I then cross the room and sit down next to him.

"Just like in the song," I say to him, "you promised you would never leave me. And you never, ever broke a promise to me...until you died."

Dad puts his arm around me. "I know. And I'm sorry about that. I wish I could have stayed longer too. But it wasn't my call. Just as it isn't your call either. But also remember, just like in the song, we had a lot of fun sailing on the lake together. And in your heart, there's always been part of me."

If I think about this for another second, I'm afraid I will burst into tears. "We're not going to discuss that again, are we?"

Dad has the same look on his face as when he'd had to tell me that a close family friend had died. He is silent for a minute. "I remember when I was sick in the hospital in Florida and you came to be with me and help your mom get through it. As I recall, she was having a tough time with the nurses?"

"Or more accurately, they were having a tough time with her."

"Correct. Anyway, you said to me that you didn't want me to die because I was your cheerleader."

I nod, unable to speak.

"And what did I say to you?"

I take a deep breath in order to fend off the tears which I hadn't noticed were already cascading down my cheeks. "You said, 'I think *you* are everybody's cheerleader.'"

Dad places his hand on my knee. "And was I correct?"

"Yes, but even cheerleaders need cheerleaders from time to time."

"And that's one of the reasons I came back to you. Just a few short months ago you were depressed. You had lost your direction, your enthusiasm for life."

"True," I agree.

"And now?"

"My life is back on track and more wonderful than I could ever have imagined. Why just last night, my agent called to tell me Sam and Robin want to exercise the option on my other two novels."

"And I couldn't be prouder of you. I'm also proud of your boys."

"Yes, wasn't Chase amazing in the movie?"

"Extraordinary! And Brock will be an outstanding father and General Manager of the Rangers. I remember when he used to collect baseball cards, watching him rip open the foil covers to see what gem he might have just purchased. And now he's reached his dream too."

I'm getting a sick feeling in my stomach with the direction this conversation is going. It sounds like he's writing the ending of my life. "Yes, and the best is yet to come… grandchildren! I have a lot to look forward to."

Dad's chocolate brown eyes are staring at me. "What's the lesson I was always trying to teach you?"

My heart drops. Maybe this is the last day I will get to see him. "That life's not fair," I whisper.

"That's right."

"Is today the last day I'm going to get to see you? Are you leaving me again now that everything is going well for me?"

"Not exactly. There's another part to the 'life's not fair' lesson I need to add."

"I know," I say with exasperation. "And the sooner I accept this the happier I'm going to be."

"Actually, no. I know that's what I used to tell you…over and over…but I was wrong."

"What? You were wrong? You mean I never really needed to accept that? Because I didn't. So, it's okay if you were wrong about that, Daddy. In fact, that's the best news I've had today. Because life isn't fair and, pardon my French, it sucks when it's not. It stinks that you haven't been here for me and the boys."

A small smile stretches across Dad's face. "Life's not fair here, on Earth. But where you are going, I can promise life will be fair…every day… because what you will learn is that love is more powerful than death. Death is not the end."

"I'm not planning on going anywhere in the near future, except to my doctor's appointment tomorrow."

Dad takes my hands in his. "Margo, it's time for you to accept that life here on Earth will never, ever be fair. In fact, very soon, it will be very unfair to a lot of the people who love you. You need to let go, let go so that the rest of your life will be fair. There are many, many souls who are waiting for you to be reunited with them."

"No," I barely whisper. "No, I'm not ready. I have too much to finish here. Don't let them take me from my boys, Daddy."

"Margaret, I'm your boy, remember?"

I'm sobbing now. "No, Brock and Chase are my boys. You are my father, remember?"

"All three of us are your boys. And we always will be. Nothing can separate us from you. But the time is coming, very soon, for you to come home with me. It's time for your life to be fair, all the time. I know you don't remember the deal you made with God, but He does. It has an ending, an ending for your time on Earth as Margo. The next time you see me, you will have no choice but to come with me. You have to accept that life on Earth is not fair, but it is fair in Heaven."

Before I can vehemently deny what he's saying, my cell phone rings. It's Brock. "Look, I have to take this call. Meredith might be on her way to the hospital." I grab my phone and swipe the bar to answer. When I look up, Dad is gone.

CHAPTER THIRTY-NINE

Brock was calling just to let me know that Meredith had her weekly check with her OB-GYN and she and the baby were doing well, but it would probably be another week before the baby arrived.

I ended the call wondering if I would still be here in a week. Then I reprimanded myself. Of course, I'd be here. I'm hardly on death's doorstep. Besides, hadn't Dad told me in one of our previous conversations that time in Heaven is different from time here on Earth? He might be done with our little visits, but it could be a good, long while before he comes back to get me.

"Daddy?" I call to see if he might reappear. Nothing. "William?" Nothing. See, I tell myself. Everything is fine.

I sit back down on the couch where Dad had been a few minutes ago. Should I get my affairs in order? Do I need to call all my friends to tell them goodbye? Maybe I should drive over to Brock and Meredith's to give them a hug? Or to Melissa's?

What should I tell Wynn when he gets home tonight? Will I even still be alive then?

Disgusted with myself, I stand up and head to my bathroom to take a shower. I want to make sure I'm at least clean, when Dad comes for me. I laugh. Good, I still have my sense of humor! Instead of focusing on death, I'm going to focus on what I have left of life, a life which now is very rich and rewarding. I look in the mirror. "It always was rich and rewarding, you idiot," I say aloud. "You just didn't recognize that it was. Dad came here to get you to see that."

Feeling better and peaceful, I get in the shower and decide what Wynn and I will have for dinner tonight.

• • •

Once a year, I have an appointment with my surgical oncologist who removed half of my thyroid seven years ago. The suspicious nodule turned out to be benign, but the pathology report did indicate a small, almost immeasurable bit of carcinoma, so small that my doctor wasn't worried about it. Since nodules exist in the half of my thyroid that remains, my doctor has me get a sonogram, annually, to make sure they haven't grown. Then, he goes over the results with me in his office. Every year, when I leave that appointment, I thank God that I don't have cancer.

Today, I'm a little on edge. Maybe the nodules have gotten larger and they aren't benign. Maybe this is the beginning of the end, what Dad was hinting at. But then I remember what I've been told about thyroid cancer: it's the best cancer to have, because only in rare cases can it kill you. And those are the cases where it has spread from another part of the body. I'm healthy! I feel fine. Today is definitely not "D-Day" for me.

Ordinarily, I drive myself to this appointment. But Wynn has a business call to make in the same building, so he's offered to take me. We are going to lunch afterwards.

When we arrive in the parking garage, Wynn tells me he will meet me in the lobby of my doctor's office. His call will only last a few minutes.

As usual, my doctor is punctual and the nurse calls me back right away. The doctor comes in and, in very technical jargon, explains that the nodules have not grown and everything is fine. He'll see me next year.

Yes, yes you will. I plan on living another year. Wynn is waiting for me in the lobby. I silently congratulate myself that I don't have cancer as we walk out of the building and head to the car.

Seeing that Wynn has just answered his phone, I quietly enter our car. Wynn starts up the engine and navigates out of the parking spot. He swipes his credit card at the exit and the gate lifts, allowing us to leave. He wraps up his business call and turns to me. "What did the doctor say?"

"All good. He'll see me back next year." *Yes, he will.*

"That's great, Margo. Let's go celebrate! Where would you like to eat lunch?"

"Somewhere outside since it's such a pretty day. How about Seasons 52?"

"Exactly what I was thinking."

After we are seated at a table for four beneath a patio

umbrella, I decide it's time to tell Wynn about my "visits" with Dad. He'll get a kick out of them, I'm sure.

"There's something I need to tell you, Sweetheart. And I'm hoping you don't think I'm crazy."

"I already do...think your crazy. So, don't let that stop you," he laughs as he takes a sip of the tea the server has placed in front of him.

"Well, I've been seeing my dad."

Wynn steals a glance at me over the top of his sunglasses. "Your dad has been dead a long time, Margo. What are you talking about?"

"I know. I've had dinner with him. He's been in our pool. He's been at the condo."

Wynn pauses, unsure of what to say. "When did these visits begin?"

"The first one was right after Chase and Libby's wedding. I was kind of depressed and I thought maybe I'd just imagined seeing him to make me feel better. But it turns out there was a purpose to his visits."

"Go on," Wynn prompts.

"Okay, this is the crazy part. It turns out that I have my grandmother's soul."

"Interesting." Wynn says. "Do you believe that? What does that mean?"

I wonder if Wynn believes *me*. Or does he just think this is my "author mind?" Telling him was a mistake. I've opened Pandora's box now. I'll never hear the end of it from him! For once I wish he would go back to checking the sports scores on his ESPN app. But I have to answer, now that I've told him. "I think it's a nice thought and that's all it is. Yesterday when Dad came by..."

"What do you mean, 'came by?' Does he ring the doorbell?"

"No, he just appeared in the living room. But yesterday he insisted that it's time for my soul to return."

"Return to where?"

"To Heaven. So, I was nervous that today the doctor might say I have cancer, but I'm fine so now I feel sure it's just been my 'overactive imagination.'" I make the air quotes with my fingers.

"Wait, you mean he told you that you are going to die...soon?"

"Yes. He said that yesterday. But I'm not worried about it."

Wynn is uncharacteristically quiet for the remainder of our "celebratory" lunch. As he finishes scribbling his name on the credit card slip, he takes my hand in his. "I don't want you going anywhere, Margo. We have a lot of the world to explore together, not to mention a grandchild entering our lives any day now."

I squeeze his hand. "Not to worry. I don't plan on leaving anytime soon."

As I start to stand, Wynn pulls me back to my seat, leans over and kisses me quite passionately. "Good. I'll hold you to that." He stands. "The next time your dad shows up, let me know, ok?"

I nod as we walk to the car. "Thanks for not making me feel like a lunatic."

We get inside and buckle our seatbelts as is our habit. Wynn does what I silently wished for at lunch and finally checks his phone briefly for the latest update from the ESPN scoreboard before starting the car.

Wynn enters Central Expressway and heads north towards our exit. I pull down the visor at my seat to check my lipstick. "Maybe we should stop at the grocery store..." In the mirror, I see my dad in the seat behind me. I take a deep breath. "Okay, Wynn. Dad's actually sitting behind me right now. Can you see him?"

"It's time, Margaret. God is calling you home. Take my hand," William says, reaching around the side of my seat.

In the split second Wynn looks in the rearview mirror to see if my father is, indeed, in the back seat, the truck in the lane to my right cuts us off. Wynn slams on the brakes and swerves, too late to avoid impact.

EPILOGUE

Heaven
March 16, 2019

I can still feel my hand in Dad's as we ascend into the most amazing blue sky I've ever witnessed. I felt no pain as my door was sheared off and I watched my body slam into the pavement of Central Expressway. I felt relief as I watched Wynn pull onto the shoulder and open his door. He was dazed, calling my name. For a few brief moments, I tried calling out to him to let him know I was okay. But he couldn't hear me. I was already dead. I wanted to cry, cry because I would miss him. That's when Dad whispered to me.

"Time goes fast where we are heading. The time you are separated from him will be brief. Remember, the love you shared is more powerful than death."

I am strangely comforted by this. As the sun shines even brighter, I look at all the fluffy clouds floating by.

"It's amazing here, isn't it?"

I look at the spirit speaking to me, the man who was once my father and who now is again my son. "William," I address him.

His spirit radiates joy. "Mom," my son replies.

"We're finally together again," I say.

"Yes, that was God's plan. He allowed you to return to Earth so I could raise you since you didn't have the chance to raise me."

I beam. "I need to thank Frances and Ike for doing that for me. They did a tremendous job! But first, what did you think of our story? The one you asked me…or I should say Margo… to write?"

"Well for those left behind, it had a very sad ending. Hopefully they won't miss our message."

"Yes, I hope not."

"But for the souls up here, it's a beautiful ending…one you had no choice but to write. Dad can't wait to see you again. Your sister, Irene, is elated. You'll see them soon."

Out of the blue I wince.

"What?" asks William.

"Someone's speaking to me…from a distance. They sound like they are in pain."

"I don't hear anything. Maybe it's your imagination. No one is in pain in Heaven," my son explains.

"This person is. And the second voice sounds familiar." I strain to recognize to whom the voice belongs. "It sounds like my son. It sounds like he is saying Margo."

"I'm right here, Mom."

"No, not you, William. It sounds like Brock. There's a woman's voice…the one who's yelling. Brock's trying to comfort her."

"I'm puzzled. Maybe I can find Angel Gabrielle and he can answer your question."

"Shh… I'm needed. They're saying my name."

"Margo?"

"No, Margaret something." In an instant I feel as if I'm evaporating, fading into the sky.

William suddenly realizes why God needed Margaret back on this particular day. "Go! We will be here when you return!"

I'm drifting, slowly like a leaf floating from a tree, back to the earth, back to a hospital delivery room where I see my son, Brock, standing next to his wife. He's holding a baby girl. I feel myself melting into her sweet, newborn body. I look up at the man who is now holding me, looking into his amazing chocolate brown eyes. He looks back at me and says, "Welcome to our family, little Margaret Grace."

In an instant Margaret and Margo are absorbed into this gorgeous creation of God's.

William's spirit remains frozen. On Earth, his heart would have been breaking into a million fragments. But in Heaven, he knows that in the blink of an eye, she'll be back. "Mom?" he calls, wondering if she can hear him. Gabrielle is nowhere to be found.

A billowing white cloud outlined in silver rolls towards William. When it comes to a halt directly at his feet, he is no longer looking at a cloud but looking into the face of God.

"Why did you take her?" William asks, knowing what God will say.

God gently lifts William's soul and holds him in the palm of his hand. "I needed her soul so she could be born into Brock's daughter."

William is more puzzled than angry. "Why then, did you insist I meet with Margo? Why did I do that if you weren't going to keep her here?"

Warmth radiates from God, enshrouding William, causing his anger to instantly evaporate. "To give her peace about your death. She was still angry with me for taking you away from her. And why did I allow her to go back to the mortal world? Margaret's soul purpose is to be with her sons. Don't worry, William, she'll be back someday. After all, love is more powerful than death."

ACKNOWLEDGEMENTS

I want to, once again, thank my faithful editing team who took the time to provide me with invaluable feedback on this story. Donna Friedel, Bonni Garrison, Melissa Glanton, Kathy Haddox, Pat Shaw and Nancy Wiginton. I am deeply thankful for our enduring friendships. Your thoughtful comments and laser-sharp eyes enabled me to publish a much better book.

I am also grateful for my new editing readers: Elizabeth Tucker, Sara Hacala, and my new daughter-in-law, Baylee. The three of you offered different perspectives: from someone who doesn't know me at all, to a special cousin who's known me all of her life, to the woman who's just getting to know me. Welcome to the Diane Cobalt editing team. You have my gratitude! And as always, all remaining errors are mine!

Thanks to all of you out there who have taken the time to read *Soul Purpose*. I have wanted to share Margaret's/Margo's story for many years because it's one that is very close to my heart.

To my sons, Chad and Gage, you are my "soul purpose." It's been an honor raising you and a privilege watching you become such fine young men! Thank you for reading the earliest version of this book and providing me with your much valued comments. I also deeply appreciate your assistance with technical glitches and your patience with me.

Last, but certainly not least, *Soul Purpose* would never have been published without my husband who took care of me while I recovered from surgery to repair my broken kneecap and resulting pulmonary emboli. I literally couldn't do anything, no matter how simple, without his help for many weeks. Thank you, Chip, for being my *soul mate* and for all the loving care and encouragement you have given me for the past thirty-seven years.